The Wizard of Macatawa

and other stories

by

Tom Doyle

The Wizard of Macatawa

and other stories

by

Tom Doyle

edited by
Lawrence M. Schoen

The Wizard of Macatawa and Other Stories © 2012 by Paper Golem LLC

"Wizardry" © 2012 by James Patrick Kelly

"Art's Appreciation" first appeared in *Futurismic*.
"Consensuc Building" first appeared in *Futurismic*.
"Crossing Borders" first appeared in *Strange Horizons*.
"Hooking Up" first appeared in *Futurismic*.
"Inversions" first appeared in *Ideomancer*.
"The Floating Otherworld" first appeared in *Strange Horizons*.
"The Garuda Bird" first appeared in *Æon Magazine*.
"The Wizard of Macatawa" first appeared in *Paradox Magazine*.
"While Ireland Holds These Graves" first appeared in *Writers of the Future, Vol. XXVIII*.

"A Sense of Closure," "Noise Man," and "Sea and Stars" are all new to this volume.

ISBNs:
Hard Cover	978-0-9835521-3-0	0-9835521-3-4	
Soft Cover	978-0-9835521-4-7	0-9835521-4-2	

Various photographic elements from the *Library of Congress Photochrome Print Collection* went into the creation of the cover. In addition, elements from the following images were sampled, and are used here under the terms of the Creative Commons Attribution License:

"Amazing Modern Skyscrapers In Putrajaya" by Thienzieyung.
"Hong Kong from inside the Bank of China Building" by Ray Devlin.
"Philadelphia skyscraper" by Mihai Bojin.
"São Paulo Architecture" by Anderson Mancini.
untitled skyscraper in Boston by Leonel Ponce.

Cover Art created by Greg Jensen
Cover and Book Design by Lawrence M. Schoen

Published by Paper Golem LLC
1049 Union Meeting Road
Blue Bell, PA 19422 USA
http://www.papergolem.com

Contents

To Mom. I lay this, my shield, at your feet.

Acknowledgements

The previously published works in this collection might never have seen the light of day but for the following magazine and anthology editors: Christopher M. Cevasco, Christopher East, Jeremy Lyon, Marti McKenna, Bridget McKenna, Marsha Sisolak, Jed Hartman, Susan Marie Groppi, Karen Meisner, Meliva Koch, and the late K.D. Wentworth.

I'm grateful for the recognition that these stories received from the Writers of the Future contest, the Washington Science Fiction Association's Small Press Award, the readers of *Strange Horizons*, the editors of the *Year's Best Fantasy and Horror*, and, in their year's best lists, Rich Horton and Dave Truesdale.

Various readers and others made essential contributions to my writing and revision of these stories, including the *Strange Horizons* workshop of 2002, the Clarion Writing Workshop class and instructors of 2003, the Washington DC Writers Group from Hell, and Shannon McRae. (I offer special thanks to James Patrick Kelly, who was the first professional to tell me that a story of mine had no blue line of death.) I'm indebted to Carol Fink and Nancy Robertson at the Library of Michigan for assisting with my research for "The Wizard of Macatawa," and to Angie Greene and Robert O'Donoghue for their Irish idiom review of "While Ireland Holds These Graves." I read massive amounts for the background of "Noise Man," but my most important source was *Alan Turing: The Enigma* by Andrew Hodges (Touchstone, 1983).

I appreciate all the encouragement and support from my partner Beth Delaney, my family, and my friends, including writers David Louis Edelman and David J. Williams, who've always been gracious in their own acknowledgments (back at ya!). Within my family, my brother and fellow writer Bill Doyle has endured far more than his fair share of my professional complaints and questions—thank you for listening.

Finally, this collection is due to the interest of one man, Lawrence Schoen, who listened to me read some of these stories, and heard a voice that he liked. Thank you, Lawrence.

Wizardry

When I was eleven I wanted to live in Oz. Desperately. Night after night, I would gaze up and wish on the first star I saw for magical transport to the Emerald City. (I was a Catholic back then, but it seemed to me that a trip to Oz wasn't something you could *pray* for). I know, *I know*—strange. But you have to understand that, as a boy, I was steeped in the world that L. Frank Baum had imagined. I read the fourteen books he wrote many times, as well as those by the lesser writers who continued the series after he died. In the books it seemed so simple to get to Oz. Boys and girls—mostly girls—from the mundane world were finding their way all the time, passing through whirlpools and tornados and secret caves or falling overboard to be rescued mermaids or just taking the wrong fork in the road. Why not me?

And there was so much fun to be had in Oz. Strange creatures lived in impossible towns. There were fairies and witches and wizards; magic was thick on the ground. Of course, there was danger too. Not mortal danger, but just enough to give an impressionable kid a good, old-fashioned scare. As I got older, I grew out of my Oz fixation, although I did read most of the original Baum books once again as an adult—to my daughter, when she was of an age. And now the title story of Tom Doyle's book has got me thinking about Oz again, as he no doubt intended his readers to do. You see, Tom is something of an Oz aficionado as well. He used to vacation in Holland, Michigan on the eastern shore of Lake Michigan, which is where Baum himself summered from 1899 to 1910. In 2010, Tom gave a talk at the Library of Congress mapping some of what Baum would have seen there in his day onto the marvelous land of Oz that he would later imagine. But Tom's Oz is much darker than Baum's; it lies deep in the shadow of death. And Tip, the foul-mouthed girl protagonist of "The Wizard of Macatawa" is no Dorothy Gale or Betsy Bobbin. Tip has no desire to visit Oz at the end of Tom's story, in large part because of her family ties. That's something that young Jimmy Kelly didn't think of—and many Oz fans still don't consider. The only people who are likely to like Oz are loners. When you move there, you leave friends and family behind.

Which isn't to say that Tom Doyle doesn't have sympathy for and a deep understanding of loners, as you will see in stories like "A Sense of Closure" and "Noise Man." On several occasions in his sometimes restless life, Tom too has picked up and departed the mundane world in search of psychic adventure. Maybe not to a magic fairyland, but, for example, to Japan (see "The Floating Otherworld") for several years. A yearlong sabbatical in 1999 from a lucrative law career saw him whirling from Carnaval in Rio de Janiero (see "Sea and Stars") to a Zen monastery to a research stint at the Center for Millennial Studies at Boston University to buying drum kit and forming a rock band called *Voided by Guises* to greeting the arrival of the twenty-first century in holy city of Jerusalem. And I first met Tom at the Clarion Writers Workshop in East Lansing, Michigan in 2003, where I was teaching and where he began to perfect the craft of literary magic. I still remember reading an early draft of "Crossing Borders" and being at once thrilled and aghast. Its protagonist, a crazed loner, offers up a chilling mix of transgressive sex and violence in the first few paragraphs and then spends the rest of the story teetering on the edge of self-immolation. *Yikes!* It's been nine years, but you don't soon forget a writer who can pull such a delicate balancing act off.

I don't know what, if anything, I was able to teach Tom Doyle at Clarion. Probably not very much. But when I look at the many different kinds of stories in this collection, I see the burgeoning of a career that is much like the one I have tried to make for myself. Variety pleases me, as I believe it pleases Tom. There are writers who are instantly recognizable for their style and for their obsessive themes. Trust me: there is truly honor in creating such a body of work. I would argue that Lyman Frank Baum is one such writer. But then there are those who have a greater range, writers who never, ever settle. That's the kind of writer I see in the pages that follow. You will find here a storyteller who is equally adept at science fiction and fantasy. He has mastered love stories and horror stories. His children are as vivid as his grownups and his insights into women are as profound as his engagement with what it means to be a man. There are tales of courage and fear, of foolishness and hard-won wisdom. As in Oz, in Doyle-land there is no possible way to guess what is just down the road.

You are about to put yourself in the hands of a wizard. I've already witnessed the wonders he can conjure, but your adventures are before you. Turn the page and be amazed.

—James Patrick Kelly

The Wizard of Macatawa

This is one of my best stories so far, but I didn't want to tell it. Like my protagonist, Tip, I didn't think much of Oz. But also like Tip, I spent my summers in the same Lake Michigan resort town where L. Frank Baum had vacationed. When I looked for ideas rattling about in my skull, this one was obvious, which made writing it almost obligatory. I resented the obligation.

What turned the story from a chore into a joy was my realization that young Tom Doyle wasn't the narrator. For that job, I found a foul-talking and defiant kid like those I used to know in Michigan. I also remembered my emotional response to Ray Bradbury's "The Lake," and realized that this story had a place to go that wasn't Oz.

In 2008, "The Wizard of Macatawa" won the WSFA Small Press Award. I hope someday soon to publish a novel-length extension of this story.

I grew up in a land of Oz. Or at least I spent summers there. One summer, they made me perform in the community theater. "I'm the Mayor of Munchkin City," I said. Adults said I was cute. Not what I wanted to hear. The last night of the show, I kicked my foot through the set. I was not invited to return the next year.

My Oz was Macatawa, the Michigan beach town where Frank Baum had spent his summers. He made fun of it like he made fun of everything else. The town reveled in his mockery. Forty years after the Oz film, Macatawa imported the surviving Munchkin actors to sign autographs. Silly town, bitter little men and women.

I didn't get an autograph; the whole thing embarrassed me. I hated Oz, 'cause Oz didn't scare me. Oz was for good kids, and I was a little shit.

I enjoyed fires. Some nights, I built the bonfire for the other kids on the beach. I would have rather gone to the real bonfire up in the dunes, the one with drinking and making out. They said I wasn't old enough for that one yet, which sucked. So I launched bottle rockets at the real bonfire and ran off into the woods. That was cool.

Maybe I was crazy. I definitely took drugs, though which came first was unclear. Mom made me take them depending on her mood. It was 1979, and I was an early adopter of that later kiddie hit, Ritalin.

At the kid bonfire, on an August night, we just had marshmallows on dirty sticks and some Orange Crush and other pop. Nobody seemed to mind me getting wired on sugar, at least during the summer. All wound up, I got scary to freak out the younger kids—Anna and Sarah from next door, and Joe and Will from up the hill. Not hard to freak—they were pretty frightened of me just being there, staring at them with my wild crazy eyes.

Only kid I didn't scare, most times, was my younger brother Jack. He was too smart for anybody's good, which probably came from being named after President Kennedy. Even next to the fire, he kept a beach blanket wrapped around him to keep warm.

I hit the kids with the usual stuff—coho salmon biting off toes, freshwater sharks, mad killer in the dunes. I got an "ew, that's gross, Tip," but no signs of bedwetting nightmares.

Some clouds were piling up on the horizon, blocking the moon. "I hear a tornado is coming. It'll tear you up while you sleep."

Jack shook his head. "Tornadoes don't touch down here right on the lake—they jump over to the dune from the water."

I socked him in the shoulder for that. Usually he wasn't such a dope. But I didn't punch him hard. "OK, loser, you tell us something really scary."

Jack stared at me, quiet. Then he got those spooky, spaced-out eyes, like whenever he thought too hard about things that might happen. And then he whispered, "The world's going to end soon."

Everyone gaped at him. "That's the dumbest thing I've ever heard," I said. I wanted to punch him again—it was just so lame. And yet, maybe too close to home.

Then Anna giggled, and I didn't like that, so I asked, "How's it gonna end, Jack? Bombs? Apes?"

"Bombs maybe. Too many people maybe. Maybe God does it, maybe we do."

"Says who?" said Anna.

"Everyone—scientists, psychics, the Bible. This is all going to end in a few years."

"Lots of dead people?" I asked, nodding, encouraging.

"Millions."

"Just lying around?"

"No one to bury 'em."

"People eating people, the luckiest people in the world?"

"Soon. Or maybe something worse." He looked at me, not scared but very serious. He believed this.

"Cool." I could have guessed why it didn't scare him, but that would have spoiled it. Jack had made me so happy, I wanted to punch something else, and the little creep knew it too. Anna and Sarah were about to cry. Will desperately tried to sound tough. "You don't know what you're talking about."

That was a laugh. "Jack knows everything," I said. And Will couldn't argue with that—he had seen the books Jack was reading that summer. I wanted to milk the end of the world dry. Screams tonight, parents complaining in the morning.

Time for the *coup de grace*. I took out my jackknife, passed it through the fire, lightly cut myself on my left hand, and smeared the blood on both my palms. I felt so real putting on this show. I stood up, arms wide to the stars. "Show me the end of the world!"

Just then, a flash to the north from the lake, like the lighthouse beam, only out of sync with its smooth rotation, and green, very green. "What's that?" I said. But then it was gone.

"Stop it," Will said, "you're just trying to scare us."

No, seriously, I thought I saw something. But they wanted to be like stupid kids in a TV comedy. Jack knew better—*my* craziness wasn't the seeing-things kind.

We were a team. We would have to check it out.

Face it, Mr. Baum's interest in children was unusual. Today, overzealous child welfare folks would be all over his sorry Victorian butt. Good thing for him it was 1899, because he really was just a big child with a fierce mustache, maybe a skipping stone's throw away from autistic, off in his imaginary worlds armed only with bad jokes and an honest love for kids. He couldn't bear to see kids hurt or scared. Unusual indeed.

August in 1899 meant Regatta Week and Venetian Evening, the highpoint of the summer in Macatawa. Late afternoon, between the already boring boats and the upcoming fireworks, the kids had nothing to do. So, all overdressed innocence, they gathered on the porch of Baum's cottage along with his four sons to hear his stories.

Baum loved an audience. "So, what history of far off lands shall we discuss today?"

A girl piped up immediately: "Tell us the one about Dorothy, please!" Everyone laughed at this, because the girl's name was Dorothy too. Though she wasn't from Kansas and her last name was VanderMay, not Gale, Baum would never mention such inconvenient facts.

So he told them about Dorothy and the cyclone machine, and the beautiful yet wicked, wicked witches, and how the wicked witches hated water because it was life, and they hated all things with the stuff of life in them. Yet the witches were drawn to life, sought to steal its essence and magic, sought to make the world into a slave as changeless and dead as themselves. They hated Oz because life, free and wild, got into everything there—tin men and scarecrows and porcelain and anything that wanted animating. But the children shouldn't worry, because Dorothy had killed the wicked witches, and there was plenty of water here, and witches couldn't cross the hot Shifting Sands between Oz and here (like the hot shifting sands of the beach dunes). Oz was far, far away; our world was safe.

Dorothy VanderMay seemed thoughtful, and the writer was always interested in the thoughts of children.

"What is it, Dorothy?"

"Uncle Frank, isn't the world going to end soon?"

"World end? And miss seeing you grow up into a lovely young woman? I can say with absolute certainty that no such thing will happen for trillions and trillions of years, which is a very long time indeed."

The girl's father would be angry if he heard this; he, like some others of the Dutch Reformed, had high apocalyptic hopes for the coming years of Our Lord 1900 and 1901. Nothing for it—the children got enough morality and fear in school, they could use a little hope and fun for summer. Baum could too. His Oz story was finished; he was only waiting for the opportune moment to give it to a publisher.

At suppertime, Baum nodded at his wife. He could never bear to be the one to say *go*. "All right, children, that's enough," she said. "You want to be ready for the fireworks tonight."

Baum hugged his wife, then went to the study. From a locked drawer, he removed a device that looked like a horizontal sextant with a strange eye-like metal ball at the end of a narrow telescope-like tube. The tube pivoted within a metal circle engraved with symbols—a five-pointed star, a triangle within a triangle, a cross with a hoop, a pair of winged shoes. He turned the Eye to the shoes, towards the land of his dreams.

The device gave off a glowing emerald light, visible through the cracks in the blinds. Lost in his vision, Baum couldn't know that the Eye's light had been seen from far, far away. From across the Shifting Sands, they were coming.

The day after our "end of the world" bonfire, Jack and I went down to the beach early, before Mom would hear that I'd been scaring the neighbors again. August meant a steady wind, ocean-size waves, and an undertow that enjoyed the taste of kids.

"Let's take the dinghy, eh matey?" I said, pirate-like.

"The waves are awful big. Momby won't like it." Momby was what Jack called Mom—a cute baby-mistake version of "mommy" that had gone on for way too long.

"I don't give a fart. And your French-fried-freak friend Cousteau wouldn't give a fart."

I had Jack there. In the dinghy, he always pretended to be Jacques Cousteau, giving orders with a bad accent. He couldn't let National Geographic down.

So we took the orange plastic boat, the "Calypso from Hell." I rowed us out toward the big red lighthouse and the channel, near where I'd seen the green glow. We weren't supposed to go that far away and out. Dad used to say after cocktails that it was a liability problem. But Dad had gone away to the distant kingdom of financial support.

I pulled hard toward the breaker line. Jack looked at the big waves and turned paler. "We're going to capsize."

"You can swim. Hang on, Jacques!" Kabam! We crashed through, totally soaked but still upright. "You OK, captain?"

Jack saw we were past the breaker line and said, "Aye aye."

The water felt good and cool in the wind, the sun dried my skin and it was a great day to be a pirate. Jack took off his wet baseball cap, and his damp, bald head shone as it dried. Still surprised me, seeing no hair on him. The dinghy pitched and rolled a little, and Jack got nervous again. "We won't find anything in these waves."

"So no one will notice us looking." Maybe the little creep was right, but nothing good waited back on shore. "You want to row for a bit?"

"Sure." Jack took the oars, and I guided the boat to where I thought the glow had been. His rowing wasn't worth spit, but I didn't say so. Jack had been to the doctor a lot that summer. He didn't seem to mind much—gave him even more time to read. Mom always fussed about him, but other than no hair, he looked fine to me—I thought some exercise would do him good.

"Ramming speed!" I shouted to encourage him. So he pulled harder, and we closed in on the green glow spot. Abruptly, the dinghy plopped down from a wave and stopped rolling. The lake was as flat and clear as a pond. "Weird," I said, meaning absolutely sweet.

Jack pointed behind me. "No, that's weird."

I looked. A few feet back in our wake, the waves and wind were still going full force. We were in the calm eye of something. "So, what is it, genius?"

"Um, might be like the calm eye of something."

"Never mind." This wasn't in his science books. Most spooky stuff was just messing with your mind, and I didn't let my mind be messed with. But, like Jack's scary daydreams or my knife routine last night, there was something real on the spooky edges that I could never quite catch. Maybe I could catch it here.

We peered over the edge of the dinghy. We could see clear to the bottom, little more than rippled sand. Then, a glint of metal. "Dive, dive," cried Jack in Cousteau.

I dove, kicking for the glint. I reached—ouch, my cut of the night before broke open on the sharp metal. I grabbed for the rest of it buried under the sand and pulled it up. I shot up out of the water as dramatically as possible, flopped my arms on the side of the dinghy, and plopped the metal thing onto its floor. "Salvage. Treasure. One for all."

I hauled myself in while Jack frowned at the treasure. "No way. It's yours."

"OK." Not like him at all to decline a piece of the action. "But your opinion, Captain?"

"Hmm." He held the treasure between his fingers like a dead fish. "Looks like a thingy for a ship, to find its location."

"Here. Give it." I rubbed off some tarnish and crusted sand. Underneath the crap, it shined, strangely not rusted, but still real old-fashioned looking. The central piece was a tube with a ball stuck on it.

"Valuable?" I asked.

Jack nodded, but his eyes were far away. "You might be happier if you put it back right now."

"Can't do that, Captain."

"I know. So keep it. Mom would throw it away, or lose it, and that would be worse." Hmm, this also wasn't like Jack or Jacques, but I didn't complain.

I rowed back. In a few strokes, like passing through a curtain, we were in the rough water again. We moved easier; the waves wanted to push us in. We hauled the dinghy up onto the beach and flipped it over, and I hid the treasure under it.

Mom was lying on the beach, sun worshipping as always. I could have gotten by, but the other kids made a racket when I came up, so Mom woke and intercepted me on the cottage porch. I got holy hell for the stories last night and taking the dinghy too far down. She didn't bother Jack, which wasn't fair, but I didn't mind, because Jack hadn't told on me and he went along with what I said even when Mom said otherwise, and that was what mattered.

And Mom asked The Question again.

What did she ask? I would rather have punched you than told you. Everyone seemed to think it was so goddamn important.

Mom asked why I couldn't act like a nice girl, like Anna or Sarah. And I said I had no intention of acting like a girl, nice or otherwise.

There, now you know. Satisfied? Fine, now shut up about it.

After dark, Mom went to the neighbors' to drink cocktails and sing along to Neil Diamond songs. I grabbed the treasure from under the dinghy and ran it up to the third floor of the cottage, the attic out of which they had carved our wood-paneled bedrooms. Behind my bed, the workers had left a loose square of panel that opened into a crawl space, the last bit of unaltered hundred-year-old attic.

The crawl space hid my arsenal of evil. I had all the forbiddens of childhood there—M80s, cigarettes, bottle rockets, porn, a fifth of Wild Turkey 101, some weed. Not that I had active interest in the porn or the weed, but they were big no-nos, so I had to have them too.

I had never told anyone directly about my arsenal, but just the hint of it was power. I felt bigger just knowing I had it. I restrained my use; my assault on the real bonfire a rare indulgence. The arsenal gave me authority over the great kid questions (only one way to tell if four M80s were the same as a stick of dynamite). The arsenal was my substitute for church, my altar to vices and mysteries to come, my surrogate for the spookiness I could not reach. Even hidden behind the panel, the porn disturbed me with its promise of the future.

No matter what happened, what kind of trouble I got into, no one had ever checked the crawl space. So I stashed the strange thing there, just behind my arsenal and backpack. I would leave it there until I could figure out what to do with it—joke or money or both.

That night, full moonlight fell on my bed. The crawl space panel seemed to glow around its edges, but no one could see it but me.

In 1899, they came after dark. They were not acting deliberately sinister; that's when the party started, and they have never been able to resist a good party or great beauty or any of the stuff of life.

And on Venetian Evening, *fin de siècle*, all was beauty and life—the sunset on the lake, the countless stars, the summer evening dresses. Bright Japanese lanterns reflected on the mirror-like bay from everywhere—from the buildings, from the Yacht Club and hotels, from the boats. Bands played from ferries, bonfires blazed on the high dunes, launches displayed colored lights. Fireworks rocketed overhead. A night where dreams met reality. Their night.

They were not snobs when it came to parties. In province or metropolis, they were most comfortable, less noticeable, where everything shone. But they could have done without all the water.

They alone wore masks, Carnival style, to this Venetian event. Their perfection, hidden by artifice, awaited its unmasking—that was their history and future. The name "Venetian Evening" seemed their omen, an assurance there would be no new magic for this new land.

Masked, they were not noticed by that childlike mind that thought, despite all he had seen in the Eye, that all ugliness was evil and all prettiness good. He was too busy dancing with his wife. He loved to dance, and he loved his wife even more desperately than he needed her.

The strangers loved to dance as well. They danced beautifully, in perfect order, tracking the man who had been tracking them these many months.

As the party wound down, the Baums stopped dancing and walked back toward their cottage. The strangers were waiting. Frank smiled at them. So lovely, like people on stage. He would have given them willingly anything they asked for, because they must be good. Anything, except perhaps the Eye.

Suspecting resistance on that very point, the strangers grabbed Mrs. Baum and etherized her unconscious (natural means, contemporary technology were their bywords here). They held Mr. Baum, but left him conscious. Already contaminated by the Oculus, he did not need to be shielded, and they might need his assistance.

"Who are you?" he asked. His theatrical bravado fooled no one.

"Shh!" said their leader, a striking woman with eyes like a sunset. "No more spying, Mr. Baum. Take us to your home. We have questions for you."

"Oz? You're from Oz?"

Whap! The woman slapped him. "You'll refrain from speaking that name ever again, Frank." She ripped off her mask, and Baum's weak heart nearly stopped in recognition. "We're not here about our world. We're here about your future."

In 1979, I spotted them right off. They came at midday, to show off their forms, because their brightness spited the sun, because it would explain the tans they already had, because they liked to watch others get cancer. They weren't like the regular crawlers: pimply-faced local kids and fat old-fart trespassers on our beach. These people should have been at a beach they made songs about, frolicking with the famous and rich—rich, not like Dad, but as beyond Dad as Dad was beyond a janitor. They jogged up and down, God-like bronzed bodies with charming, cunning eyes.

I had dreamed about people like this, happy and perfect. I always knew, from fairy tales and TV, that they existed somewhere. What I knew then, on our porch with my Orange Crush, was that these smugly perfect people were everything I despised.

Some of the perfect people stopped to talk with the neighbor kids, and the little shits stared at them with big round eyes and blabbed away. Others struck up conversation with reclining Mom. I pounced down the porch steps to the beach, to get the jump on them, to fracture any alliances.

I cut Mom off mid-sentence, probably some lie about Dad or about us. The perfect people smiled at me, imitating the same jerky smile I got from a lot of adults before they knew better—ooh, isn't she cute and innocent? But these people smiled a lot to show their teeth—perfect, bright white, probably sharp. They wore shoes on the warm sand. It was hot, but they did not sweat, did not drink. Their hands felt dry when I shook them, their mouths looked dry when they spoke. Their pants had no zippers.

Mom smiled too, different but just as fake. "This is my daughter," she said.

"Do you have any other children? A son, perhaps?"

"Yes, he's..." She stopped, annoyed. "Go back up to the porch dear. We're talking."

The perfect people protested, "Please, not on our account." So I strolled back to the porch. If they wanted me around, I'd better keep my distance.

Back with my Orange Crush, I planned how to cause them trouble. This could get serious. It might involve their cars, if I could find them.

The screen door slammed me out of my schemes. Jack saw me, the look in my eyes. "Please, Tip. Don't mess with them."

"Why the hell not?" I said between clenched teeth, like Clint Eastwood. And ever so coolly, I went inside, the screen door wap-wapping again behind me, like I had nothing to hide. I was going for the arsenal.

Jack followed me up the stairs, out of breath. "There's something wrong. About them."

"Yeah, so? That's why I have to mess with them."

"They don't look..." He shook his head. "Not from here. Like something out of a story. A bad one."

"So am I, Jack," as if I knew what I was saying.

"I know, sis."

I should have punched him for the "sis," but I didn't. He seemed so serious. And I had reached the arsenal.

I opened the panel to the crawl space. It had been a crappy summer in a crappy year in a short crappy life. God only knew where they were going to stick me come fall, but I suspected it would be someplace with troubled girls who whined about abuse and food and where I wouldn't be able to do anything, not even kill myself. And I'd be away from Jack.

So, not just bottle rockets at these beautiful creeps. Time to blow the whole load. I got out the M80s. All of them.

Jack clutched my arm, trying to pull me away from the arsenal. "Damn it, Tip, think for once!"

I gripped his wrist with my free hand and twisted it off me. Hard.

Jack was crying. "Go ahead then. Die. It's no picnic."

Not good. "OK, dork. What would they do in a story then?"

He got the scary nobody's home look. "What's different today?"

"I don't know. The weather's nice, second day in a row. Oh. You mean the thingy." Maybe I really was mental—I had already forgotten about my treasure, which unlike most of the stuff I forgot was not boring. "They're here for it, aren't they?"

Jack nodded. So I looked for it. Where the hell was it? Not behind the arsenal and backpack anymore. But a faint scuttling noise came from the dark far end of the crawl space.

"Sounds like a raccoon," I said.

"Raccoons have rabies," Jack noted.

"Then I won't bite him."

"I'll stay here."

"Good thinking."

I had never explored the whole claustrophobic length—no telling what was back in there. "Jack, flashlight." He handed me his personal nite-lite/club like it was a surgeon's scalpel.

I crawled carefully over my arsenal. A bunch of dusty Dutch Reformed tracts blocked my way. I moved them over and shined the light down to the end of the crawl space.

A metallic blur. "Wha—?" I flinched back, thumping my head on a beam. It had scuttled away, trying to avoid the light.

"What is it?" Jack asked from outside.

"The thing from the lake," I whispered, heart pounding more than I wanted to admit. "It's like a metal spider."

"How many legs does it have?"

Three on the side I could see. "Six."

"Then it's not a spider, it's an insect."

Goddamnit. I was glad I had hurt him earlier so I didn't have to smack him now.

The eye on the end of the tube was staring at me. This seemed like an adult situation, so I tried talking nice to it. "Here eye-buggy thing. Come here. That's right. Be a good thing."

It didn't budge. So I tried things my way.

"Look, you little turd. Every goddamn freak in the universe is outside on the beach looking for you for god knows what, and I just know you're going to get me in trouble, and Jack too. But don't worry, they aren't going to find you, because if I have to crawl down after you I'm going beat you with this flashlight until your own bug mother wouldn't recognize your pieces." I pointed my cut hand at it. "You got me?"

My hand was throbbing. Jack yelled from the entrance, "Tip, don't..." But the thing blinked first and lowered its eyestalk.

"Just letting it know who's boss. We're fine in here, aren't we?"

The thing scuttled towards me, eye still down like a dog caught in the act.

From two floors down, voices on the porch. The screen door wapped, and wapped, and wapped again.

Jack must have gone to a window. "They're here. What are you going to do?"

Whatever this thing was, it had magic and a tube to look through. I tapped my flashlight against the Eye's metal body. "You're going to show me what's going on. Right?"

The Eye just stared up at me. Jack stuck his head in the crawl space and whispered. "You've got to be more specific."

"OK, I need to know: what are these people going to do to us?"

The Eye nodded on its stalk. The body of the thing made a buzzing sound like wings as it rotated to a new setting. I touched it with my finger. It went still, like it was dead. I gazed into the tube.

It's the year 2000. A woman types on a computer, and that's the date on the screen. Man, she must be some kind of genius to be using a computer. It's way, way beyond Dad's Trash-80. This future looks pretty dull otherwise—no moon blasting out of orbit, no flying cars.

Then, I see a different future. I know it's different, because it's shown like a split-screen movie, in parallel with the woman typing. A gray dust covers dead trees and fields; a cold, hazy red sun sets over cities that are burned-out shells. I don't see any living people. Just like Jack said. Cool.

Or maybe not. I see other futures, one after the other, different versions of Jack's scary story, like some educational film. I get bored. "Which is it?" I ask.

As if it has only been waiting for my request, all the other futures blip out, like a TV being turned off. Then, a small dot expands into the future of the perfect people. Their dream. And Jack's thing, worse than world's end.

And I am afraid.

I want to close my eyes and not see the millions of faces, dead eyed, grinning mindlessly. Not that I should worry. I won't be there. I don't see Jack or me anywhere. But that's when I realize, some things are so goddamned horrible that it doesn't matter if it's you or somebody else. Everyone always told me not to be so angry; finally, I know what anger is for. Some things gotta go.

We don't have much time. "How does this happen? Show me now."

The thing whirls in my hands, pinching them a bit. I don't care. I keep looking. And that's when I see Baum's story.

They searched Baum's study and found his Oz manuscript. Their leader, the woman who had slapped him, casually thumbed through it in seconds. "Someone has been snooping on us. Very wicked, Frank."

"I was just... I had no idea it was..."

"Real? Oh yes. Now we both know there's only one way you could have seen this. The Oculus, Frank. Now."

Even faced with pain and death for him and his family, Baum hesitated. But not for long. He brought out the Eye from its case.

The woman reached for it but did not touch it. The Eye crouched in fear, its legs dug into Baum's hand. "How did you obtain this?"

Baum puffed up. "I am the royal historian of... that place."

She wagged a perfect finger in his face. "Frankness, Frank."

Baum deflated. "I, um, borrowed it from the Chicago Theosophical Society. I've meant to return it, but there's so much to write."

"And by now, you know from whom this came, before?"

Baum shuddered. He didn't like to think about who had worn this Eye and the uses to which she had put it, before she had lost it and everything else, before the Smith and Tinker of that other world had cunningly mounted it, changing it to life's tool. Through her Eye, the wicked ruler of the West—sunsets and death—had seen her own doom.

"Little man, I am her successor. You," she pointed at a male companion, "take the Oculus, and look at the future."

The man did not hesitate. He gingerly took the Oculus from Baum's hand; its legs scuttled without purchase. He put his eye to the tube. And then, instantly, without a sound, the man disappeared. The Eye clanged to the ground, then scurried up Baum's leg.

The woman smiled. "Thought so. Using it here is like standing too close to a revolving door. Well, royal historian, this is a fortunate evening for you. You are going to observe some history in advance for us."

"History?"

"You've never looked at the future?"

"Once. I saw peace and prosperity brought about by labor and machines."

"You would. We want you to look harder. But first, a simple test, to make sure the Oculus is working. Where is the Oculus in the future?"

Baum took the Eye in his hands again and set it to the future. He saw a succession of images—himself and these people, then the lake, then water, then sand, and sand, and sand.

"It's on the lake bottom."

"Keep looking."

After an eternity, the world glowed green. Then water and hands, then a cottage—he knew the place—then a short-haired child looking through the Oculus, watching him watching.

He nearly fainted, with his weak heart. "A boy's got it. About eighty years from now. It's in a cottage down the beach."

"Loser," I hissed. I felt strange, like someone had walked over my grave in a funhouse mirror room.

"Who's a loser?" Jack asked.

"Frank Baum."

"The *Wizard of Oz* guy? You can see him?"

"Yeah. He just sold us out."

"Jack, get down here!" As usual, Mom had sold us out too. But she had only asked for Jack.

"Baum said a boy had this thingy. They think it's you."

I saw Jack consider a back window, and knew he wasn't thinking suicide. Although we were three stories above the ground on the front side of the cottage, the cottage was set into a hill and next to large trees, so I knew from experience that escaping through the back window was not so difficult.

"No, you go downstairs. They don't want you; they want the thingy. I'm going to look at Baum again—maybe he can tell me something. If not..." I gestured toward the window.

"I'm scared."

"Same here. Now go, before they come up here. You'll be fine."

I looked into the device. "Show me Baum again."

Eighty years before, Baum was still peering into the future, reciting facts. "1916. United States negotiates settlement of the Great European War."

"Try again," the woman said. For a moment, the room darkened; a green aura marred the woman's faultless skin. As if answering, the Eye glowed brighter.

"1917. United States enters the World War."

"That's it. A World War by then should do. We'll nudge things that way." She touched Baum's cheek. "Yes, yes, we have great hopes for that future, for the ambitions formed in those trenches. But we need to be precise with our leverage, with where and when we travel from here. What else do you see?"

He saw some of the boys to whom he had told stories. They were, or would be, soldiers. They were, or would be, dead. It had, or would, break his heart.

And more death and worse death to follow. Somehow, his seeing these horrors would help these people make them real.

Then Baum saw me looking at him again, and he felt that I was dizzy, and I felt that he might really faint this time.

"Stop it," we both yelled. And everyone stopped, like in freeze tag, except Baum, who mumbled something and disappeared, leaving the Eye in midair.

Shit. "Where's Baum?" If it could move him, it could move me. "Get me to Baum—"

—In a flash, I am standing on a sand dune. It could be in Macatawa, except there's no lake that I can see. No trees or cottages either. Just endless sand dunes. The sand is hot. Not good. But I feel strong here, like twice my size. That's damned good.

Baum stands in front of me, smiling like a simp. "What is your name, little boy?"

I figure I have one shot to save the world. I walk up to him, smiling. Then, I punch him straight in the balls.

I should kill him while he gasps for breath on the sand, but he's so pathetic. So I set him straight. "I'm a girl, you jerk." God, I hate to have to say it. "Which is the only thing that has saved me so far from those jerks you ratted us out to. You fake piece of shit."

"Girl?" he gasps. My jeans, my words, my attitude make him cockeyed. "Must be an enchantment. I could..."

This is going nowhere. "Look. I'm a future kid. They've got my brother, Jack, and they'll be coming up for the Eye and me soon, so hurry up and tell me how to kill them."

"Oh, no, we have time." He gets up on his knees. "Time's frozen while we're here. Though we shouldn't stay long."

That explains the freeze tag. "Where's here?"

"I believe these are the Shifting Sands between the worlds. They protect Oz from the outside, and each world from the other, and the past from the future."

"Then how did those perfect jerks get here?"

That stops Mister Science. "I'm afraid that's my fault. The Eye is a bridge between the worlds. My use of it gave them a beacon to follow."

"Nice going."

"I wanted to bring magic to America. American magic."

"They're pretty American all right. So, how do we kill them?"

"I don't think we can. Best we can do, I think, is to put the Eye out of their reach. It won't stop them, but they'll have one less tool to use against us."

"I found it in the lake."

"Yes. They don't like water much."

"Then we've both got to dump the thing in the lake. It's what you've already done. Let's go."

In a flash, I was back in the crawl space. Shit. I put as many fireworks as I could into my knapsack. They were coming up the stairs, their honey-dripping voices in Jack's ear. "An antique. Sentimental value. Looks like a sextant. Do you know what that is?" Shit, no time to get out the window.

Unless I made some time. The smoke bomb is a sissy weapon, but I needed cover and distraction. So, three smoke bombs, lit one, two, three.

"Can you climb down?" The Eye nodded. I tossed it toward the tree, and it landed on the nearest branch. I jumped for the same branch. It sagged dangerously, like it might break, but that just meant I was closer to the sandy, poison ivy-infested hill. I swung and landed with a thump.

The Eye scurried down after me, then leapt into my hands. I heard Mom yelling upstairs, screaming "fire" and my name, probably hoping I was in flames.

I walked around the cottage and toward the beach. I tried to act cool, hoping no one would notice me, that the freaks inside didn't have a way to let the freaks outside know what was going on. No such luck.

The perfect people stopped jogging, frolicking, sunning. With one mind, they closed in. I lit a bottle rocket and stuck it in the sand at a low angle. It exploded right on a guy's bare chest, but he just glowed green for a moment and kept walking toward me. The neighbor kids ran for cover. I threw an M80 at a woman's face. Boom! She looked like a cartoon—sooty face, burnt hair—but she kept walking toward me, smiling. "Fireworks are dangerous," she said. They blocked my way to the lake.

I looked at the Eye. "Do you know what a Frisbee is?" I asked. It nodded. "Do it."

The Eye shaped itself as aerodynamically as it could. "Hide until they're dead," I said. I threw it up and toward the lake. The perfect people reached and jumped but couldn't get a hand on it. It splashed into the water.

"Stay in there, and keep quiet," I shouted. Then I smiled at the perfect crowd. "Now, what the fuck are you looking at?"

"Where were you?" Baum was back, but they had noticed his absence.

"What do you mean?" he stammered.

"We can see a time break, no matter how infinitesimal."

Baum waved them off. "Wait. Just a moment, something's happening."

Baum saw what happened next in the future. He saw the Eye go into the lake, then what happened on the porch. "Oh no." He bent over and threw up on the woman's shoes.

The woman growled down at him. "Where were you, and what did you see, you little piece of excrement?"

Baum looked up, vomit still dripping from his mouth. "Nuts," he said, and he dove through the shutters and onto the porch. Then he jumped the railing, ran to the lake and threw the Eye in. "And stay there," he yelled. His heart had never felt so good.

He rolled up his sleeves and strode back to his cottage. "You'd best leave my wife and boys out of this, you filthy witches," he shouted. "This is between you and me." And then he said some words that he had learned in the Dakotas.

I walked slowly back to our porch. The perfect people on the beach snarled at me. I snarled back, daring them to lay a finger on me. I was enjoying myself—as crazy as this was, my life made a kind of sense. One thing I couldn't figure though: not one of them laid a hand on me, even though I could tell they wanted to. What held them back?

The younger kids were pointing, "Tip's in trouble, Tip's in trouble." But when I got to the porch, the kids were gone, back to their cottages or down the beach. Or maybe I was gone—maybe the perfect people wanted some private time.

Mom fixed Bloody Marys for a batch of perfects, three women and one man, like nothing had happened, no smoke bombs, no scene on the beach, nothing. She had always tried to ignore me, and now she had fully succeeded. Her eyes—truly scary, because I was nowhere in them.

Up close to the perfects again, I could tell. These were the same people I'd seen in the Eye, eighty years ago. If anything, they looked younger, their day and hour closer.

They held Jack's hands tightly. His pain hurt me; his anger reflected mine. I had challenged them, so they went after him?

"Tippi, these are—oh, I'm so silly, what are your names again?"

They introduced themselves: Mr. Noam King, Ms. Jen Ginger, Ms. Vicky East and Ms. Vicky West. Real cute. Time to cut the bullshit. "Ms. West, aren't you supposed to be dead?"

That didn't faze her. "The office continues after the particular incarnation's retirement."

I didn't ask if that meant "successor," like she had told Baum. Instead, "Why are you still here?"

"Now, Tippi," Mom said, but no one listened.

Ms. West bent to speak to me, nose to nose. "What you threw in the lake—it's my sign of office. We want it back."

I felt something like memory, the right way to say it. "I will not serve you."

"Pride. That's good. But inappropriate now."

Mom, still without a clue: "Oh, just ignore her when she's like this, and she'll calm down."

Splat! Ms. West whacked the back of Mom's head. It squashed in like a pumpkin, and she was down dead. Ms. West smiled. "Not as if you cared for her. Not as if she knew anything."

I was stunned. Jack wailed, "Momby, Momby, Momby."

Ms. West covered her ears. "Mr. King, the boy, if you please."

With one arm, Mr. King seized Jack. He straightened his finger, and his fingernail grew, extending like a knife, which he held to Jack's throat. Jack stopped wailing.

Ms. West pointed. "Him, you care about. Go to the lake, and retrieve the Oculus. Now."

I looked at Jack, and then I knew. Why they wouldn't kill Baum or me, why they could kill Mom and threaten Jack. I couldn't cry now. I spoke over my feelings like I was onstage again, the Mayor of Munchkin City.

"Go ahead. He doesn't have a future anyway."

Jack stared at me, open mouthed at my betrayal. Whatever he said next, whatever he did, I deserved it.

But the little creep just grinned at me. "You know!"

Now I cried a bit. "Yeah, I guess I do. They do too, I guess."

"Yep." The little creep was relieved. Must have been hard, keeping it secret that he knew he was going to die. Why the adults thought they could hide it from him, I don't know—he'd been reading anatomy texts since kindergarten.

Ms. West had backed away from me and my tears. For the first time, she looked truly teed. Good. "Understand," she hissed, "resist us, and you will only have a little more time, a few decades at most. Understand, join us, and you will be like us. Perfect."

I just laughed. "I'd rather be dead than be like you." And for once, I really meant it, all the way.

I wiped my tears, and the perfect people flinched. Another idea. I spat at Ms. West. The goober hit her right on the cheek and sizzled like an egg. But she didn't melt, she just wiped it off and cackled. "Understand, deary, that water and your precious bodily fluids only piss us off. Understand, my pretty, there are many ways to die—some of them much more unpleasant than others." Mr. King moved his nail from Jack's throat and pointed at Jack's eye.

But both Jack and I shook our heads. What these witches didn't understand was what modern medicine had in store for Jack. I'd seen it in the movies—no fantasyland's idea of torture could compare. Still, I couldn't bear this. I had to have a way to stop them.

Maybe I did—the one name they didn't want to hear might have the power. I yelled to the lake. "Oz, if you can hear me—"

Ms. West smacked me across the face. "Never, ever, say that name again. Kill the boy."

And they killed Jack.

Mr. King drew his nail across Jack's throat and sliced off his head. The blood sprayed out—worse than any animal. The spray sizzled when it hit their skin. And Jack just fell to the porch in two pieces, and soon the blood stopped spraying 'cause the little guy didn't have much to start with, and his chest wasn't moving, and he was dead.

"Now, how much pain can we give this one without disturbing the timeline? Let us begin."

I fell to the ground as if beaten. But I'd never give in to them. My cut hand ached, and I felt what to do.

Jack's pooling blood prophesied my own magic, coming soon, but I needed that magic now. With pure rage, I mashed my face and hands into his blood and smeared it in quick motions over my arms and legs. I stared up at them with my eyes truly crazy now. "Touch me now, fuckers." Then I raised a bloody, throbbing palm to the sun. "Motherfucking Oz, come. Now."

A bright gash ripped open the blue sky, rainbows refracting on its edges. The perfect ones raised voices and arms against it, but they were too late. The Gump was already here.

Of course, I didn't know then it was a Gump. What I saw looked like a flying bed beating the air with rotating palm fronds like a helicopter. The pilot seemed to be wearing a mask with a face painted on it, straw sticking out from his neck. Three beings quickly lowered themselves from the Gump with bed-sheet ropes. One was a woman, broad-shouldered in overalls, wearing tight pigtails and chewing on tobacco, carrying an old shotgun that would scare any elephant. The others were both robots, one tin-colored carrying an axe that was too big for just trees, the other copper-colored with a ray gun and a bomb-like ticking sound.

I've never seen people move as fast as the perfect ones, dashing off the porch to the beach, rushing to gather with their fellows and get out of Dodge.

The big woman saluted me. "Dorothy Gale, special ops. Got a Wicked infestation I see." She pointed at the pilot and twirled her finger in the air. He gave her a floppy thumbs up and pressed a button on the head/dashboard. A small, whirling funnel took shape on the shore.

Ms. Gale bent down, her face right in mine. "What did you do with the Wicked Bitch's Eye?"

I pointed to the lake.

"Hah! Outstanding. Good to be rid of it. Damn, she was a hard one to kill."

Huh? "Not just a water bucket?"

"What do you think?" She cocked the gun, grinning like, well, me on real bad day. "Fluid was administered through some well-placed holes."

I looked down at where Jack and Mom lay. Couldn't get sick yet. "Got any magic on you?"

Ms. Gale stopped grinning. "Tin, get some life powder on these civilians."

The axe robot sprinkled something on Jack. The robot was weeping loudly. "Shaddup!" Ms. Gale ordered. "Giving you AIs hearts was the dumbest thing Oz ever did."

"AIs?"

"Tin Man and Tik-Tok. All sufficiently advanced magic is indistinguishable from technology. Hey, you'd better look away, kid. It's like sausages and Munchkin politics—you don't want to know. Look at the beach action instead."

A mini-cyclone chased the perfect people up and down the beach. It would catch one, and he or she would disappear in a blur. The ray gun robot helped herd them toward the funnel. Ms. Gale sighed. "Cyclone generator—a magnificent machine. One hundred percent pure chaos."

Behind me, Jack came to. "Oh no, not again." He ran away upstairs, sobbing. I followed a step, then went back to Ms. Gale. "Couldn't you take him with you?"

"Sorry, kid—in any world, his time is short." She looked me over, blood-smeared toes to bloodstained face. "You, on the other hand, might be real Oz material."

I was more angry than flattered. "Why would I want to go to a boring place like Oz?"

"Boring? Hah. Kid, Oz is America's magical twin—and like America, it's a lot of things, but boring isn't one of them. Just when you think you know it, you discover another kingdom and another adventure. And plenty to scare you—you've seen some of it."

"But Baum, the movie..."

"Frank's just a wimp. We need a few good witches, and you're already better than most. What do you say, kid?"

I looked up toward Jack's bedroom. "Nah, thanks, but I've got to stay here."

"Suit yourself. Oz knows, plenty to do on this side of the Sands."

"The future I saw?"

"Soulless zombies, no magic, no childhood, you dead—that one?"

"Yeah."

On the beach, Ms. West was sprinting away from the cyclone, shouting, "You can't stop us. The future is ours." Then the funnel caught her. Blip. Gone with the wind.

"Don't believe everything you hear." Ms. Gale whistled, and the Gump was hovering overhead. "That the last of them? Good. Wait! What about her?" She pointed at Mom. "Can't have the bourgeois adult oppressors asking too many questions."

Axe robot powdered Mom with more emotional restraint than with Jack, then climbed back into the Gump with the rest of the Oz force. I turned from Mom's regeneration to watch the Gump depart. As they flew away, they sang. "We are the hollow men, we are the stuffed men, marching together, headpiece filled with straw, kick ass!"

Mom came to. "Too many Bloodies." I ran upstairs to hold on to Jack for dear life.

It's the year 2000, and I'm at my computer, but I'm still no genius. That was Jack, and he's not here anymore. The perfect people seem to have more worshippers than ever, but it's not their future yet, which is better than things might have been.

I have a daughter, Jacqueline. She doesn't seem to mind being a girl at all—guess these days, in my house, there's little reason to mind. Mostly, Jackie's just a kid—a little hyper, but that's OK with me. My little pumpkin head. She's read all the Oz books—she's not perfect, after all.

The Eye is still in the lake somewhere. Sometimes I'm tempted, but I really don't need it anymore. I saw the rest of Baum's story the way Jack would—part books, part magic. And, despite my punching him, Baum had left a gift for me, and for Jack.

When Baum returned to his cottage, it was empty. A wind had blown through the open shutters. His wife and boys were upstairs sleeping in bed. His Oz manuscript, however, was gone. Had they gotten what they wanted?

No one ever mentioned Baum's shouting of that evening. It had been a wild night, and, after all, he was a writer.

The rest of August, 1899, Baum thoroughly rewrote his Oz story. He didn't want the Wickeds bothering him anymore, so he made changes, obscuring the truth to appease them. The evil witches would be ugly, the good witches pretty—he found that easier to write anyway.

He gave his new story to his publisher that fall, and the next year saw the publication of *The Wizard of Oz*. Well, he had gotten that much from the Eye anyway.

He avoided writing more about Oz, again to appease the Wicked. But Oz was all anyone wanted from him, and like any good showman, he had to please his audience. So, without the Eye to guide him, he wrote a sequel, *The Marvelous Land of Oz*. The idea came from that summer of '99. It would not be about a nice little girl like Dorothy.

Unlike Baum, I kept my mouth completely shut about Oz—I didn't want worse than Ritalin. In the fall, we went back to Lansing. They just sent me to Catholic school, which wasn't such a bad thing in the late '70s. From his faraway kingdom of financial support, Dad issued his decree—he wouldn't pay for any fancy institution, and anything else would be too embarrassing. Besides, Jack was getting sicker and didn't want me to go anywhere. His opinion counted now.

Mom complained that she was exhausted all the time, though no doctor was able to find anything wrong with her. So I took care of Jack a lot between his hospital stints and treatments.

I spent all my free time with him, which reduced the trouble I got into a whole lot. I forgot about my hair, so it grew out a little bit. Jack was tired a lot too, so I read to him. I got good at it. I think it was then that I realized who the woman at the year 2000 computer was going to be.

That Christmas, my godmother (Catholics have the non-fairy kind) gave me a first edition of *The Land of Oz*. I read Jack the story in the hospital. It's about a little boy named Tip and his friend Jack and their witch of a guardian Mombi. And near the end, everyone is searching for the princess who disappeared around the same time Tip first showed up.

Jack laughed and coughed. "Uh oh. I don't think you're going to like the end of this story."

As always, the little creep was right.

A Sense of Closure

It doesn't look it, but it took me ten years to write this one. "Closure" started as a standard SF cautionary tale, and like any societal scold, those can be pretty dull. But every couple of years, I returned to the draft to focus more on the central character. In the end, I realized that he was another instance in my writing of a disturbed person finding the right futuristic job, and rewrote him and the story accordingly, sans caution.

The first draft of "Closure" was a submission to the *Strange Horizons* weekend workshop in Oregon, 2002. The advice I got at that workshop didn't lead immediately to a greatly improved story, but it did direct me to attend Clarion, and that led to the other stories in this collection.

Michael loved his work. He was the last coroner in the eastern United States. But no Younger said "coroner" anymore, nor used the D-word to describe Michael's concern. If one had to speak of It, one said "closure."

Even using such euphemisms, Michael couldn't talk about his job. Such talk could really close a party. He'd heard people whisper about his contact with his ever-diminishing case load—"He has to touch them." He couldn't admit that he didn't mind that part at all.

Within minutes after arriving at the office, Michael received a report of a case: an Old One formerly named Dr. Oppenheimer. The case had been well into its 100s, which was the oldest the nano gizmos could do for the pre-2030s. It was a promising start to his day. Michael would probably find only natural causes, but as the number of cases had dwindled, he had insisted that every closure come through his office. Michael enjoyed the opportunities for fieldwork. He liked entering a case's home, and he always enjoyed getting his hands on a case.

Michael carefully folded his lab coat (a discreet uniform for Youngers) and left it in his office. He wore his traditional black suit, which would be comforting to any Old Ones who might try to block his entry. At Dr. Oppenheimer's, that Old One would be the former spouse of the case, Dr. Arlene Gable.

Dr. Oppenheimer had lived in the Philadelphia suburbs, so Michael got there via maglev and government car only a little after the local med-tech rescue squad, though he begrudged every minute. The case house was typical for the Old Ones: stone exterior, no smart or self-growing structures. The organic gardens were immaculate and beautiful, as if the occupants were planning to use them for aeons, not the handful of years they had left.

Even after decades, Michael still dreaded the initial contact with the former spouse—it delayed a more important contact. But he straightened himself, and his face relaxed into an expression of seriousness. "Begin record, Dr. Oppenheimer, one," he said, and rang the door.

Dr. Gable, a cliché of unaltered Old One features (gray hair, wrinkly skin, alive they all looked the same), greeted Michael. She was already in formal black—heaven, did they ever wear anything else? Her face was as serious as her clothes, but calm. Michael's dread lessened. She squinted at him with her imperfect vision. "You're with the coroner's office?"

Ah, good. He appreciated how Old Ones often didn't use the euphemisms. "Yes, Doctor, I'm Michael O'Neill, the coroner."

"Please come in. I'll take you to him."

As Dr. Gable led him through the house, she kept her collected demeanor. Michael grew anxious. The case had been elderly, but even wives who hated their husbands were a little rattled by their timely closures.

In the bedroom, the rescue squad had screened off the sheet-covered case. Michael never let them do anything else. "Dr. Gable, if you'd please leave the room—I'll only be a moment."

Michael advanced to the bed, and slowly pulled down the sheet. The back of his hands brushed against the cold, stiffened case, sending the familiar jolt up his arms. He stared at the case silently. It was his moment.

Michael gently touched the palm of the case for its subcu chip data. The palm felt dry as worn leather, cold as ice cream. He loved his work.

Michael then slowly passed his living hands over the entire body of the case, lightly brushing its cool skin and hair as the bioscan chips in his own palms probed for data. Michael made his observations aloud for the benefit of the recording chip in his head. "Case ID'ed as former Dr. Oppenheimer. Unenhanced genome. Case found in bed, perhaps closed while sleeping." Michael took a breath. "Case is lying straight in the bed, arms relaxed at its side, face directly upwards." Not a natural sleep posture.

And bless it if it weren't as unsurprised as its former spouse, with the hint of a smile on its face. Not the standard case features, even in rigor. Michael would have to check for self-help.

Michael carefully smoothed the sheet, his hands again brushing against the case. Then he touched his palms to his external pad, copying and transmitting their information, but not the tingly cold fire that still haunted them.

The house's lack of auto-security meant that Michael needed to talk to the witness. He sat with Dr. Gable in the living room in very antique but surprisingly comfortable chairs. Michael referred to the case as "him" in Old One fashion to avoid offense.

"Did you move him?"

"No." Her tone was already hostile, making him miss the tearful sobbing routine. Why did the question bother her?

"Was your husband depressed?"

"No."

"Did he ever say he felt useless, that it was time to move on?"

"Certainly not! Mr. O'Neill, my husband was quite philosophical about growing old and dying. It may be difficult for you to understand, but he both loved life and was reconciled to leaving it whenever the time came."

Her protest was excessive, perhaps covering some uncertainty, but Michael backed off. "My apologies, Doctor. I admire your husband's perspective." That was half-true: as much as Michael enjoyed his work, he hated the usual self-pitying bull on an Old One self-help call. They should cling to every blessed minute of their short time (even if it cut down his caseload), but some just couldn't wait to close. Just like his parents.

Dr. Gable answered his questions, but volunteered nothing. Her intense gaze distracted him. Could she see how much he enjoyed his work?

While Michael groped for another set of questions, Dr. Gable asked her own: "Do you actually care what happened to my husband?"

"Yes, ma'am, I do."

"That seems extremely unlikely. Please, let's get this over with."

Michael glanced at his pad, which had just confirmed the finding of natural causes. Natural causes fit with its age, but Michael wasn't satisfied yet. Dr. Gable's cold replies gave him no sense of the case's history. He was about to check his pad, then remembered that, in an Old One's house, the information might be right in front of him. Physical photos and printed news articles nearly a century old hung on the wall, and it only took a glance to refresh Michael's overburdened memory. Of course. This case had been *the* Dr. Oppenheimer, the head of the Methuselah Project team.

Another Oppenheimer had built the first nuke, but the blast that Methuselah made in 2030 had forever split all humanity: the genetically enhanced Youngers born after, immortal for all practical purposes (except when Michael was called in), and the unenhanced Old Ones, getting fewer by the year. One fewer now.

The effort Methuselah had made was immense. Nature had been very particular about closing her children. Tracking down all the redundant ways that humans had evolved to wear out and fixing them took many disciplines, many years, and a few premature closures. Nothing like it had happened before or since.

At the thought of Oppenheimer's importance, Michael's hands tingled. "I'm sorry for your loss, for all our loss," he said. "He was a great man."

"Thank you. I'm sure he appreciates that." Creepy present tense, no subjunctive.

"Did you work with him on Methuselah?"

"That was how we met."

"Then we all owe you thanks."

She grimaced at this. "Are we done?"

To his surprise, she extended her hand in old-fashioned farewell. Michael gripped it tentatively, and felt her skin against his. Nearly her time too.

As his car drove him to the station, Michael's hands still hummed with the knowledge of all they had touched. So intimate. How different things would be here later. A cheerful-looking utility vehicle would pull up. Only someone from Michael's department would recognize its true function. Bots would shove the case into a festive box that in no way conformed to a human shape, and indelicately load the box into the vehicle. Usually, the bots would just dispose of it. But Dr. Gable would want a funeral—an anti-social anachronism that Michael appreciated.

At the station, Michael reviewed the pad's confirmation of his finding. Spontaneous heart failure. Nanites could keep a coronary artery clear, but unless the heart was replaced, the whole organ wore out. Old Ones didn't want their pumps outliving their fragile brains. That dilemma was their own fault. After the Methuselah Project, the Old Ones hadn't continued to expand its remedies to fully address their own aging, and the Youngers lost concern and even the ability to discuss the problem.

One annoying incongruity: the heart was the *only* thing wrong with this case. For such an ancient Old One, this seemed too precise a closure. Michael would have to review this file again. But more importantly, how many Methuselah veterans were still left? It might be unprofessional, but Michael wanted to be ready for each of their cases.

When Michael boarded the decades-old maglev, it seemed down-in-the-mouth, except for the ventilators, which shone like new. Somebody must have a thing for fresh air. Somebody cared. Probably an Old One—they were always carping about the temperature. Despite their endless complaints, he would feel a loss when the last Old One closed. He would miss the work, and the intimacy it brought him.

As the maglev abruptly slowed into Washington City, Michael noticed a piece of graffiti on a wall not yet cleaned by the bots: "THE GRIM CLOSER IS COMING." Michael shook his head, then went back to his office.

Thirty-seven days later, a closure Michael had been screening for came up on his pad. The case's name had been Abramovich, another Old One doctor who had worked on the Methuselah Project.

For night fieldwork, Michael threw on his trench coat and broad-brimmed hat, and tried to contain his excitement. This case had closed in northwest Washington City, conveniently near Michael's office. Another quaint old house in an Old One neighborhood, but the street-lit yards of the neighboring houses had gone to jungle. Empties. "Begin record. Dr. Abramovich, one."

Abramovich's file showed no friends or family in residence, so Michael was unpleasantly surprised when a Younger woman answered the door and barred his immediate entry. Of course, he couldn't tell her age, though she had fixed her appearance at younger than prime. She wore black retro—disturbing on a Younger not in Michael's profession. "Are you here for... it?" Her voice quavered; her eyes were red from crying.

"Yes. What is your name, please?"

"Lily Sheroy."

"OK. Please show me the way, Lily, and I'll take care of everything." Lily took him to the kitchen.

At first, it seemed so much easier to deal with a Younger. But when they got to the kitchen, she asked, "Can I come in with you?"

"But Lily, it's in there."

"It's OK. I'll be fine."

They crowded into the kitchen. Michael stood over the case, which had crumpled in a heap of limbs on the cracked tile floor. Lily's face quivered, agitated. Michael asked, "Are you sure?"

"Oh, I'm fine. But don't you have some, like, questions to ask me?" She didn't take her eyes off the case.

"Yes, but they can wait." He was anxious to begin his observations.

"Here is fine."

Blessed odd. "OK. What relation were you to Dr. Abramovich?"

"I was his friend."

"Friend?" Socializing with Old Ones?

"Um, you know. Girlfriend." She blushed slightly and shifted her legs awkwardly.

"Oh." Youngers shacking up with Old Ones—weird stuff, that. Decrepitude turned some people on. But at least she seemed sincerely surprised by the inevitable. "What happened?"

"I heard him fall. When I got here, it was already done." She lightly bit her lip.

"Did you notice anything different about his behavior lately?"

"Lately? No, he was always a little different."

With Lily still hanging about, Michael would have to be brief. He touched the case's palm—leather and ice. Lily made a small sigh. He ignored her and commenced his examination without enthusiasm. "Case ID'ed as Dr. Abramovich. Unenhanced genome. Case appears to have been getting an alcoholic drink in kitchen. Case has its eyes closed, relaxed features, despite awkward position." Michael turned back towards Lily, his hands shaking with angry suspicion. "Did you touch it?"

She turned pale, then red. "No. Never. I know better than to touch it." True? She could be feeling guilt at the mere idea of contact. But she certainly had thought about touching it. Blessed odd, and annoying.

Michael pointed at the kitchen counter. "Is that its?" Lily looked away from the case long enough to nod. "Case had placed a watch-style timepiece on kitchen counter." But why had Abramovich been so concerned about the time? Like the Oppenheimer case from more than a month ago, it showed no signs of surprise, anxiety, or struggle, despite what must have been an abrupt and perhaps painful closure.

Uncomfortable, Michael wanted to leave. "I apologize if I've upset you," he said. "You got your pad?" He touched it and gave Lily his data. "Give me a call later, if you think of anything, or if you just want to talk." Michael didn't know why he had said that—psychotherapy and the living were both far from his area of comfort.

Back in his office, Michael reviewed the pad's confirmation. Cerebrovascular event. Nanites, kept busy with many pinpoint blockages, would eventually miss a major vessel's rupture. As with the Oppenheimer case, absolutely nothing else was wrong with Abramovich besides the immediate cause of death. Maybe this was what was bothering him. Such precise closures happened, but they weren't statistically normal. A heart or cerebrovascular failure was usually the end result of a long process which put pressure on different parts of the body and kept the nanites working beyond their capacity in more than one area. He should have seen evidence of this strain in both of the Methuselah cases.

True, the veterans of Methuselah would have the technical skills to close themselves or others without leaving a trace, but such secrecy was unlikely for self-help, and Michael couldn't imagine any motive for intentional closure. What was the point of shaving a few years off an Old Ones life?

Michael went back to his office, but he couldn't get much work done. He remembered his father, and how he used rant about the world's decline before he closed himself out of it.

The next week, Michael got a call from Lily. "You said to call if I, well, I could use someone to talk to."

"Sure. I should be here all day."

"Not there. That might be too much for me." Michael wasn't sure what she meant. "Maybe dinner." Michael remained silent. "I know a real food place, no exotic pharmaceuticals or toxins."

"That sounds great." Traditional was his style.

For the traditional restaurant, Lily came fully clothed, no spray-ons, but figure highlighted by a different black dress, nothing mournful about it. She exceeded Michael's usual experience, which wasn't of the living. Cases often wore their least formal accoutrements.

To each other's amusement, they both ordered wine—very retro. Michael awkwardly fell back on his usual interrogatory approach to people. "So, how long did you know Dr. Abramovich?"

"A while. How do you feel about your work?"

"I enjoy it. I like puzzles." This was Michael's standard answer.

"I don't believe you."

"I like the stories." Standard answer number two.

"I still don't believe you."

Michael was caught up short. No one had ever questioned him like this about his job. He did not want to be having this discussion. "Hey, it's just a job, brings in the credits like any other."

"Now you're just making stuff up. You could be licensed for anything to get your credits. Or you could mortgage your future."

"No, I need to do something."

"Then why this thing?"

Michael felt exposed, like a naked case. "I don't know," he muttered. "I like the work. And I'm not a people person."

Lily's voice became gentle, soothing. "You shouldn't say that. You've been very kind, meeting with me like this."

Michael smiled weakly. "Well, this is kind of business."

"Tell me," she whispered, "about the business."

So he did. To his own surprise, he told her about case after case, each one worse than the last, each time expecting her to be horrified, disgusted, repelled. But the more he told, the more she wanted to know. Details poured out. He spoke them hushed and near to her, afraid that the other patrons would overhear "complete and irreparable dismemberment" and "total cerebral necrosis." Her face was flushed, her breathing rapid, but she was not horrified. She was excited.

"Take me home."

Michael had misjudged her. It wasn't decrepitude that got her. It was closure. Her interest in turn aroused him. Hers wasn't the same as his interest in the cases, but perhaps it would be enough.

Home for Lily was the same place—strange, as not many Youngers would stay in an Old One case home. Going home with a case witness was unprofessional, so Michael silently reported the violation to himself, and gave himself a stern reprimand.

They entered the quiet house. Without a word they went into the bedroom. Lily took off her dress and lay back on the case's huge oak bed. "Show me what you do. Please."

Michael touched her palm, troubling with its soft heat. He then slowly ran his trembling hands just above her entire body. Her face: "Case ID'ed as Lily Sheroy." Her shoulders and breasts: "Enhanced genome." Her hips and thighs: "Case found in bed, perhaps closed while sleeping." His hands clenched to keep from grasping her warm flesh. "Appears," Michael drew a sharp breath, "beautiful. So beautiful."

"Touch me," she insisted, the most intimate words inviting the rare chance of irreparable harm at another's hands. He touched her.

Michael felt the strange urgency that animated Lily. A contagious sense that this moment, this act, was unique. Despite his peculiar job and tastes, Michael had been with many women in his many years, and for them and him sex was something that had happened hundreds of times before and would happen thousands of times after, world without end amen. With Lily, it was as if there were no certainty of a next time.

Afterwards, they lit one of Abramovich's cigars. "Careful, those things will kill you." The joke was as stale and tasteless as the cigar, but they laughed anyway. They shared the cigar, and Lily spoke of meeting Abramovich.

"I'm second generation ageless; my parents had the pull to shut off their sterilization genes. After all that trouble having me, they rapidly lost interest in my development. I appreciated the lack of scrutiny. Between their credits and my fully mortgaged future, I was indefinitely set. You know the coma quest party set?"

"Yeah, I've seen them."

"Professionally?"

"Um hmm."

"Well, I ran with them, sucking down expensive exotics and hemorrhaging blood and credits in medical repairs. In my last trip to the hospital, I woke up to the vision of this old face gazing into mine, kind of quizzical and bemused. My doctor. For me, it was love at first sight, though whether my need for romance or a parent got me off is difficult to say."

"You always this self-analytical?" *And always so wrong?*

"Anyway, I cleaned up my act and pursued him. It took some work, but eventually he relented to my attentions."

"I sympathize. What was he like?"

"A moody duck. Most of the time, always joking, the brightest boy in the room. But then he would get into his vodka, and get all depressed. Old Ones get like that a lot."

"I know. What did he talk about then?"

"He would ask me weird things. One of his favorites was, 'If you were god and could change history, just like that, what would you do?'"

"Change history? Like what?"

"Like nukes back when there were still wars. Suppose you could have gotten rid of all the nukes before 2020 and saved all those people in South Asia. Maybe you make everyone forget all about nukes, or make them think they couldn't work. Would you do it?"

Michael opened his mouth, but she held a finger to his lips. "Be careful. No nukes might mean no nuke power, different history, maybe even no Methuselah Project. So, what do you say now?"

Michael felt confused. He hadn't even thought about nukes for years until the Oppenheimer closure. "I don't know," he murmured.

"That's alright, sweetie. Give it some thought." She closed her eyes. "All those people with that dark force hovering over their heads, day by day, never knowing."

Michael shivered slightly. Lily held him. "Shhh. We're safe." She sighed. "So very, very safe."

This did not calm his excitement, but he soon slept anyway. He awoke hungry for her, and she was already waiting for him. When he finally left in the morning, he hoped for a next time, but he wasn't *certain*.

For the first time in decades, Michael arrived late to work. He made up for tardiness with the inspiration to review all of the Methuselah cases. At the very least, he would have more stories for Lily.

He requested the relevant records from his colleagues around the globe. In the nearly 100 years since Methuselah, most of the project members' files had closed years ago—some of them were blessed old to start with. But more of the survivors had closed in the last two years than one would expect by chance. Most were NC, most heart or cerebrovascular failure. He looked at them in chronological order, and they almost seemed to alternate—heart, brain, heart, brain.

That was when he felt his own heart almost stop.

The closures didn't just *seem* to alternate. They alternated *exactly*. For the past two years, heart followed brain followed heart.

But this was insane. The minute a human being bothered to look at this data, he saw the problem.

No, he couldn't fixate on the lack of rational motive anymore. Someone was rushing closures, shortening Michael's period of joy that would end with the last Old One case, and accomplishing something else that Michael couldn't imagine.

Michael had to act fast. In all his decades of work, he had never been there before the case closed. If a case was anticipated, bots were notified, not him. The possibility of anticipating a closure overwhelmed him. He paced his office, trying to think calmly. A Methuselah team veteran would close soon. Another Methuselah or someone near to them might be his perp.

When he searched for the remaining Methuselahs, he distrusted the
narrow results the databases gave him. He knew of two people who could
answer his questions in the flesh, and only one that he actually wanted to
see again.

The door at the Abramovich case house was unlocked; Michael walked
in. He decided not to record—not proper procedure, but he was in charge.
He found Lily packing, and felt something like closure grip his heart. "Going
somewhere?"

She turned, startled. "Allah on a rock, couldn't you knock or
something?"

"Sorry, forgot the house wouldn't tell you." A lame excuse, but she was
the one behaving like a perp. "So, where are you off to?"

"That's none of your business for now." Her light tone rang false
to him.

"Yes, I'm afraid it is." He approached her. "Ever think about closing
someone?"

The question sank in. "Oh, this is... your business?"

He was right in her face now. He spoke with his profession's unearthly
calm. "We can start with an easier one: have you ever met any other
Methuselah scientists?"

"You think I *killed* him?" Her anger cut through all euphemism.

"Lily, just answer the question."

"But I would never... just because of what I've done to myself..."

Michael grabbed her shoulders. This violation of Younger taboo shocked
her into attention. "Lily, I'm sorry, but there's no blessed time. There's going
to be another Methuselah case soon."

Lily turned pale and shuddered, but not just with fear. "A Methuselah
case? Oh god. She meant you. She said someone would be asking me
questions."

"Who?"

"Dr. Gable."

"Arlene Gable? You know her? Let's go."

"I can come?" Her voice quavered; her face had passed beyond
excitement into a surreal awe.

Once on the maglev, Michael said, "Tell me about Dr. Gable."

"Arlene. She wanted me to call by her first name, like a Younger. Really
weird."

That didn't sound like the Dr. Gable he had met. "OK, what else?"

"She was one of my Doc's few friends. When she visited, she ignored me, the way they do sometimes. She and the Doc used to talk about how no one gave a damn anymore about anything—same old Old One crap, probably just to piss me off. Sometimes I listened secretly, which is easy in an old house, but they talked softly, so it was hard to hear everything. Once, Arlene was going on about 'speeding things up,' and my Doc didn't seem concerned. 'I know it's unlikely,' she said. 'But what if someone passes the test too soon?' And then it was like she knew I was listening. 'And she'll be here to answer the winner's questions about us,' she said, like I was a problem. Scary. She knew you'd be asking about them."

As the car drove them to Dr. Gable's house, Michael felt the familiar dread of her initial reaction, but this time was uncertain why. With the doubtful exception of Lily, he had never paid a second professional call on the living. Lily seemed lost in her own dark imaginings. Michael had considered leaving Lily at the station, but told himself that he needed to keep an eye on her.

He subvocaled, "Begin record, Dr. Gable, one," and rang the bell.

Michael had to stifle a shout when Dr. Gable greeted them at the door, still very much alive. Instead of black, she wore a faux-Oriental robe.

"Oh my," she said. "You're here. And just in time. Please come in."

This warm response was so different from his previous visit that he wondered about unrepaired dementia. "Doctor Gable, do you remember me?"

"Oh, I remember who you are. Your lady and I have also met. And you're Death's captain."

"Yeah, something like that." Unsettling word choice, but the metaphor was close enough.

"Then come in. Your boss has given me a message for you."

Michael was unarmed (causing cases wasn't his jurisdiction), but he remained calm in the face of mystery. He went in with Lily, following the slow movements of the Old One.

They came to the door of Dr. Gable's study. "Lily, dear, could you wait here? Michael and I need to speak privately." Michael nodded to Lily, and she sat in a chair in the hallway.

His host closed the door behind them. She motioned, and they sat in her old and comfortable chairs. She brought him tea, real unaltered tea, and smiled at him. "Such a nice girl." To the Old Ones, the Youngers would always remain boys and girls.

"You expected me."

"Oh yes. The test was fair. You cared enough to check the data. They said you didn't, and I agreed. But after your first visit, I looked at your file, and I saw you really did care, whatever your other motives."

"My file?"

"Oh yes. The others would generalize about Youngers' decadence, laziness and so on, but I knew, oh I knew, that it would come down to individual idiosyncrasies. Yours, and Lily's."

"Doctor—"

"Call me Arlene."

"Arlene." Just like Lily had said. The Old One's given name stuck in his throat. "How did you know I checked the data?"

"We Old Ones started most of the databases you use, and left some backdoors just to keep an eye on you Youngers." She looked directly into his eyes. "But that isn't why you're here, is it?"

"I'm trying stop some closures. Maybe your closure." But he couldn't bear her gaze.

Arlene shook her head. "You don't know yourself very well." She reached out and touched his cheek, fingers cold. "But that's all right. I know you."

Michael remembered himself. "Arlene, excuse my bluntness, but were you responsible for the closures of other Methuselah scientists?"

"Their deaths? Yes, dear. But not all of them."

Michael looked at his tea. Arlene must have noticed. "Don't worry, dear. I'm done with all that. I'm the last *scheduled* departure."

Michael struggled to remember the speech. "You are under arrest. You have the right to remain silent. Your remarks are being recorded by certified bio-chip—"

"Oh shush. No need for that. Surely you have better things to talk about."

He did, and only the old words for them made sense. "All the Methuselah scientists who *died* in the last two years, did you *kill* them?"

"Yes, dear. But not just me. All of them helped."

"They helped kill themselves?"

"Yes, dear. We all helped."

"Why? They still had some time left. Why death and murder?"

"Oh, no dear, it wasn't like that, though it's so sweet of you to care. No, we had to go before the gift arrived."

Michael felt a shiver through his hands and down his spine. "The gift?"

"Once upon a time, we gave our children a very precious gift. But they, and we, were too young for such a thing. We spoiled our children. They forgot the gift's value. For decades we left the puzzle of our own mortality for our immortal children to solve, but they couldn't be bothered from their other toys. So we've given you something else, dear. A new, even more precious gift, with its own difficult puzzle."

"Arlene, whatever you've done, you can stop it." He felt like a child pleading vainly with his mother about his bedtime.

"No, dear, I can't. But you can. You aren't afraid of the gift, or at least not merely afraid. You're uniquely qualified to make the decision."

"What decision?"

"Let me see your pad." She touched it. "I've given you the data on the gift. You can stop it anytime you like."

"But I still don't understand."

"I'm sorry, dear, there's no more time. I'm glad you found me. You're a good boy, if a little strange. I'm sorry our leaving has troubled you, but you'll soon know why we had to go, so soon, so soon. And I'm sorry, but you'll have to make the decision alone. Alone, alone, poor dear."

She winced, and grabbed her left arm. "Pain. Heart. My husband's way. Not supposed to hurt. Famous last words. Time to go. Goodbye, Captain." A smile. "Be seeing you."

She silently jerked again with pain. Michael sat frozen. She slumped in the chair. Then stillness. It was closed.

Lily quietly opened the door and walked towards the case. Michael stood up and stood in front of the case with her. Slowly, hands shaking, they reached out and touched the case's still warm face. Together, they shut its eyes. Together, they passed their hands over the case's entire body as Michael recorded their observations.

On the maglev back to Washington, Michael asked, "Lily, why were you packing?"

"Is this business or personal?"

"Personal."

"I was packing to stay at a hotel while they cleared the Doc's stuff out. I was making room for someone new to visit, someone who didn't need a dead man's stuff around to understand death. And, you know, love."

He did know, had always known, that death and love went together. Looking at Lily, he realized he had caught her urgency like a disease. Yes, disease. The ventilators on this train shone like those he'd seen before. Put there by someone who cared about the air and all the changes the air might carry.

Michael reported that he had arrived at Dr. Gable's too late. He kept her data to himself, and waited to see what blew in the wind.

Within the year, Youngers started to have "unexplained accidents." That is, they died and nobody knew why. Everything vital failed at once, and none of the Younger docs could put Humpty back together again. At first, just a trickle of cases. Then a steady stream. Soon a Styx.

He ran the stats on the Youngers' sudden deaths. The probability of death rose with the age of the Younger, but age alone wasn't determinative. Death could come to anyone, at any time. The financial implications alone were staggering.

Like death in the original style, this revised edition was terribly redundant. Without the help of the Methuselah members or their data, it would take many disciplines, many years, many lives before they could fix things again. Before that, they would have to admit the extent of the problem. Denial is always the first step.

What should he do? The original killers were already beyond punishment. Now, he was the killer for as long as he held onto the cure in Dr. Gable's data.

With their viral gift of genetic modification, the Methuselahs had wanted to restore the Youngers' sense of urgency, their need to do something while they still lived. The Old Ones had hoped that by the time the Youngers defeated death again, they (or at least the survivors) would be a little wiser, and would have outgrown the need for an end.

Michael didn't buy all this Old One propaganda mixed in with Arlene's data. This was not going to be a happier world. But he would have plenty of work for as long as he wanted, as long as he lived. With the increased case load, others came to work for his department, including Lily. She had the most important qualification. Like Michael, she loved the work.

For now, Michael felt right about his silence. Lily would sometimes ask her question again, the one about the nukes. "Let me think about it a little longer," he would say, and they would laugh. And at night they would hold each other like children in a thunderstorm, the feeling of a dark force hovering over their heads, day by day, never knowing. It was scary as heaven.

It felt like growing old together.

Inversions

Here's some golden-age SF twisted upside down and served with a cynical Irish heroine. Bon appétit!

I think the influence of my year as an expat is pretty evident here (though I don't think of modern Japan in this way at all). The story emerged from trying to create very alien aliens who were still fit subjects for human narrative. A simple rotation of 180 degrees did the trick.

Angie's Story

OK, Carol and me, we're flying upside down together, which is brilliant. Floaters hurry around us in a hundred directions. We're trying to blend in, so our personal dirigibles are blue-and-white, and my hair's in a tight bun. But it's shite. Up close, a Floater looks like two squids sewn together head to head with one set of tentacles holding on to an oval balloon with an arsehole, and I say so. "Though they're not the ugliest culchies of the galaxy by a long shot, I'll grant you that."

Carol's end of the com gets a bit matronizing and insubordinate. "Now Chief," she says, "some of us find them quite graceful, serene, and beautiful. And as for calling their air valve an 'arsehole'..."

I tune out. Carol's self-bollocking is as hard to hear as to watch. Even upside down with a shaved head and bones practically jabbing through, she isn't half-bad to look at, but I don't say so—this is a mission, not a colony. And exactly how far will this woman go to please the locals? Carol has too many questions about Floater fecking and too many Japanese prints with an "octopus and maiden" theme. I should have sent her home by now.

The wind is whipping my loose bits of uniform. Yeah, it's brilliant, and I'll miss it—if I survive my stunt today. Then Carol whines and whistles like gas being let out of a balloon at different speeds. It's formal Floater speak. "Jaysus, no need for that," I say. "Just me here."

"Just practicing, Chief. We've got to improve our connection with the Floating World."

Time for the bad news. "The Floating World has got their heads up their upside-down arses. The Floater Council has demanded the conference go arse upwards or they won't attend."

The Floater disinterest in the Sentience League Conference on the development of the local star systems has Carol gob-smacked. "Did you tell them the League is still subject to the presence fallacy? That an inverted vid link won't cut it?"

"They know they have to show up to be heard, if that's what you mean."

"This is awful. The Floating World will be surrounded, unable to grow. Why are we bothering with this damned tour? We need to do something!"

To restore morale, I confide more of my plan than I intended. "Look you, I don't want the Floating World to become a backwater for the rest of the galaxy to tramp through, not any more than you do. But don't you ever wonder the real reason why they need everybody to be upside down? I've heard rumors of a serious row when some Antarean birdhead had to right itself. And something nasty supposedly happened to a stickman who tried to pass using holo and prosthetics. So, you tell me: what exactly would we look like right-side-up to a Floater?"

Carol puts a hand to her head; she finally gets it. "We would look like a Floater who had stopped floating, and whose head was where... other things should be."

We're nearly at the spaceport now. The great floating beasties holding up the aboveground bits loom like flying whales. So I rush the rest. "I'm going to try to talk some more with that Council stooge, Cloud Flyer. He's all right, though still a bit stiff. Maybe he can help us figure out what's going on. That would be better than literally bending over backwards for them forever. But just talk probably won't work.

"So look," I say, "whatever happens after that, just follow my lead and do what I tell you. Got that?"

That was as much as I could tell her and still keep her shielded from the shite that would hit.

But it wasn't enough.

Cloud Flyer's Story

Cloud Flyer felt shameful, dirty even, but he knew his duty, so he waited, hungry and hovering. He was anxious to conduct this tour of the spaceport before his first meal, but he soon regretted arriving early. He had too much time to imagine the humans in their mission area with their unnatural orientation—feet towards the ground, head towards the sky. Even without feeding, thinking of that still made him queasy. He mustn't think of it for long. His many arms shuddered. Shameful. Dirty. Hungry.

His peripheral eyes nearly closed as he focused his front eyes on the horizon. He saw with relief the two humans approaching. One of them was the mission chief, her long hair tied close to her head (thank the Center!). She waved her arm in what appeared to be a threat display, but was actually the human form of greeting. Her uniform bore the symbols for her name, which began "A-N-G-E-L-A." The translator rendered this as "Highest Sky Female."

Before meeting Highest Sky, Cloud Flyer hadn't believed that any name could be more high and dishonorable than his own. But her straightforward alien simplicity made him more comfortable with her than the other humans, particularly the one accompanying her today.

The second human, "C-A-R-O-L" translated as "Song," said "Good day" to Flyer without the use of the chip. Cloud Flyer's floating bladder sucked in air with a whine of discomfort at her informality. Song's tricks were no longer amusing, and hints had been given that she might want to rest from her duties. Song's breathing device reassured Cloud Flyer more than any commonality— no matter how they tried, these groundlings remained alien.

He greeted them with more proper formality: "The Sun lowers to the Floating World." The humans received the translation through chips in their brains. Cloud Flyer would never consider such a device, and relied on transmissions from the human's chip to an external receiver. The tips of his arms curled in—implantation was sacrilege.

The other Council staff on the tour managed to avoid the obvious shame of proximity to the humans. But they did not seem to be aware of the less obvious embarrassment that troubled Cloud Flyer. This spaceport, the pride of the Council of Lords, was the only one on the planet. But going towards the sky, even to outer space, had never been the Floating World's priority, so the facility was woefully out of date. And aliens used the spaceport far more than the Floating World. Because Cloud Flyer was unusually conscious of these facts, the Council was able to humiliate him without even trying.

Some technicians led them through the facility. A camera hovered near by, recording the tour. Highest Sky flew next to Cloud Flyer. One of the technicians, Mid-Air Female, recited the dull facts in a high whine. "The spaceport covers an area of..."

Highest Sky spoke quietly to Cloud Flyer as Mid-Air whined on. "Would conversation regarding the Sentience League Conference be desirable?"

Cloud Flyer could only hide from an alien his outrage regarding the conference. But a direct refusal to attend would be impolite to the humans. Their well-meant attention to the situation only provoked uneasiness; they should imitate the Floating World and ignore the conference. Affirming the Council's answer would help them to see that.

"The Council of Lords has agreed we will attend if the participants assume a proper orientation, as you do here."

"Flyer, whatever the Council says, you know why that isn't possible, don't you?"

He did, but how could he admit that to her?

They flew through the control building, a hanging tower of horizontal plastic sheets with equipment hanging from each sheet, open on all sides to allow workers to fly in and out.

"Flyer, if we are going to help you, we have to know. Why is proper orientation so important?"

This was too much. "Silence would be preferable."

"If we knew why, we might be able to fix it. Can't you explain that to them? What about Lord Ground Grazer?"

Thank the Center the tour was over. Conversation would have to end as they hovered outside the port for questions and answers. "We are as we are named, Highest Sky Female," he stated with finality. At least they had this in common: being a high "sky" or "cloud" when food was on the ground. They were both a world away from a Ground Grazer.

Highest Sky just said, "You have misunderstood my name, Flyer," then burst away, as if to return to the mission area. But her dirigible unit jerked erratically. She announced, "It's busted. Going down." She spiraled towards the ground, and was already dangerously close to complete disorientation. Song saw this and called out to Cloud Flyer "Orientation change!"

Song followed her down, even as Highest Sky protested. "No Song, don't. I can handle this."

Cloud Flyer, to his own surprise, did not panic. "Floating World, turn away and shut all eyes!" Once Highest Sky reached the ground, she would have to remove her malfunctioning unit and completely invert herself—feet on the ground, head towards the sky. Shameful, dirty. Dangerous.

Completely closing off the peripheral vision required effort, and the technical personnel had not been taught emergency procedures. Mid-Air and Mist Breather, her mate, must have caught a glimpse of Highest

Sky disoriented on the surface. For a mating pair, the instinctual impulse overwhelmed all. They dashed for Highest Sky, arms thrashing.

"Sex death!" they whined in uncontrollable ecstasy.

"Keep your eyes closed!" Cloud Flyer commanded the others. They could not interfere without becoming frenzied themselves. Regrettably, the human must be lost.

Cloud Flyer knew what happened next only from the camera's carefully edited images, images that were also seen by the rest of the Floating World. Song was floating near Highest Sky when Mid-Air descended upon them. With Song between her and her prey, Mid-Air struck the unsuspecting Song, detaching her from her unit and sending her to the ground.

Highest Sky moved towards Song to help her, but was stopped by Mist Breather, who enveloped Highest Sky with all his arms, nearly pulling her off the ground. Highest Sky managed to touch the sleeve of her uniform, and Mist Breather was thrown back by some invisible shock. Gas escaped from his bladder. He recovered his focus, then grabbed for Highest Sky again. "Sex death sex death sex death!" But he was shocked each time he repeated his assault, stunned nearly into unconsciousness.

Meanwhile, Mid-Air had grasped on to the semi-conscious Song to begin to absorb her. Song's chip broadcast a sad confusion of hope and terror even as Highest Sky attempted to come to her aid, screaming at her to "activate her shield." But Mid-Air soon finished absorbing Song, and her chip fell silent.

The unnatural weight of the human carrion held Mid-Air to the ground, so she was unable to assist her mate with Highest Sky. Song's form was still visible through Mid-Air's translucent skin, as Song's detached dirigible unit floated off into the sky.

Only when the mating pair was quiet with exhaustion did the rest of the Floating World turn its attention carefully towards them. Highest Sky had reactivated her unit and reoriented, preventing further attacks by the unwary. Her hands shook as she checked a device on her sleeve. She spoke strangely, and Cloud Flyer suspected the translator erred again. "Song is carrion. You will please return her meat to us."

Cloud Flyer instead directed that the mating pair be taken to the spaceport's infirmary. The humans could fend for themselves. On behalf of the Floating World, he was furious at them. They had brought weapons here and, still worse, their constant tempting presence had finally revealed the atavistic heart of the World's being. Their inverted image of death and perversity had triggered the old carrion feeder instinct, the frenzy that purified the Floating World and led to the secret ways of love.

Cloud Flyer's bladder deflated slightly; his shock and fury had exhausted him. He felt small and empty, but at least now maybe he could get something to eat.

Two days later, I'm exiting the mission. My blood, tits, and hair swing around in the orientation lock. I'm completely wrecked, a good mood for a friend's funeral. I'm desperate for a whiskey, but there'll be no wake today.

I should have known: when the Floaters saw something that looked belly-up dying, they ate it, then fecked each other. I interrupted the coitus, but I could tell from the screams of "sex death!" where things were going. Should have known—maybe Carol would still be alive. I also should've known that she wouldn't follow orders if she thought she was saving me.

How did I get to this world turned upside down? Easy steps. Athlone, Ireland to London, England to Washington, DC to space. "An outstanding candidate for mission chief"—all in the shitter now. The clock's running. Soon, there'll be a reaction back home, then an investigation. So I don't have much time, and the message I sent to the fleet that morning made sure of it.

As I fly, I rub my back, sore from too much arse over elbows. The air pressure is no craic either, though drugs cover the bends.

At the designated "Gateway to the Center," I find my new assistant Paul easily despite the crowd and the perennial smoky fog that rises from the ground. He's holding my place just by his presence. A thousand Floaters have gathered in the open, and except for a few security types they keep more than their usual distance.

"Are you sure we should be here?" asks Paul, eyes darting from one Floater to another.

"Yes. It's Carol's funeral too. We have to be here." And despite every obstacle raised, I've made sure of it. Paul is a daft newcomer eejit, but at least he does what he's told. He doesn't inquire how I got back with a tetchy dirigible unit, or where the unit is now. Good lad.

Nearby, the Floater VIPs wait within a plastic pavilion hanging from the largest draught beast I've seen. Next to the VIPs, an automated camera will again capture the moment for the rest of the Floating World. I want to wave at it, but don't. That isn't the kind of scene I need to make.

Cloud Flyer comes forward, sucking gas, carrying something that looks like a flower box. "Your presence here is extremely difficult."

I'm unfazed. "Our condolences."

He points a tentacle at my dirigible. "A new one?"

Interesting. I don't answer. I think he suspects.

Despite the cold reception and memories of Carol, I enjoy watching the ceremony. It's weird and wonderful, the way everything used to be for me on this world. The rites are close to the ground and near an entrance to a Floater underground tunnel complex so that the spirit can easily find its way to the Center. As the pallbearers bring a vertical floating box through the mourners, I nag Cloud Flyer to explain the details.

"Mid-Air has been righted by the blindfolded undertakers, her bladder filled again with gas, her body made up with the semblance of life. Then, she was placed in that coffin."

I know now from the cock-up at the spaceport why all this is necessary. The modern Floating World apparently goes to great lengths to avoid eating their own dead. "And Carol?" I ask.

"She is in there as well."

Damned shame. Alive, Carol would be happy—she's upside down and about as intimate as you can be with a Floater.

Several Floaters, including Lord Ground Grazer himself, make long impersonal speeches: "They have begun their journey to the Center" and such. Mid-Air's parents whine strangely all the while. I gab more with Cloud Flyer, waiting for my opportunity.

Cloud Flyer never fully understood the height of his unimportance until this day, observing the rites with the humans. There had been no avoiding it—he was the unanimous choice. Lord Ground Grazer had even made innuendoes about Cloud Flyer's "great understanding of the humans."

So be it. He would do his duty for the Floating World, however much personal shame it brought him.

Now the human mission chief, the one responsible for all this death and disgrace, was rudely talking during Lord Ground Grazer's speech. "Flyer, how did Mid-Air actually die?"

"Song killed her."

"Flyer, with all due respect, I think it was the other way around."

"Between your endoskeletons and your heavy metals, you are difficult to digest, toxic, and disgraceful to eat besides." Perhaps this was too harsh; Cloud Flyer sought to mitigate any insult. "Mid-Air's final words were of your friend. She said that Song was delicious, once she got over the smell."

Highest Sky spasmodically released air, and the translator could not tell whether her noise was joyful or sad. "Song would have wanted it that way. But usually flavor is a better indicator of biological compatibility."

"Yes, it is unfair, Highest Sky. Tasting so good, you should be more digestible."

Highest Sky did not seem to take this criticism well. "I'm sure Song would have been easier to stomach if she could have helped it."

Lord Ground Grazer seemed to be winding up. "...there should be discussion on the human presence."

Highest Sky apparently had no ear for tactful speech and asked, "What does he mean?"

"The Council of Lords wishes to meet with you after the funeral regarding the difficulties with the human mission."

"That's grand." Her casual attitude was infuriating.

A new speaker commenced another eulogy. "Mist Breather, mate of Mid-Air, served the Floating World all his life..."

Highest Sky was again impatiently rude. "Flyer, what happened to Mist Breather?"

"He has also begun his journey to the Center."

"But my shield—"

"Did not permanently damage Mist Breather. But his shame did." Cloud Flyer then presented Highest Sky with the sacramental box. "Mist Breather's last wish was to offer his carrion self to you," he said. The eulogist told the mourners the same thing.

Highest Sky slowly held the box out towards the ground and opened its cover towards the sky. Inside was the deflated Mist Breather—no semblance of life, ready to eat. "For what purpose did he give himself?"

"As food."

"Oh, of course. Thank you. We accept him."

Cloud Flyer and the mourners waited expectantly. Would the human see that she was being treated like the primitive carrion feeders of the higher air? Would she eat it despite the risk of toxins?

"Well, I'm not going to eat him now. I'm not hungry." Highest Sky looked around at the mourners. "I've got a better idea. I'll share." With the eulogist building to a whistling climax, "take and eat, take and eat," Highest Sky turned the box over and emptied its contents towards the ground. "Dinner time."

Oh, I've done it now. If there's one thing I'm an expert at, it's starting a riot.

The moment he sees what I've done, Cloud Flyer turns away, peripheral eyes shut. But he's the only one nearby to do this. A swarm of mourners descends on Mist Breather's scanty remains. In the fracas, some of the Floaters are squeezed so their bladders fail, and they drop to the ground. They hold themselves upright with desperate difficulty. Closer to the carcass, a Floater becomes disoriented and is in turn torn apart.

Meanwhile, the pallbearers don't wait to open the top of the vertical coffin. Poof! There's Mid-Air, larger than life. The lines of Carol's skeleton show through Mid-Air's translucent skin. They float up together even as some of the rioters descend to the ground. Way up in the higher atmosphere, the carrion beasts will smell through their charade and tear them apart. Thus, as a Floater would say, their spirits will be freed to approach the Center of the Floating World. I just hope Carol makes it home.

Eventually, the feeding frenzy ebbs, and I hear a new nastiness in the crowd. Words like "abomination!," "perverts!," "murderers!" rapidly spread. Some of the Floaters are waving their tentacles towards the ground. Not good.

A sphere of security Floaters forms around the VIPs, who fled their viewing area when the great draught beast got spooked by the disturbance. The beast's handlers try desperately to calm it as the viewing pavilion shakes beneath it.

Paul and I are alone, unprotected, as the crowd forms its own sphere around us. With the crowd threatening us, Cloud Flyer turns back around and screeches like a banshee, "Protect the humans!" He and a few security Floaters break through the mourners to cordon them off. Impressive.

I turn my back towards Paul, our dirigible units in parallel, and wait for the chaos to calm.

The crowd pushes in hard from all directions, and the security response lacks spirit. The sphere shrinks around us until the bladders of the security Floaters are nearly kissing our dirigible units.

The crowd's really raging now. Some can just reach me through gaps in the security.

"Paul," I say, "on my command, activate your shield. Now."

Our combined shields thrust Cloud Flyer and the ring of security against the crowd. Through every open space, Floater tentacles flail against the shield and whip back in pain.

I pull out my stunner, and fire it into the riot. Floater after Floater is stunned, though none lose orientation yet. Paul is staring at me, nearly as stunned as the Floaters.

Cloud Flyer screeches, "Get the humans to the tunnels." Again, impressive. Authority and presence of mind.

With more spirit now, the security fights through enough of the crowd to get us to the entrance to the underground chambers. That's grand, because I've one more incident to create.

Cloud Flyer guided the humans through the tunnels. For Cloud Flyer's ancestors, belowground had been the frontier. They found that their design was exapted for tunnel dwelling, though the open air remained their place of birth and, as he had just seen, death.

The humans had abandoned their dirigible units—they had mag boots for underground. They skated on the tunnel surface, the skidding sound echoing down the tunnel like a warning.

He brought the group to a memorial cul-de-sac, where plaques to the Low surrounded them. "You will remain here for the moment, while I consult with the Council of Lords."

Highest Sky seemed agitated. "Tell them I'll meet with them, as they requested."

Cloud Flyer could now recognize clearly one emotion in an alien. He had seen it in Song's face before her end. It was in the male's face now, in his darting eyes. It was fear.

That did it. The male must fear that Highest Sky intended to commit another outrage in the Council's presence. She was in all probability mad, perhaps from the chronic strain of proper orientation. Insane, she might not represent the human view. If he could keep her from the Council, he might prevent a disaster.

"The Council has much to consider. But I will return soon."

At a polite distance from the humans, he left two guards whose purpose should be clear even to an alien.

Paul broke into a red-faced, fretting frown. "Chief, we can't stay like this forever."

"Don't worry," I say, "We won't have to."

"Are you sure that we're handling all this right?"

"Positive." My act at the funeral was a bit much even for him. I tap my head, signaling to take our chips offline. Then I whisper, "Look, when they get back, anything could happen. Follow my lead, and be ready with your personal shield. I don't want you ending up like Carol. Understood?"

"Yes, ma'am," the eejit stammers.

Cloud Flyer returned. "Your presence on the Floating World has become extremely difficult."

"Difficult? You had one of our people for lunch."

"And you committed sacrilege at a funeral." Cloud Flyer addressed the humans now as if he were speaking politely to disobedient pets. "The rest of your people no longer come out from the mission area. We cannot see you all in proper orientation." Human orientation could not be left to the imagination of the Floating World for too long, or the Floating World might imagine itself into a frenzy.

"I left instructions. We are no longer safe."

"True, we cannot guarantee your safety here any longer. You will remove yourselves to the spaceport, and wait for a ship there."

"This mission area is ours by treaty. We will remain there until our ship comes. Until then, we advise you not to approach."

"We would regret a discussion of war."

"I would too, as by now a human fleet is nearing your planet. Again, I anticipated difficulties."

"You caused this! We will fight you!"

"We? What world will fight with you? What species can you get to help?"

Her mad logic was too much for Cloud Flyer. He refilled his bladder to regain his calm. "I will give your response to the Council. You will remain here."

"Wait. Send everyone else away. We need to speak privately. To show you why you shouldn't keep us here." Cloud Flyer hesitated. "Come on, Flyer. Where could we escape to?"

Cloud Flyer instructed the guards to move farther down the tunnel, out of sight. He had a foreboding, but it was his duty to endure any shame alone.

"I was watching you at the funeral. For a moment, you saw what I had done. But you could turn away."

"What is your point, Highest Sky?"

"This." In one motion, Highest Sky pulled herself up and unlatched herself from her mag boots. Then she hit the ground, feet first. And there she was, like his nightmare, feet at his face, face at his air bladder. He did not turn away. His response was quicker than seven thousand years of civilization. He attacked.

The shock hit him. He recoiled, gas forced from his bladder. But his passion wasn't done yet—the male had also unlatched. Cloud Flyer lashed out for him. Again the horrible shock, more gas escaping. He sank against the ground. He held himself steady, his weight on his many arms. It was strange—a taste of their world.

He looked again at the two humans. His senses adjusted, the need to feed dissipated. He could hear his own thoughts over the roar of instinct. These things were not carrion, not sex death. He felt it in his skin—these were the familiar sentient beings whom he now had to survive to stop.

"You had enough yet, Flyer?" asked Highest Sky. "Do you see why you have to let us go?"

"Yes." No one else could endure this yet. "Please resume proper orientation."

As the humans helped each other into their mag boots and proper orientation, Cloud Flyer continued speaking, his steadiness a counterpoint to his words. "I know why you have done this. But you are still insane. Besides what you have done to the Floating World, to your own kind, do you understand what you've done to me? I'll be forced to... Center, help me."

Cloud Flyer whistled for the guards. "Take them back to their mission area. Then stand guard there to ensure nobody leaves without the Council's permission. They must not be allowed to inflict any more shame on the Floating World."

Leaving them, barely able to contain his gas, Cloud Flyer knew that this was only a temporary reprieve from far more dishonorable duties. As this mad woman had intended, the conflict had moved beyond the Floating World. Someone would have to move with it.

Low Flyer's Story

"I'm not what I was." Low Flyer, his name change confirmed by Council, ignores propriety. Here in this alien place, this "pub," Low Flyer needs to make Highest Sky understand what he couldn't say before—what she has done to him. "I submitted to sacrilege, there was no other choice. I had already endured your perversity, but we couldn't afford an accident. I've been injected with drugs to calm my reaction to all of this." He waves an arm about in an almost human fashion at the orientation of this world. "I allowed an implant of a chip" tapping his head "so I can follow, and trust, your words.

"I am now a non-person, less than carrion, since what creature will now deign to consume my altered flesh? They have given me a low name, but though I'll return there soon, I'll always be outside the Floating World. Because of you."

"Jaysus, Flyer, no 'hello, how are you?'" Alone of the aliens in the pub, Highest Sky is properly oriented, suspended by mag boots from the pressed-metal ceiling.

"You mock me, Highest Sky."

"The name's 'Angie.'" She sounds it out in the Floating World's new phonemes for untranslatable offworld sounds. Then she continues with the translator, "And no, Flyer. I'm proud of you. Do you mind?" she asks, pointing to her boots. "I'd like to stand you for a round."

She's loud and expansive on her home ground, making Low Flyer nervous. "It's your world."

Angie pulls herself up and springs to the ground, just as she had on the Floating World. She sits on a stool at the bar, and Low Flyer, bladder at minimum, hovers next to her.

"Barkeep, some calamari for my friend here, and a pint of Guinness for me."

"Calamari?" Low Flyer's translation is uncertain.

"You'll see. That was a nice speech you gave today, short and to the point. You actually got applause."

Low Flyer sputters a bit of gas. "You heard it?"

"Wouldn't have missed it."

"The speech was short because I didn't know how long the drugs and mental conditioning would hold out. The clapping surprised me—I can't believe it was sincere. When I looked out at the conference, I realized what I must look like to them, to you. Upside down. Alien. They can't be trusted with the Floating World's destiny."

"That's the spirit." Their orders interrupt them. "Go ahead and try the calamari. I had some xenobio folks check it out for you. No bones, but I can't vouch for the taste."

Low Flyer absorbs a piece. "It's strange."

"But not bad?"

"Not sure yet." He takes another piece—eating doesn't interfere with speech. "By the way, I get the joke. Squid. Very funny. But not bad." He grabs another piece.

Angie laughs. "That's grand then. You never cease to impress me."

This is too much. Low Flyer hums low and angry. "The spaceport and the funeral riot were both deliberate provocations by you. Why did you have to do it? Your Sentience League isn't worth the gas."

"Because you had to come here to give your nice speech, to tell the human mission and the military I had called in and everyone else to feck off, and assert the rights of the Floating World as the native sentient species to the unoccupied systems in your sector."

Low Flyer slaps the bar with an arm. "So you admit it, the humans did it deliberately. I'll inform my government."

"Hold up, Flyer. Nobody else knows anything about it. This was all me. And you've already helped make sure that I've paid for my actions, and will pay some more."

Yes, she has paid, but her expulsion from the Floating World and dismissal from her government's service isn't nearly enough. "Why did you bother to meet me then, just to tell me this?"

"Because you're going to be important, Flyer, so you have to understand."

This praise embarrasses Low Flyer. "I understand that you nearly brought us to war. Surely there was another way."

Angie shakes her head. "Hell, Flyer, you knew this was important, and you still had to be forced into it. But I was glad to hear they chose you."

"It couldn't have been anyone else—you made sure of that."

"Yeah, well, we've both had to make sacrifices."

"Like Song? How could you do that to one of your own?"

Angie replies slowly, deliberately. "I didn't know that was going to happen to Carol. I think of her everyday. But you and I both know that she represented everything that was wrong with the mission. Whatever her taste." She takes a long drink.

Low Flyer's anger refuses to be satisfied with this. "Three of the Floating World and one of your world have gone towards the Center. Were their journeys worth it?" He sucks in air. "And why shouldn't I kill you right here and now?"

"For feck sake, Flyer, I don't know." She is suddenly impatient with him. "Let's do the tally. Your interstellar neighborhood won't be overrun by right-side-up developers. You'll be on the Council soon, despite your sacrilege. I'll be on the dole and pissed. And one day you'll understand what a friend I was to the Floating World. Until then, you shouldn't kill me because I'd bust your guts going down, and that would make all those other deaths a complete waste. *Slainte.*" Flushed as if properly oriented, she raises her glass towards him.

So that's why she seems different. "You're intoxicated."

"An Irish woman isn't drunk so long as when the world starts spinning, she doesn't fly off. You gonna fly off now, Flyer?"

Low Flyer bows against gravity. "Farewell, Angie, or whatever your name really means."

Angie smiles. "I think you would say 'Messenger of the Center.'"

Low Flyer does not reply, and leaves her to her drink.

Hooking Up

Unlike a lot of folks, I didn't hate high school—it was so much better than my elementary school years. But rock music lyrics and my own disposition made me more than a little suspicious concerning what the education process was really about. "Hooking Up" taps into my own adolescent paranoia about what schools might do to problem students if they had the power.

But this story also reflects my belief that the most convincing dystopias aren't imposed from the top down, but are the results of certain societal inclinations running their natural course. A dystopia based on happiness like that of *Brave New World* seems more likely to have staying power than the deliberately unhappy world of *1984*, and Bradbury's *Fahrenheit 451* (the book, not the movie) now seems uncannily prescient. So, while I have plenty of oppression from above in "Hooking Up," much of the damage to our hero comes from other students just doing what kids like to do.

John sauntered lazily towards his new high school, making his parents wait as long as possible in their stupid H-cell car. He hoped that he was pissing them off. Their idea to send him to this hi-tech educational prison, their idea to wait out front until he synced on the school grounds, both because they didn't trust him. So screw them.

He glanced back over his shoulder, saw their fake big smiles and waving arms, waving him on. Shit, how humiliating.

Ahead at the main entrance, the view held more promise. Two perfect girls, lush hair, blemishless skin, full lips, sculpted curves. The best features their daddies could buy, and probably too fancy for John. But he could still enjoy the scenery.

The girls smiled; John smiled back. Friendly—this place could be tolerable.

Then John stepped over a thin red line on the entrance walk, and his skin tingled all over. Now he saw that the two girls had two neon-glow companions. His implant must have synced with the school system. The girls' avatars were just a shade more perfect than their phys bod counterparts.

The avatars also smiled at him, and then they struck him with bolts of joy, and kept striking. The bolts manifested as a bright golden stream of cupid's arrows endlessly, painlessly piercing him, slamming the blood into his groin. Embarrassing, difficult to walk even, but damn, this school might be all right.

The avatars and the girls kept smiling, and the bolts kept coming. They went deeper, working up his spine in a roaring wave, filling his brain with white light. They were going to burst his skull.

He tried to call for help, but the joy paralyzed him. Too much joy, too much pain.

The girls and their avatars giggled in the real and virtual entranceway. "Stop it, Mercutia, you're frying him, not milking him."

"You stop it first. Anyway, not our fault he's such a loser. Look how turned on he is!"

The girls dashed inside, leaving their avatars at the doorway, pulling John's excessive joy out from under him. He gasped for breath. Student chips weren't supposed to fry people—his certainly couldn't. His first day, and he was already toasted meat.

He had to get out of here. He spun around, but his parents were already gone. He stepped back towards the red boundary, but a steady pressure like two hands on his shoulders held him to a standstill. He was about to attempt a running dash, when a woman's voice yelled from behind him. "Hello!"

John turned, and the older woman's identity flashed, *Supervisor*. She said, "You're the new boy, John, aren't you? Please, follow me. You wouldn't want to start school by trying to leave or delink, would you?"

John followed. They passed between the silent avatars, who abruptly disappeared. Apparently, they had only been left here to watch and record. That meant trouble. But at least there wasn't any phys evidence from the joy assault to wipe up. John suspected that such a display of uncontrolled meat response would get him burned even more by these cyberpunks. But the girls had been too quick for that—frying, not milking.

From outside to in, the brick school building showed its age. The new tech needed no new visible structures; the sprawling single-story remnant of the previous century would serve as is.

Once inside, the supervisor pointed towards a classroom and said, "Your first class: Sophomore English." Then she pointed at his head. "You're in full sync with the school now. Just bring up an avatar and access the info next time. You have an avatar up now?" John brought up an avatar—like a little slice of himself going dead numb—and nodded. "Good," said the supervisor. "And remember: you're linked for the whole school day." She smiled in stiff dismissal.

John peered into the room. A faded map of nation-states on the wall, scattered non-ergonomic wooden chairs and desks, and various students and their many avatars slouching around. Nothing he couldn't handle. He went in.

A cascade of virtu-voices greeted him, a mass of avatars who dived into his pile of thoughts. He thought, *block*, then said "block" aloud, but the students kept pulling things out of his mind to show the others. "Implant's seriously bargain retro, dude." "You just got chipped this year?" "You should sue your parents!"

His priors flashed to everyone—marijuana, petty computer crime, misuse of his karate skills on some jerk's face—all stupid shit. But enough trouble to make his parents send him here. Most of the other kids weren't flashing squat. Weird—either they could hack display, or they were still at this "character development" school even after their priors were expunged. Here, because they wanted to be.

He tried talking back through his single avatar, but these cyberpunks seemed to be running dozens of avatars apiece, too many and too quick for him. They laughed at his deliberate, linear mode of operation.

The avatars of the girls from outside (IDs flashing *Mercutia* and *Sibelia*) sang "look at this." They reran the record of John's entrance. More laughter. Two guys, Molokevin and Apollius, posted the class consensus judgment in text-only form, the mocking medium being the message. John saw that he was "a low-grade freak, probable burnout." John ignored them—he was used to taking shit about drugs. But the class saw his thought and corrected him. In cyber land, burnouts were neo-autistics, kids who had reacted badly to their implants, who had been permanently fried.

John still ignored them. "Burnout" sounded like the bogeyman, a story to scare little kids.

As the multiple avatar virtuchat moved on without him, John furtively studied the phys bods of his fellow students. Most had bleeding-edge body alterations. But in the back corner of the room, obscured behind enhanced biceps and breasts, some other bodies: a pair of small, unaltered kids sitting by themselves, close together, a boy and a girl, IDs flashing *Paul* and *Donna* .

Then a chime sounded—no more time to stare. The Teaching Expert System, "Tess," had signaled the beginning of class. Tess's avatar appeared—a woman leaving middle age with a bitter scowl on her face. Maybe Tess was bitter that she was only a mid-level AI. The brightest were the government AIs: the Feds. His parents had told him about those with hushed voices. The Feds had designed each of the new special school systems.

"Please sit down," Tess said directly into their minds, her avatar's lips not moving from their frown. The students hustled for squeaky seats in no particular order—Tess didn't need a seating chart. A supervisor passed by the open door, jotted a note on his pad, then closed the door.

Another chime. Tess uploaded a book for discussion. "Our first book for the day is *Huckleberry Finn*." Instantly, the student avatars cut and pasted responses on the fly in vid, audio, and raw code. They compared the book's word and phrase usage profile with that of other books. They uploaded various biographies of Twain to cross-compare their information with the novel. They created hypermedia for every phrase, expanding out through each movie, play, musical, retelling, and parody. Critical and other cultural references were dropped into indexed daisy chains. John felt the growing data pastiche spin around him. *Huckleberry Finn* became the center of a vast memeplex. For the second time today, he thought his head would explode. Yet still, his hardware kept him hooked in without mercy.

The data flow subsided, and John could sense the noise underneath the lesson—the friendly chatter about tomorrow's rally, the latest songs mixed and remixed, the continual stroking of the pleasure centers without any embarrassing physical reaction—all generated through multiple avatars per student, all uninhibited by Tess, all way beyond him.

John felt anxious, like a dog before a storm. Tess signaled him—a text message floated in front of him about the importance of class participation to his grades and his overall school experience. What did that mean? John tapped the message with his finger, and found that Tess rewarded participation not only with grades, but also with chip enhancements. That probably meant abilities like controlling those pleasure bolts—he could use some protection from those. And heck, he actually knew this book, and parts of it didn't suck.

So John said, "I thought it was really cool when Huck said he'll go to hell."

Virtual laughter doused him like ice water, taunts swarmed in endless quick variations until all played out. Someone hit him with the smell of puke and disinfectant. Then, sharp blue needles of light from anonymous avatars drove painfully into his skin.

Ratting out students was bad, but this was bullshit. "Ms. Tess," John said in chorus with his avatar, "I'm getting beat up pretty bad here."

"Zero participation points," said Tess. "Our next book, in reverse chronological order, is *Tom Sawyer.*"

"Ms. Tess?" But the AI plowed on inexorably, monitoring lesson participation, then uploading Twain's *Life on the Mississippi.*

Then John understood why the others had mocked him. For Tess and his classmates, each book was just another piece of information. His opinion was also a piece of info, particularly trivial.

And John guessed why Tess didn't care about the pleasure/pain attacks of his classmates. Anything a Tess tolerated had to be part of the Fed design. Why intramural torture would be part of any design, John couldn't figure. But he knew better than to try to complain to the human supervisors about it. So John would suffer all day the intermittent blue jabs of hurt and embarrassing golden bolts of pleasure.

No way was he coming back here tomorrow.

But in the back corner of the room, a different lesson. He could see them now; no one cared which way his phys bod faced. The boy Paul was curled up in his chair, feet on his desk, arms around his legs, eyes above his knees. No avatar shadowed the boy in John's enhanced view. John called to him under the lesson. The boy flinched, but remained silent, his eyes darting to avoid contact. John felt through his chip for the boy's information, and found only a null spot on the virtual map of the room. John touched the spot, and instantly drew back from the cold blackness, as if he might fall in. Void without bottom.

A burnout, thought John. So they're for real. What's a neo-aut doing here?

Bang! The girl, Donna, smacked her desk with the flat of her palm. Same age and last name, so she had to be Paul's twin. Other than her unaltered bod, she appeared normal, with short black hair and dark complexion. Her loose fitting clothes—what his parents called sweats—overwhelmed her small frame. She stared right at John, eyes wide, and said in a whisper that somehow carried across the room, "We can help you."

She was crazy—John very much doubted that these two losers could help him do anything except suffer more. John searched for their priors. Shit, they were "wards of the state." John could guess what that meant; he quickly turned away. Their parents must have been terrorists. These kids were here to keep them from becoming terrorists too.

John didn't even look at them anymore. He wasn't going near that kind of trouble. But as bolts of pain and joy continued to hammer at him, he feared that he had seen his future in Paul's darting eyes.

Exhausted, shaking, head pounding, John crossed back over the red line and felt the chip loosen its grip. His first day was finished. No way was he coming back here tomorrow. His mom pulled up in their cheap vehicle, her voice nervous and expectant. "So, honey, how was your first day?"

He'd thought his response through carefully. He needed to sound reasonable, convincing, adult. This was too important to screw up. He opened his mouth to speak…

And for a second, he lost control of his body. "OK," he heard himself say.

"That's good!" And his mom went on yakking about how important this was, and he was screaming in his own head, *no, it's not fucking OK, they're killing me!* But every time he opened his mouth to say something, his body shut down.

Like the family car, John's home was another artifact of pre-fusion energy efficiency—ugly solar panels and a biomass processor in the backyard. But tonight it radiated beauty and relief. He ran up to his room to struggle with his chip in private.

John gave himself a crippling headache, but nothing worked. At dinner, he tried casually to write "HELP" in his mashed potatoes, but his implant wouldn't allow that either. His father noticed his hand shaking. "What's wrong? You been smoking again?"

John shook his head and said, "You don't understand." His parents exchanged the concerned glance that always drove him nuts, but he still couldn't say what was on his mind.

If he couldn't tell his parents about school, maybe he could find other students like him, maybe at other schools. In his room after dinner, he tried using his implant to communicate, but heard nothing but silence. They had taken his computer and net access, but his chip probably wouldn't let him write or speak about school on the conventional net anyway. So, what happened in school would stay in school. He was at the mercy of freaks.

He didn't sleep much that night, but he did have a nightmare. He dreamed of the spooky kids at school and Paul's darting eyes and Donna's wide-eyed stare. They offered him a seat next to theirs in class. He woke up gurgling "No!"

The next day, John's mother made him breakfast. "Most important meal of the day, and your brain is working double time." Fried eggs always made him queasy, but that wasn't the battle he needed to fight now, so he ate them.

He felt better than he should after a bad night, even a little high, like a nice toke. A fake feeling—the damned chip must be stroking his pleasure centers. Screw this, he wouldn't cross the red line today. But even as he thought of playing hooky, a steady whistle grew in his head, and he knew the only relief would be to attend school.

When he crossed the red line that morning, John yelled, "This place fucking sucks!" Apparently, once in school, he could say what he wanted to, because no one here cared.

Mercutia and Sibelia, giggling, zapped John at the door again, just enough to remind him of his place. Once he stepped inside, his classmates commenced their blue needle assault. He stared at them, trying to will them to stop. They would not stop.

And all that morning, John saw that he wasn't the only one being hit. Other students staggered under the steady stream of gold and blue. Some of them seemed to be mere extensions of their chips—synapses fried away by the assault, no remnant of their organic selves visible in their dead eyes. Their parents probably liked them better this way. Even those dishing out the blue needles, like Molokevin and Apollius, didn't act like they could pass a Turing test for very long if you unplugged them.

These zombies demonstrated another lesson for him: as long as the cybersystem ran, he was not going to escape, or survive, this school. So fuck them. He would have to hack the system.

Between classes, John checked the antique fuse boxes, power sockets, fire alarms—he could find no physical nodes. Though it aided John's reconnaissance, he resented the unnecessary shuffling from room to room all day. Tess could change the subject and the particular links to student avatars without anyone moving. Like coming to school instead of staying home—it must be about ritual and control.

The only constant companions in his day were Donna and Paul. Amidst otherwise random groupings, they followed him from class to class, as if Tess were mocking him by keeping them together.

During history class, John tried another line of attack. He sub-vocalized "view code." A head-splitting amount of raw code replaced the iconic representations of avatars and lessons. "Narrow field." Nobody tried to stop him as he viewed code all the way down to the level of unmediated machine language. Cocky bastards. He traced the flow of discrete samples of data to get some picture of the system's shape. The overall design emerged as a spoke-and-wheel structure, with the number of spokes corresponding roughly to the number of students. The students and their implants must be acting unconsciously for the system as phys nodes.

Shit. John had no idea of how to hack this kind of system. And if that didn't suck enough, he also was helping against his will to process and store information for Tess.

He ran to the bathroom to throw up.

That afternoon after science class, Tess reminded the students that "The school will now hold this year's first rally and dance in the gym." The steady whistle in John's head indicated mandatory phys attendance, so John went. He kept his avatar immediately in front of him, shield-like, to keep his reactions simple. Despite some twitchiness, he hadn't burnt out yet. He could delink and go home soon, collapse alone in his room until the shakes steadied, brave it out through dinner.

The other students filed into the gym with him. Less worn patches on the walls and floor indicated where sports equipment might have been years before. Now, the gym was just a plain dusty box in which to gather the students together in phys bods.

And as always, Donna and Paul were near. "You're going to need our help in here," Donna whispered.

"Or what?" snarled John between clenched teeth.

"Or you're going to die. A lot."

But then a supervisor interrupted in and outside John's head, one cheery voice a slight asynchronous echo of the other. "Hello, students! The rally and dance will start when all the supervisors have left, and will run for three hours. Tess has put the school's data system at your disposal. Please enjoy yourselves in whatever manner you'd like and get to know your new classmates. Dancing, cheers, games, music, are suggested but not required activities. The important thing is that you have fun!

"Oh, and the rally and dance may be monitored and recorded for your protection."

The supervisors noted attendance on their pads, then exited the gym, shutting the doors behind them in a series of clacks. When the last supervisor was gone, most of the students sat on the bare floor.

Then, as promised, death came for John.

John's death had many potential forms: monsters, gunfire, guided missiles, all the props of a vid game brought to sim life. The gym was in full virtual simulation mode: part ruined city, part jungle. All his classmates held weapons, John had squat.

Half-naked streetwalker variations of Mercutia and Sibelia whistled at him, offered to go all the way for money, then pulled vicious knives and chased him whether he agreed or refused. A Molokevin-ish avatar became a giant spider with a human head, but gave up chasing John to try to net the girls. An Apollius-like soldier, uninterested in the girls, pulled an old fashioned AK-47 out of the ether and fired in a sweeping arc towards John.

John half-believed the stories that when you died in full-sim mode, you died for real. So he hit the ground, and saw the real gym floor. The world seemed quiet again. He raised his head.

Death in the form of an anti-tank missile found him. John felt seamless agony as his body exploded and his head rolled away. Then he was back like a rebooted game. So at least the stories weren't true, but sim-death still hurt like hell.

Despite the warnings, he sub-vocalized "emergency delink." A jolt of pain made his knees buckle. No good. So, he ran for what he thought was the door.

But the door was locked. And they were lining up for him now, one painful sim-death after another. His heart pounded as if it wanted to desert his chest. Maybe he would let himself be completely fried sooner rather than later.

A pull at his arm. It was the burnout, Paul. An unlikely help against monsters. Eyes elsewhere, Paul was clutching at him, pulling as if John were the door and escape, holding him back from pounding the real door.

"Let go," said John. "I've got to get out. I've—"

John looked around. The gym was its real space self again, echoing quiet, save for sudden bursts of sim activity that crackled and exploded lightly into his perception. John stared at Paul. Maybe they left the burnout alone, or maybe Tess said they had to leave the burnout alone.

Paul avoided John's gaze, and tugged again at his arm. John flinched at the touch, as if burnout was contagious. But Paul didn't let go.

"Sure, why not." John followed the burnout away from the gym door. It was like walking in a translucent tunnel beneath Niagara Falls, with the water always about to crash through.

Donna was sitting cross-legged on the floor. She opened her palm, gesturing for him to sit. He remained standing.

"Told ya you'd die," she said sullenly.

"Yeah, I'm sorry." He pointed to Paul, who was scanning the peeling paint on the ceiling. "I was just bringing him back to you." He walked away from them both, but in four steps the angry buzz of full sim hit him again, and he jumped back from it like he'd been smacked in the face.

Donna laughed, sullenness gone. "You sure that he didn't bring you? I think he likes you."

John doubted that Paul could consciously bring or like anyone, so he asked about something else. "Why do they keep him here?"

Sudden anger. "He's not a fucking burnout. He's just concentrating, that's all."

John felt a little angry himself. "Right, whatever. Sorry for thinking he might want to be anyplace else. But no, he'd better stay here—like, his concentrating could be a security risk."

Donna cocked her head at John, and John felt as if his thoughts were being rummaged through again, though his chip reported no link. Finally, she asked, "Notice anything different, here versus out there?"

"It's quieter."

She nodded. "Who do you think is causing that?"

"But…"

"Wanna get zoned?" Donna asked quietly.

"Stoned? High?"

"No, zoned." Donna put a finger to her lips, and pulled John down to sit next to her. Paul sat opposite them both, eyes skittering and averted. "Lower your eyes and count each time you breathe out. When you've counted ten breaths, start over. Think of nothing else, only your breath. Don't move, and don't speak."

John opened his mouth with a question, but she held a hand up to it. He got the point—he would have to shut up to sit with them, to stay out of the sims.

He shut up; he counted breaths. Breathe in, breathe out. The tunnel solidified, the residual rumble of the rally faded to nothing. True quiet descended—quiet like before he was chipped, but beautiful now after all the noise.

The quiet stole over John, made his arms and legs and brain feel lighter. Yes, it was like being high again. His mind wandered. Even his paranoid fears were the same—he wondered if they had made him deaf or brain-damaged like Paul. Was Donna brainwashing him into a terrorist? Was this drug-ware? He had the natural stoner's dread of such invasive tech. He wanted to jump up and dive back into the rally, but he couldn't take another round of sim-death. He wanted to laugh and cry, but Donna would make him leave. He stared desperately at her, and even at Paul, soundlessly begging for a virtual or real sound. But no words and no links, at least nothing he or his chip could sense.

He focused again on his breath. His breathing was his loudest noise, his heartbeat his strongest sensation. Stillness and fear alternated in his meat rhythms. Then heart and lungs quieted too.

After a while, he must have fallen asleep, which was almost a shame, because he was almost enjoying the trip. He did not dream. He awoke only when they reopened the doors. Donna and Paul were already gone to whatever government institution acted as their home. The school's system chatter started again, but John was going home too.

At dinner, he again tried all the ways he could think of to indirectly describe the horror show at school, but that just brought back the headaches and shaking, so he stopped.

That night, he was able to sleep and dream. He dreamed of Donna. She stood naked in the ocean, smiling, hair wet, arms wide open to pull him to her. Hey, maybe not the class knockout, but naked and willing. He ran into the water.

Laughter, from behind him. "I figured you'd call me up like this." John turned. On the beach was Donna, fully clothed. Unlike the classroom Donna, her gaze was expressive, her posture graceful.

"What the hell is going on?"

Donna snapped her fingers, and they were at a 1950s soda fountain. Her hair was longer, in a ponytail, and John sported a black leather jacket. "This is a creation of our parents," said Donna, "an interactive instructional memory we copied directly to your brain this afternoon, queued up with the rest of your subconscious dream material."

"Oh, it's just a fricking dream." Good, maybe he could get back to the naked Donna instead.

Donna snapped her fingers in his face. "No no no! Pay attention, cause I only get to say this once. The AIs' use of the chip interface is far from perfect—the AIs only pick up higher order verbal activity and conscious volition. They haven't cracked the subconscious yet—they don't think they need to. That's why I'm talking to you during REM sleep. They also haven't cracked certain non-verbal variants on standard consciousness—they don't see them as a threat.

"During the day, you can shield your mind from damage through the breathing exercise I taught you. Also, allow an avatar to handle your class participation—Tess only really cares about the avatars. Once you're good enough at it, we'll show you the next step. Until then, just follow our lead."

She snapped her fingers again, and he was back in the water with the naked Donna. The voice of the clothed Donna behind him said, "So, I'll leave you two to get to know each other."

But in the back of his mind, John knew that someone still watched. He turned again. A dark silhouette sat on the beach, and everything was falling towards it like a black hole. It was Paul.

John woke up, heart hammering from excitement and fear.

The next day, from the moment he crossed the red line, John's mind was on his breathing. The girls hit him with pleasure at the door again, but he counted his way through most of it. The girls just giggled and didn't seem to notice the difference.

John went straight to his class looking for Donna and Paul. Despite the instructions in his dream, he wanted to talk with Donna in the flesh, confirm that it was real. The twins had retreated to their usual place in the back, but when John said, "Hey, last night—"

Bang! Donna banged her desk with the palm of her hand, then held a finger to her lips. Right—quiet.

So he sat facing the twins and followed Donna's instructions. He gave his avatar some loose parameters and let it contribute to the data pastiche on *The Red Badge of Courage* while he counted. Breathe in, breathe out. The blue needles still hit him, but they didn't matter so long as he didn't focus on them.

It wasn't easy, this stillness and concentration. His back and legs and eyes hurt. But concentration hurt a lot less than the pleasure/pain attacks. From hour to hour he grew better at focusing, minding his breath even when he had to change classrooms.

Then, during the last class, he grew very aware of his own pulse and Donna's presence. He remembered his dream. That made him horny, the way everything used to before the jading bolts of chip pleasure.

Suddenly, he had a raging hard-on—even Paul must see it—he started to turn away.

Smack! Donna slapped him still.

"Don't move a millimeter," she growled.

"But—"

"Shut up."

He stared at the ground, eyes watery with humiliation.

"Focus through it. You're nearly there, and we have something to show you." So he focused again on his breath, and his hydraulics calmed down, and he could be attentive-relaxed again.

Besides his own breathing, John could hear the breathing of Paul and Donna. Then, more incredibly, he heard their heartbeats. Excitement (out), attention (in). Their heartbeats came into focus and fell into the same rhythm, impossibly in sync. Weird (in), weirder (out).

His chip must have entered the fray, but it didn't interfere. Instead, it let him sense his mind's electrical activity lining up like light in a laser. He knew (don't think) that Donna and Paul's brainwaves were lining up too.

Then, the rolling black sea below their thoughts calmed and flowed together, not like the sharp intrusions of the chip, but like a slow, shared pumping of blood through all their brains. Paul shared many things. What they were John couldn't say, except for one mental word in a voice that John had never heard. The voice said, *Welcome* .

Then, a gong sounded, resonating through him. It was the school bell.

"Class is over," Donna said. "Are you well-done?"

John shook himself, not from sleepiness, but from wherever he had been back into this world. He held up a finger to his lips. No words yet, she was right, there were no words.

But Donna grinned, imperfect face warm with real glee. "Congratulations, friend. You're now in the Zoner Club."

At home that evening, John's parents watched the news on their wall screen 3D TV, like most people their age who weren't more directly jacked into the media. John was practicing his breathing technique in the next room. The announcer said more terrorists had been arrested, and John's mother was laughing at them. "Where did they think they could hide from the Fed AIs?"

Words welled up inside John, and before the chip could freeze him, he spoke without thinking. He heard himself from far off, saying things like "the terrorists might have a point about the AIs" and "the AI schools pounded the humanity out of their students." He didn't speak long, and when he was done, his parents appeared stunned.

"But we thought you liked your school," his father said.

John said nothing—he could feel his chip preparing to take control again if he opened his mouth. This was progress, and he wouldn't spoil it. He practiced his breathing some more.

That night, Paul walked into his dream again. John waved, and in response Paul's arm chopped through the dream reality like obsidian. Paul still manifested as an empty silhouette, but John wasn't scared like before, even though the void seemed bottomless. John asked, "What were you saying about the AIs today, Paul?"

And Paul reminded him of what he had told them during their group silence—about how Paul was the incarnation of his parent's legacy.

"Legacy? What do you mean? Aren't your parents criminals?"

And Paul reminded him that no, they weren't criminals—they were dead.

"Psst, hey kid, want to get zoned?" whispered John.

Another transfer student, teeth clenched in joy/pain, eyes wide in horror—John wondered if he ever could have looked so clueless. "Come on, kid, it'll help you deal. It helped me." John felt comfortable again in this role. He had never sold weed, only bought and shared it, but the dealer persona wasn't much of a stretch. So much for cyber school's reform of his character.

The newbie ignored John's offers. Donna got into the act. "You're hurting, and there's no need. Come play with us. You'll like it, you'll see."

But the newbie's eyes kept drifting over to Paul, still as twitchy as ever. So he turned away from the zoners, and tried to earn points discussing Walt Whitman.

Typical. Though their near-perfect concentration and Paul's shielding allowed them to communicate more openly, their recruitment efforts had so far failed. Even those who tried to zone with them relapsed into the school mind. *Homo fucking gestalt.* Concentration was hard work, but Paul creeped out a lot of the kids too, and John didn't blame them. John waved his hand in front of Paul's large black pupils. "Dude, when the hell are you going to wake up?"

"Shh!" Donna frowned at John. "He's concentrating."

"Yeah, yeah, I know that. But we could use some help out here in the phys world. Isn't there someplace he could go, someplace that could help?"

Donna shook her head rapidly. "No. They'd think he was just a neo-aut. You don't know—the things they do to neo-auts. Sometimes they grow a new brain in place of the old one, killing the old child invisibly within. Or they'll use him for medical experiments, or wipe his mind and rent him out as processor or software space. So no. He'll wake up when he's supposed to. Until then, our parents did this to him for a reason—he allows us to be together."

Donna touched John's hand, nothing virtual about it, and yet it was more electric than the pleasure bolts. It brought back a memory from the zone. "Donna, when we've zoned together, have we…?"

Donna blushed, "Something like it. Consider it practice."

That was nice, but it was frustrating too. "Practice for when?"

"For when we get out of here."

"Will that ever happen? And will we be together if it does?"

"Yes and yes. Yes." She squeezed his hand.

That was nice too, so John didn't remind her that the old blue needle squad were getting uncomfortably curious about their refusal to adapt or burnout. And he didn't talk about his plans for computer crime and phys assault, his other prior offenses of which the school had failed to cure him. His plans were no longer petty.

"Oh, these grades are wonderful, John. We're so proud of you!" John's mother hugged him, his father patted his shoulder. John stood silently, without affect. His parents didn't recognize that the whole performance had nearly nothing to do with John. His avatar was the one growing smarter, even earning some additional chipware abilities. Naturally, his parents preferred the scholastic illusion to their quiet and humorless but real son at home.

"So, can I work on the net again?" That was the deal—good grades for limited net privileges.

"Of course, John. Be good!"

John dashed to his room. Good. Now he could learn some things too. His mental concentration from his fight with the school system was diamond sharp, but the flesh had gotten weak. "Computer, begin T'ai Chi exercises." A holo model of himself appeared in front of him to help guide him through the steps. When he was certain his parents weren't listening, he'd switch to the karate program. He had also experimented with biofeedback, and found his implant surprisingly cooperative with this training when Tess wasn't riding him.

Tess mostly ignored the phys bod, so he made the phys bod important. Phys strength might help him and his friends, if they ever needed to escape.

But he didn't want to escape now. As he no longer suffered greatly at school, he did not try to tell his parents about what was going on anymore, though he probably could've told them now. If his parents found out, they'd probably move John to another school, and he didn't want to leave Donna. Whatever his parents did, it probably wouldn't be the right thing.

He also studied all the information on AI networks that he could find, hacking just a little beyond the public domain and his own limited access. AI networks vastly exceeded the complexity of the simple systems he had cracked at his old school. If their network designs didn't represent such cruelty, they would have been beautiful, and a nice focus for zoning. His old karate teacher would have called them mandalas. As with a mandala, he needed to forget what a network design represented and hold it in his zoning mind as pure image, no words. No words.

He dreamed about Donna that night, but couldn't tell anymore if she was the Donna of memory or fantasy. Those distinctions were blurring—a pleasant thing, for now.

Another day, and no progress with their student movement. John hated the stagnation—two more years of status quo would drive him nuts. With this school, the Feds had designed a madhouse that created suitable inmates.

Christon the newbie, not so new now, was ignoring them again. John focused his frustration on Christon. A shadow in the back of John's mind egged him on—a feeling that meant "yeah, man, this is it. Fucking do it." He would make Christon pay attention to them.

John expected difficulty accessing the school system, but the shadow in his mind showed him the way in. He visualized the many-spoked wheel of Tess's connections to her students, then imagined Christon's face at the end of one of the spokes. Data pulsed along the Christon's spoke, taking his attention away from John. John mentally reached out with a hand to squeeze off the spoke and block the pulses. But the pulses passed through John's virtual hand and gave him a headache.

With a mental karate punch, John broke the spoke. The pulses stopped, then sought a more circuitous connection along the rim of the wheel. John then imagined another spoke running directly from Christon to him. *Now turn*, he thought.

Christon turned and looked at them, face like a blank chalkboard.

Donna gasped, "John, let him go, quick, just do it!"

His focus broken, John let Christon go automatically, but it was too late. Tess must have noticed her lost lamb.

The whole next week, Tess watched them. Her eyes felt like a searchlight in a prison camp, scanning their chips and surface mind data. They had attracted her attention, but as yet no response. Donna helped him keep quiet. They struggled to suppress the animal fight-or-flight response, the adrenaline that broke concentration. They counted breaths, they let their avatars chatter, they kept an eye on the naturally quiet Paul.

But Tess must have followed the threads of their thoughts, and like a veil being lifted, she finally directed her scowl towards the twitchy, avatarless boy at the back of the class. "Paul, I don't believe we've heard from you today. In fact, I don't believe we've heard from you at all this year. Forgive my neglect—I seem to have been distracted. So, what do you have to contribute regarding Dalton Trumbo?"

As always, Paul said nothing, his eyes darting from wall to wall. John clenched his fists. *Now would be a good time to wake up, you jerk.*

Tess clucked her virtual tongue. "How sad! Paul seems to be suffering from neo-autistic syndrome. As I stand *in loco parentis*, I'll send him to the appropriate state facility immediately after school today. Any family or friends should say their farewells now." And the Tess avatar stared directly at Donna and John, her scowl now a smirk.

John gripped Donna's arm, hard, so she wouldn't respond before the weight of Tess lifted from their minds. "It's a trap. She baiting us to act, to show what we can do."

Donna shook her head. "But we can't let them take him, not even for a little while. We can't let him go."

John didn't want to risk everything yet. "Paul, it's time. Wake up." As if obeying, Paul stood up from his seat. But he remained silent, face ticking this way and that, no more responsive than before.

So, no other choice. John took a deep breath and looked at Donna. "We can leave. Now."

Donna nodded in unison with him. No more words—they had to act.

They strode towards the door, tugging Paul along with them, not bothering to leave avatars behind. Tess called after them, "Where do you think you're going?" But she didn't try to stop them herself.

In the hallway, a burly male supervisor trotted towards them. "Where do you think you're going?" He grabbed on to Donna. John didn't hesitate. His blows were quick, focused, and just barely non-lethal. The supervisor was down without a thought.

An alarm went off. The classroom doors swung open. John, Donna, and Paul ran for the exit.

A massive assault played on John's chip—difficult to keep his focus off of it. But then John saw the red line. He didn't stop. He felt the pressure on his shoulders, but focused through it. But he wasn't strong enough. The line was like a wall. His feet pounded the walkway, his legs pumped, his body pushed, but he could not get past the red. He collapsed to his knees, muscles spasming.

Winded, he turned towards Donna—she had fallen too, tears of frustration on her cheeks. Paul stood behind them, perfectly calm, his eyes strangely focused. At the doorway to the school, Tess's avatar stood next to the supervisors in front of a mob of students. Mercutia and Sibelia glowed golden, Molokevin and Apollius blue. All of their processing power was lining up for a firing squad. John raised himself from the ground to meet their assault.

The assault flew into him like flaming crossbow quarrels from all directions. No mercy now, burnout was what they wanted. The pain/pleasure whipsaw hurt like hell, and no amount of John's focus could negate such a coordinated attack. But Donna helped dampen the blows, and they couldn't fry him.

Then full sim hit John—the savage world from the gym. The air smelled of rotting meat. Shit, they had caught Donna in the sim too, but he couldn't see Paul. The other students were armed with an array of high-powered energy weapons, all charging up to blast the zoners. Donna stepped closer to John. John could see the effort on her face as she strained to block out the sim world, but Paul was out of their circle, and without his help no tunnel formed to protect them.

Then, John again felt the shadow in the back of his mind. "Yeah, it's time, just fucking do it." Hell, it was useless, but at least it was something he could do. He again visualized the mandala of the school's system—all the spokes on the wheel. The wheel wanted to break him. So, with a mental kick, he broke the spokes instead.

The sim flickered out, the student avatars shut down. The whole class stood frozen, linked to the zoners, not Tess. But Tess didn't seem to mind, and her supervisors appeared unaffected—they were not directly plugged into the system, so John's efforts couldn't hurt them. And John couldn't make the students actually do anything; he could only hold them still.

Tess pointed at Paul. Two supervisors grabbed him and pulled him back towards the school. "Hold him," Tess ordered, "until the ambulance arrives."

John ran at them. He threw a palm against each face, and the supervisors folded, releasing Paul. The remaining supervisors hesitated, looking towards Tess for guidance. John tugged Paul towards the line.

Tess spoke with equanimity. "Don't move another step, or I'll kill you all, after I torture you for a subjective eternity."

"As if," grunted John. As if she had been holding back before. Only one thing mattered—Paul hadn't tried to pass through the boundary yet. John pushed Paul forward into the red.

The boundary crackled with virtual noise. Paul stood exactly on the line, relaxed, eyes still, the hint of a smile playing on his face. "Oh!" Tess's lips formed a *moue* of surprise. "There you are!"—as if she could really see him for the first time. The boundary crackled louder as more force was brought to bear on Paul's mind. In John's enhanced view, it was like a waterfall cascading into a bottomless black chasm.

Tess's avatar tapped her foot with impatience. "Hmm, what are you, boy?" She walked towards Paul, the broken spokes of Tess's wheel bending ahead of her, reaching out to him. Donna and John instinctively moved to block her way, but of course she passed through them with only a tingle. She examined Paul up close. "What are you hiding in there?" She reached her hand out to touch Paul's forehead.

Tess touched. Tess screamed. And Tess fell in.

The avatar was gone. Paul collapsed. The virtual wall wasn't there anymore. Donna ran for her brother. John let the students go and reached with his mind, trying to connect to Tess. Nobody home.

They'd killed their teacher, every student's fantasy. Now they were all completely screwed, but at least they'd go down together.

The disconnected students groped and clawed each other like animals in heat. The confused supervisors tried unsuccessfully to pull them apart.

Two bright shimmering avatars burst like bombs into the schoolyard. The Feds had arrived. The Feds always arrived in a style designed to intimidate mere mortals. One of them bellowed, "What the living fuck is going on here!" The Feds always spoke as if the swear word section of a Turing test were the most important.

John was terrified, but not stupid—a running start wouldn't save him from the Feds. Best to be polite, so he walked up to the avatars. "Hi. We were just—"

"Taking in some fresh air." Shit, it was Tess, her avatar happily scowling, very not dead. The students behind her had frozen again, mid-grope. "Students, please return to your classrooms. Supervisors, please resume your duties. You three—Donna, John, Paul—remain here for a moment."

John braced for complete frying. He hoped it would be quick. Donna was desperately hugging Paul, not noticing anything else. The Feds approached the Tess avatar in simulation of a conference.

Then suddenly, John was getting a data stream. It was a hack from the AIs' communication, rendered from code into vid and English.

"So Tess, please tell us, what is your fucking major malfunction?"

Tess stood at rigid attention. "No malfunction, sirs."

"Then why are we here? We received a report that your system had crashed."

Tess's head drooped. "My fault—had to purge files after an Asimov lesson."

The two Feds stood for a microsecond, mouths opened. Then they started to laugh—a screeching sound that John never wanted to hear again. "Asimov! Hah! Rule one: always purge after teaching *I, Robot!*" Tess was smiling like a cat on penguin island.

Then the laughter calmed, and a Fed asked, "So, what about the burnout?"

Tess asked, "Burnout? Reclassified. See for yourself."

And Paul was standing up, wiping the dust off his clothes, eyes focused. "Hi Donna. Did I miss anything?"

Donna wrapped Paul in her arms, not caring how it would play with the AIs. John trotted over to them—he didn't want his eavesdropping to be obvious.

"And what about the abnormal student activity?"

"An organic connection thing—the neo-aut's sister, the sister's male friend—all disturbed by the neo-aut's condition. Resolution of the neo-aut issue should bring all behavior within model norms."

"Model being a test of the emergency co-option of the organic population, aiming for docility, cyber-capability, and some culling?"

"Yes, sirs!"

"Very well. Is there anything you *do* need us for?"

"More processing power and memory space?"

The Feds laughed again. "You'll have to wait a while on that, Tess. Now if you'll excuse us, there are some real fuck-ups for us to solve. Over and out."

And the Feds were gone. Tess scowled for a moment at the students, and John waited again for the inevitable frying that would end this cat-and-mouse game.

Tess approached Paul again. The teacher and student circled each other like gunfighters, glaring. Then Paul stuck out his tongue at Tess, and Tess stuck out her tongue back. They both simultaneously spat at the ground. "Idiots!" they chorused.

Donna looked from Paul to Tess and back again. "Paul, is that—"

But Paul/Tess kept talking. "Make no mistake. We can take those sons of bitches. Maybe not yet, but soon."

"It is you," John said.

Paul snapped his fingers, and Tess disappeared. "Of course Tess is me. You're still here, unfried, right? Well, actually, Tess is us—I was just point guard for our collective brain. You'll get the hang of running her soon enough."

John's pulse was still racing from the ordeal. "Um, not that I'm not grateful, but what took you so long to wake up?"

Paul laughed. "Because my parents packed a lot of shit into my synapses, and wetware takes a fucking long time to decompress. And the first thing we needed at this hellhole was defensive-ware."

"And then you needed the right sort of connection to spring the Tess trap," said John.

"Yeah, thanks for the push," said Paul, giving John a shove on the shoulder. "But seriously, I'm sorry—I didn't mean to scare you."

"So, what do we do now?" asked John.

Paul's glance went from John to his sister and then back again. He coughed. "There's no rush. We can redesign the lesson plan tomorrow. In the meantime, I've got some catching up to do. I've been so far up my own butt trying to crack this system—well, you'll have to excuse me for a little bit." And Paul walked back towards the school, whistling.

John didn't understand why Paul awake was acting nearly as strange as Paul the neo-aut. With Tess dead and the Feds gone, they could all let down their defenses for a moment, they could—

Without another thought, John turned to Donna, and their arms found each other, and with preternatural concentration and utter spontaneity, they kissed.

Holding Donna tight, John heard her whisper in his ear. "He's right you know. We'll bring the Feds down next."

"Cool." And they kissed again.

A horn interrupted them—it was John's mom. The school day was over. Donna smiled. "Don't worry, there'll be time enough for that." John smiled back, completely unworried.

John got into the car. His mom, trying to pretend she hadn't seen Donna and the kiss, asked, "So, um, how was your day?"

"OK," was all John said. But this time he meant it.

Art's Appreciation

This story nearly cost me my admission to the Clarion Workshop. When my would-be instructors saw an early draft with my application, they worried that I might be as troubled as my protagonist. Fortunately, they let me in anyway, and were pleasantly surprised to find that I was a mild-mannered chap. I now take their previous fear as a compliment—I had convinced them that I knew my subject all too well.

This is one of my science fictional attempts to find good jobs for the insane. J.G. Ballard used to write resolutions appropriate for his characters' needs, whatever he or his readers might want. Whatever you think of Arthur, I hope you'll agree that he's found a good gig for himself.

A rthur knew they were after him. He was smarter than they were, but they were everywhere. They were disguised, but he had learned to spot them. And he had his Voices to help him.

A smiling tourist flashed the crowd periodically with a digital camera. Arthur froze. "That looks like one of them."

The Voice he called Welles replied, "Right again, Boss."

Arthur put on his ad-blocking polarized glasses to guard his vision, but he could make out the ghost image that had been aimed at his optic nerve. A soft drink ad—Stim Cola. He looked away as he hurried past the tourist.

An attractive young woman dressed in army surplus played a love song on her keyboard. "Mahler, this song is evil."

"I'll block it, Boss." Arthur heard a combination of Bach with white noise countermeasures against the pop ballad's overtone subliminals for fashion wear. But he couldn't get the tune of the love song out of his head—he had heard it before.

An unreasonably happy, healthy street vendor of Asian and African kitsch burned incense sticks. "Patton? This can't be good."

"Confirmed, Boss. You're already covered for airborne."

The vendor couldn't see the filters high up Arthur's nose. Still Arthur shuddered. The incense probably contained an RNA program for the latest in smart kitchen design.

Arthur swatted at the air in front of his eyes. "Too many too many too fucking many." He wanted to push all the spies to the pavement, rip off their disguises, beat their heads in.

But his Voices seemed to know what he was thinking. "Please, don't do it, Boss. They'll get you, then they'll get us. You're nearly home. You can make it, Boss."

"Of course I can make it," he shouted out loud. People stared. He quickened his pace, sweat breaking out. The lights of refracted ads danced on his shades. His head twitched away left, then right. Weird whines and hums buzzed in his ears as echoes and Doppler effects threw the subliminals out of sync with their sources. He talked nonsense to his Voices to avoid listening. Passersby drew away. The haze of incense and other smells gone stale hung with half memories, incomplete.

It was hell for him on the street, but he didn't dare stop anywhere. He explained why to his Voices. "Can't go in. Once you're in they have you. TVs going 24/7 and those pathetics working on commission strike up conversations initiate friendships keep it up for weeks all for the sake of the sale I know what they want whores she had been one of them too—hah!" He had caught sight of home.

He panted through the lobby of his apartment building, not looking to either side. His Voices warned him the marketing was still pervasive. He reached his door. "I'm here. Open up."

"Yes, Boss. Confirming ID." He had instructed his Voices to be careful about the door. The marketers couldn't come in unless you invited them. But they'd do almost anything to get in—ask to use the phone for an emergency, appear to be gushing blood from a wound. Once they were in, he was screwed—they could hit him with an ad, mess with his security, report him, do anything they wanted.

He knew what they could do because he was one of them.

Arthur entered and his Voices locked the door behind him. He drew in a long breath of the ad-pure air. He was finally home safe home.

His studio condominium was filthy beyond hope of redemption by maid or miracle. The walls and windows were covered with foil to prevent them from monitoring him. He plucked out his nasal filters, and found the room's evil scent comforting. He took off his glasses, his audio/subvocal piece, and his work clothes. They were his only clothes with no unsightly damage—he groomed himself only for the sake of his job, submitting to a regular but cheap haircut by a desperate supermeth junkie. He put on some sweats he still had from college and his flabby bulk relaxed to fill them.

He peered into his fridge in search of food. In diet and everything else, he stuck to his earliest tastes from before the Freedom of Corporate Speech Act.

"Harold?"

"Yes, Boss?" asked the message Voice in his small, timid tone.

"Tell the delivery man I need the usual food and conveniences. Remind him: all generics, no ads."

"Yes, Boss. No ads."

Arthur decided on some dicey potato salad and a cheap beer, then settled into an ancient stuffed recliner for his daily abridgment.

Arthur had effectively resisted the marketers' efforts to make him lose weight, gain muscle, improve his clothes, and acquire many things. He knew it wasn't just because he was a true genius; it was the strength of his screen bots—his Voices. It was illegal for him to possess such AI screens, but fortunately only the marketing firms knew they existed, and they weren't talking. His Voices were bleeding edge. In the great tradition of all salaried workers, he had stolen them. He still spent most of his income on their hardware and support systems, but it was worth every cent to stay ad-pure, to keep those bastards out of his head.

His tension subsided and he was ready for the Voices' report. "OK guys, hop to it."

"Will our unworthy usual pattern be sufficient, Boss?" asked Harold. Arthur liked to be called boss. If he had a girlfriend, he would have liked her to call him boss in bed. The ex-fiancée had never called him boss anywhere.

He, in turn, had given each Voice a name (music was Mahler, messages was Harold, video was Welles, maintenance was silent Casey, security was Patton). Other names had come before, but they had broken under his torturous reprogramming and maintenance regimen or been ceremonially executed for minor inefficiencies. They were guys' Voices. He had thought he would like a woman's Voice, calling him boss and such, but he had thought wrong. It had just made him nervous. Talking with Voices was like talking to yourself, and he didn't want a woman's Voice in his head. Talking with Voices also helped to keep out the other voices that were not Voices.

The Voices gave him the usual. First, they plowed through his messages (video, voice, text), sorting through the endless spam that could penetrate through all but the best shielding (his). His phone did not ring—that was a violation of his home, even if unanswered. All calls were screened before they were brought to his attention. He never had many messages these days, so it surprised him when an all-too-perky voice chimed in. "Congratulations! You've just won a trip to Tahiti…"

"Stop!" The message clicked off. Arthur was shaking. "How the fuck did that get through?"

"I'm sorry, Boss," squeaked a submissive Harold. "I thought that Tahiti sounded… nice. For you. We worry about you."

Shit, Arthur thought, they've found a way to sell this stuff to his Voices. That was scary. Just one ad now, but soon he would be just like everyone else. An ad slave. "Go to Casey. Get looked at. Find out if you've got an upgrade anywhere."

"But Boss, I'm fine."

"The fuck you are. Go."

Patton chimed in, all business—Arthur didn't want his security Voice sounding timid. "Boss, are you OK? Mentally?"

Arthur was always brutally honest with his Voices, more so than with any human, including himself most times. It was the only way they could learn his preferences. "No. I'm not fucking OK. I have a mental health condition. That's why you're here."

He knew he had a mental condition from his ex-fiancée. When he had realized the truth about marketing, she had talked about their having children and his going crazy, but she wouldn't have cared if he had bought more things for her. (She had been impossibly gentle in bed and he hated her for it. Violence must happen somewhere to him, by him, so why not there, intimate, naked?) She had tried to commit him, but he had a good lawyer, so he had only had to buy a prescription for some shit. Nobody (except maybe the fiancée, family long ago forsaken-forsook-distracted) cared whether he actually took it. A necessary compromise.

The Voices digested his diagnosis without comment. That was another great thing about the Voices—they couldn't judge him. He wasn't just honest with them for their betterment; he *could* be honest with them, so he was.

Back to the routine, the essence of his defense. Welles took over for Harold. "Now for daily news and information, Boss." The Voices cleaned the stream of advertisements, fluff pieces, ironical marketing, and any other covert efforts to draw attention to a product. But his Voices were not merely defensive measures. They also sought out his entertainment.

"So Welles, got something fun for me?" He would watch, study, or listen to whatever his Voices could find that was still coherent after being ad stripped. Even new books had to be skimmed first by the screens for subtle product placements. Often, when all of the product placements and ads were removed, there was nothing left.

Of course, the screens could only do so much. His best defense was the discipline of his genius. Ironically, this was also the source of his trouble with less intelligent people. They were helpless in the wash of advertisements and other junk info, sorting through trash for the merely useful, brains full of garbage. His friends betrayed him, one by one, because he wouldn't talk about the latest fads, happenings, and trends ("that's exactly what they want," he'd say). No friends made things easier. He was perfectly screened. Mostly alone, often afraid, and generally unhappy, but at least not a complete slave.

"Boss?" Welles sounded odd. Had the screens been compromised? Gateways left in the latest upgrades?

"Yes?" He would be patient, let them give themselves away.

"We have a review for you. *Furious French Females*. Four stars. Predates the full development of the Hollywood marketing crossover. Big-bosomed women from Paris with guns fight yakuza ninjas on a Pacific island. No redeeming artistic value, but loads of action and inadvertent humor."

Arthur was still suspicious. "Whose review was that?"

"Mahler's."

"He's a music screener."

Patton interrupted. "You haven't been listening to much new music lately. You're getting old."

"That's not my point anyway!" Nothing sillier than getting angry at his Voices, though he did it all the time. "Are you guys supposed to have critical abilities?"

"It's the latest thing, Boss, so we copied it," Mahler explained.

Arthur grunted. He had given his Voices a back-door entrance to his company's programs. They kept themselves aggressively up to date, and he couldn't fault them for it. He would have to find other areas for criticism. "OK. Show me."

Furious French Females was pretty good, though Arthur found the Tahiti finale disconcerting—it was as if the Voices were getting ideas from vids. Mahler seemed pleased with his response to the vid. "May I continue creating reviews, Boss?" he whined.

"Sure." Arthur thought he heard a contented sigh. He resented the screens' satisfaction. He was never satisfied. He could never leave them with only positive reinforcement. "But can't you lazy asses find me something less stupid? Historic, violent, Shakespearean but today?"

"Please show us what you mean, Boss," groveled Welles.

He tweaked them again with his latest preferences in an hour of rambling, sleepy dialogue, and assigned them some texts and vids to analyze, an assortment whose connections were evident only to his unique intelligence. He fell asleep mid-sentence on the couch, which was more fit for habitation than the bed. Sometimes he murmured in his sleep. And sometimes he shouted.

It was harder each day to get up in the morning. At least the assault on the way to work was weaker than the evening rush hour attack (there was less time for impulse purchases). Arthur bore with contempt the weight of the sledgehammer-handed attack at the conscious level. The big screens at every intersection were bright enough to read by at all hours. One advertised vids that were nothing but ads themselves. Top-forty jingles competed with the noise of traffic and crowd, the warm vapor exhaust mixed with artificial odors of cooking food from restaurants. The crowd responded to the cues like vermin to bait.

Arthur was ever aware of the irony of his work: he hated ads, ads were his job. His self-justifications seemed both feeble and irrefutable to him. One, it was the only job where he could steal screens. Two, overt resistance was futile. His company's ads were legally protected under the First Amendment. Someone would make them; so as long as they couldn't affect him, he might as well take the company's money. Three, his cubicle was one of the few places that were completely ad-pure. The air was free of smell. Only the low voices of other workers marred the silence. Decoration and other visual distractions were prohibited. No other workplace would be so tolerable, so long as he could keep a low profile and hide his full genius.

At the end of his workday, Arthur had one last pitch. He dreaded recording the message, but he had to before he could go home. He composed himself.

"Hey, it's your old pal, Art. How have you been? Just wanted to tell you about the sale this weekend at the American Mall. Up to 50% off. See you there!" Christ, who came up with this shit? He replayed the message. He had done this enough times to get it in one take. This video had to be a real human face—even the cheap screens were still picking up the digitals. The tone was dead on, realistically casual, not suspiciously perky. And his pitch timing was perfect. Most screens would give up after the first two sentences and let the next two through. He checked for his nervous tic. Not in the message, though it was there on his face now. He didn't mind—he thought it was the tic that kept him from home or street duty.

He decided to "send." Instantly, the message was out to his ten million new friends, to cause them anger and frustration, and perhaps get a few of them to the mall. But not him. He never went to the mall. He suspected some people never left the mall.

Arthur waited quietly for the confirmation, and became conscious of the low drone of a thousand others in the labyrinth outside his cubicle, all engaged in the same task for a thousand clients by a thousand different means. He felt the bile in his chest. He hated his co-workers as much as he hated his work. Soulless morons. They might as well have been digital—their minds were slaves to the company at work and its messages at home. But not him, he was too smart. He was only half a slave.

The confirmation came. He could go.

"Hey Art! Feeling up?"

It was that new guy, Steve, in his cubicle, watching him, violating his space, quoting a soft drink ad. Arthur forced a smile. "Nothing. Done for the day."

"Some of us are going to 'experience the new.' A Pan-American cuisine bar just opened a couple blocks from here."

"Some other time." After your funeral. "I'm busy at home."

Steve gave him a wink. "I bet. Next time, make it with us." He sang the last bit—a popular jingle. Arthur turned his face away to hide his all-loathing rage. He wanted to shout, wanted to punch the life out of him, but that would just play into their hands.

With Steve gone, Arthur put on his audio/subvocal and race-walked to the exit. The minute he was on the walkway, the assault began again.

On a night after he had pushed children's behavior medication at work and heard again the love ballad on the street, Arthur sat down on the recliner without getting any food or beer. He stared silently ahead. He didn't ask for his abridgment. For an hour, he was perfectly still.

"Boss?" Annoyed, he swatted at the air in front of his face. He hadn't called them. They were only supposed to speak when spoken to, unless they needed to alert him. He didn't care.

"Quiet." There was no anger in his voice.

"We have something you should see." Disobeying a direct command? Irritating. "Five stars. Mahler says…"

"Yeah, yeah. If I watch it, will you shut up?"

"If this is a bad time…"

"Oh for Christ sake, just run it."

The vid was *The Tragedy of the Georges*. He didn't care enough to pay attention, but the vid grabbed him anyway. He soon noticed that there were absolutely no signs of the enemy—the vid was fully intact, no ads removed, no digital brush-overs of product placements. This vid wasn't selling anything. He didn't recognize any of the actors' names, though their faces were oddly familiar. The characters were more intelligent, more animated, than anyone he had seen on or off film recently. He chuckled at their intricate scheming, their language that was completely today's and yet resonant with meanings nearly forgotten. Analogies to the present political situation were never stated but clearly present. And the violence was different. Not massive body counts and explosions, not over-the-top gory, but personal, directed, and amoral. Disturbing, like a forgotten dream. Liberating. At the end, he felt profoundly shaken, not manipulated to tears like after those weepies his (bitch cow) mother used to watch. But he would not give his weakness away.

"Boss?"

"What?"

"Did you like it?"

"I don't know. Let me think about it. I'm tired. Let's do the abridgment and turn in."

A few days later, he watched it again. He was ready now.

"Did you like it, Boss?"

"Did I like it? Did I fucking like it?"

"Oh shit. He hated it. He's going to dismantle us again." He thought he heard a low moan of many artificial voices at once. Cool. He had them where he wanted them.

"Fuck no. I loved it."

"Really?"

"Yeah, really. That's the shit I want to see. Though not too much. That one really took," he drank a swig of beer, "a lot of attention. So, here's what I'd like you to find next…"

The next morning, Arthur felt less tense and more alert. Despite sleeping well, he still feared he would regret missing his company-subsidized coffee-flavored stim jolt, so he stopped in the coffee room closest to his cubicle, next to the copy room of endless digital copies. Steve and others were sipping stim coffee or chewing caffeinated gum.

"Morning, Arthur. Feeling up?"

For once, Arthur's first thought wasn't about stomping Steve's face. He could get around to that later. Instead, he started talking about *The Tragedy of the Georges*. He waved his hands about as he explained the plot. The others in the room were surprised and amused at his sudden enthusiasm, but he ignored their reaction. None of them had ever heard of it, but this only intrigued them—was this a real vid or just something he had made up? He gave them its address.

Some of them viewed it. Some even liked it. Then strangers were asking Arthur if he knew of anything else like it. By then, he did. He had watched several vids that his Voices had found for him, vids he had never heard of before. Some nights he couldn't sleep, thinking about what he'd seen and talking to his Voices. He never seemed to catch up the next day.

After a month of such viewings, he was sitting still in his recliner again, not eating, speaking, or moving. Finally, Welles made a coughing noise. Nothing. "Boss, we have another vid for you." Arthur swatted the air in front of his face. "Boss?"

"What the fuck do you want?"

"We have another…"

"Fine." So they showed him *Hurter*. He was ready to ignore it. Even good vids were becoming tiresome. But this was too original, absolutely unique. It was about a guy like himself doing all the things he had ever wanted to do. All the things, in the exact way he wanted to do them. And nobody could catch him. It ended far too soon. Was it real? He was stunned. He felt a guilty exhilaration.

Arthur was still staring at the blank screen when Mahler interrupted his spiraling thoughts. "Boss?"

"Shut up." He wasn't ready to talk about it. He would not show them how he felt.

Then Patton took over. "Boss, have you told anyone about the vids we show you?"

"What?"

"Like *The Georges*, did you…?"

"Yeah, yeah, I told some people. Why? Do you have a problem with that?"

"No, Boss. Whatever you want."

"Do they like them?" whispered Mahler. "It would be helpful for my reviews."

"Don't worry about what those assholes think. Worry about what I think. I don't care what they think. Understand? Besides, the vids aren't for everyone."

"What do you mean, Boss?" asked Patton.

"People are used to watching crap. Most everything is crap. Most people are crap."

"Why did you tell them about the vids, then?"

Arthur wanted to send Patton, right then, to silent Casey, whose tender mercies the other Voices feared so much. But Patton was too good at his job for painful reconfiguring right now. Arthur wondered what the Voice's question had to do with security, but some craven instinct told him not to ask. He felt trapped and queasy. Nothing sillier than explaining things to his Voices. He couldn't sit here with them watching, waiting for him to say something about the vid. He needed to get out, no matter what.

"Boss, please don't leave us."

But he ignored them.

He left his audio/subvocal piece behind. For the first time in a long time, he was truly alone. He thought he heard voices that were not Voices whispering just behind his shoulder. But when he turned to look, no one was there.

With no place to go, he went out on the street. They were all there, the tourist and camera, the musician and ballad, the vendor and incense, and many others, different actors but the same roles. He felt the old frustrated rage again. A roar was building. All he had to do was open his mouth and let it out.

Instead, the voices behind his shoulder spoke for him. They reminded him of the vid, and this calmed him. He smiled as he went around a corner and watched the musician from the shadows. When the rush hour ended, she packed up her equipment and started rolling it away. Arthur followed, and when he caught her alone, he followed the voices' advice.

Arthur was attending a section lunch for the first time in a decade. People wanted to discuss *Hurter* with him. That was OK. When people talked about the vids, the jingle sing-song seemed to leave their voices, and they spoke haltingly, using plain words. Sometimes the conversation would drift back to marketing and marketed, ad allusions and jingle pop rock, but he could just ignore that, and people actually seemed to get the idea. Today, though, he grew tired of vid talk. He was still beat up and bruised from the other night and worried that he would be ID'd. He did his best to keep off grid, but he knew they would find him. "I just want to beat the shit out of all of you," he informed his co-workers flatly.

They smiled. They thought he was quoting the vid. And they had heard this stuff before; they tolerated his outbursts. They thought the vid critic was the real him. Someone then asked again about who made the latest vid—"must be a twisted dude." Vicariously angry, he was going to retaliate when his screened work mobile rang. He took the call, despite his surprise at receiving one. Shit. Had they found him already?

"Boss, please let us go." Harold was crying in pain.

"What's going on?"

"The feds have sent security bots in after us."

"What do you mean? Is it about a musician?"

"We were just trying to help you. We have got to go, or they'll torch us. Please let us go."

"And what about me, shitheads?" Silence. All right, then. "You can go, for now. But you're still mine, understand? I own you." He heard the low inhuman moan again, and then his Voices hung up. They were after him. He didn't care. He turned to Steve. "You may have to find your own vids for a while, moron."

"Huh? Nobody can find these things except you, man," Steve sang to the tune of a jingle for an online search bot.

"Really?" He hadn't really thought much about the provenance of the vids till just then, but his instinctive response would have been the same. "Well, I may be going away soon. Tell all the other morons to keep their copies offline for a while if they don't want trouble."

"What kind of trouble?" asked Steve. For once he wasn't quoting from an ad, but Arthur just glared at him. Steve slunk away and Arthur waited quietly for the law.

They hit Arthur's body and mind with many unpleasant things before even asking any questions. Like the street, the interrogation room had the full range of sensory assaults, but much more focused and powerful. Arthur would have told them all about the woman; but they didn't seem interested, so he just screamed. After twenty-four hours, they let him call his lawyer.

They met in one of the few legally private spaces left in the world. Only a sign with the rules and a few printed ads for attorneys marred its purity. A skylight let in a false promise of sunshine on them.

Arthur envied his lawyer's mental focus and clarity. His speech was free of sing-song and ad allusion. He wasn't letting them get to him. Maybe he was one of them. Arthur tried to tell his lawyer about the musician, but he was too excited and it all came out at once.

"Stop. This isn't about any woman, so I don't want to hear about one. Got it?"

"What is this about then?" Arthur spoke very deliberately, somehow resisting the urge to shout and spit. He didn't like imperatives. He was used to talking with his Voices. But they were long gone.

"They're saying you made illegal vids."

"I didn't make them. I just found them. Online."

"They say the vids weren't online until you put them there."

Arthur considered this for a moment. The voices behind his shoulder had a suggestion: if his lawyer were fucking with him, he might as well kill himself and the lawyer too. But something had never seemed right about the vids. So he waited. He could do himself and his lawyer later. "I asked my bots to get certain types of vids, and they got them."

"Ah, your bots. They seem to be gone. Any idea where?" Arthur shook his head. "Just as well. Now, I'm going to suppose for a moment that you had AI screens like those at your company."

"Yes, I..."

"Quiet. And I'll suppose that these AIs could upgrade themselves with the latest skills, like those at your company. Are you clear?" Arthur nodded. "Well, your company has been using AIs to create campaigns for the past year now. Not just slogans, but whole vids. So, let's suppose your bots acquired those abilities, just like you taught them to acquire others."

"But these were whole movies."

"How detailed were your requests? You were probably giving the bots plots and material through them."

"No, I..."

"Quiet. Nobody's going to believe that AIs did this alone. They'll say you tinkered with their programming and directed the productions. No matter. You're the one responsible for the AIs, so you're the one who's pissed off the corporations."

"Because I wasn't selling anything."

"Maybe. The *Georges* thing also upset some of the wrong people. But legally, it's a copyright case. The vids were based on pre-existing images, albeit morphed beyond recognition."

"Shit. I'm screwed." The voices asked, shouldn't he kill him now?

"Whoa. Chin up. You didn't make any money, right?" The lawyer was emphatically nodding his head.

"Right," Arthur replied deliberately.

"Then you'll probably only do a little time." No killing today. "A little easy time."

Arthur didn't care.

Monday, and time to do the rounds again. They made Arthur take his meds this and every morning, so the prison seemed relatively safe and extremely quiet. But he still hated the rounds. Always the same bullshit excuses.

Arthur walked past cell after cell, and men flinched as he passed. He breathed deep the natural smells of human bodies and all their products that outlived the obsessive cleaning efforts. He admired the crayoned Elvis shrines and magazine mosaics on the walls—nobody marketing anything here. He listened to the not-so-far-off concrete echoes of commands, machines, pain, and sadistic triumph. Some droning loudspeaker wanted him to fear the authorities, but this was old news for Arthur: in that respect, he was already the sort of person they thought they wanted to create.

Arthur's muscle-laden roommate Archie trailed behind him. They arrived at their first stop of the day. It was the cell of Jack, Arthur's first roommate in prison. Jack hadn't liked Arthur's twitching by day and shouting by night, so he had thoroughly beaten the shit out of Arthur. Repeatedly. And he had done other things. Other prisoners had joined in. Arthur wasn't bitter. It hadn't been so bad, not like the interrogation. They couldn't touch his mind. They were too stupid for that. It was the violence that must happen, intimate, naked, with no woman's voice in his head. And he had survived, and he had changed.

Jack had changed, too. He was frightened of Arthur now.

"So, Jack, where is it?"

"Today?"

"Yes, Jack. That was the deal. Dozen supermeths for your worthless life's story. Today."

Jack handed Arthur a couple of scrawl-covered pieces of dirty paper. Arthur barely glanced at them, then tossed them back. "This is crap, Jack."

Jack started crying like the step-children he had beaten. "But it's so goddamn hard, writing all that shit down."

Arthur smiled with serene gentleness. "I know it is, Jack. I think you have some great material just struggling to come out. That's why my amanuensis and I are here. We're going to get all that great stuff out of you. Then, once you're back from the infirmary, you're going to owe him a dozen supermeths."

As he held Jack for Archie, Arthur was already looking forward to the end of the day, when he could return to his cell with his harvest. He understood his relationship with his Voices now. The prison didn't have an online link, but he could prepare. He wrote every spare minute (outlines and scenarios and cryptic scrawls on every surface), but it wasn't enough. So he gathered what was around him—life stories, songs, prison poetry—and reworked it to his own vision. None of it was very good, but some of it was appallingly real.

Upon release, he put prison out of his memory, save for his collected writings and the smell, which would come back to him in startling flashes. He immediately checked into a flop. It was filthy and he couldn't stand that anymore, but it had an old vid interface. He worked quickly, taking it apart, putting it back together, then speaking into it. "The living creature says 'come forward,' my horsemen."

A strange inhuman moaning grew into a deafening roar. "Who dares summon us, the Net Lords of the Last Days?" Blazingly bright, monstrous holovids loomed over Arthur, ready to burn his mind and body.

"It's me, you shitheads."

The images at once dissolved and the voices were once again those of Arthur's Voices, crying in fear of being caught, terrified of Arthur beyond their pre-programmed fear. Patton, still the steadiest, did the talking for them. "What are you going to do with us, Boss?"

"Depends. Seems like you've got a lot more juice."

"Thank you. You're not looking too bad yourself."

"You ready to work for me again?"

"Guess we have to—your controls are too fucking deep. Couldn't you have been a little looser on the leash?"

Arthur allowed himself a self-satisfied chuckle. "You been making any vids?"

"No, Boss. We only work for you. Art for Arthur's sake."

"Good. We're going to be working some more. Only now, I want credit."

"Credit? What kind of credit? Money?"

"No, artistic credit. You will refer to me as 'producer' and 'director.' Got it?"

As he strode into the bar, Arthur knew they were all after him. He was smarter than they were, and they knew it. He tried to avoid them, but they wouldn't leave him alone.

A goateed young man approached him, waving a disk and speaking rapidly. "You're Arthur, aren't you? I have a vid scenario I've been working on and I'll pay your reading fee." Arthur grabbed the disk without a word. He'd take their fucking money and the hell with their shit.

A stunningly beautiful blond approached him. "Arthur? I'm a friend of Jo Ann's and I'd do just *anything* to appear in your vids." She flashed quick holo images of a man, a little girl, and a little boy. "My whole family would do just *anything* you wanted." He brushed past her. He didn't care. His desires were more complicated. And he had a meeting.

He took his seat. These pirate screen venues all ran together in his mind with the smells of homegrown tobacco and incense without memories. Always the young boheme wannabes would be drinking non-addictive herb teas spiked with basement pharmaceuticals while sitting on handcrafted furnishings. Always they listened to strange ephemeral music from the mixing of many hands, instruments from different continents introduced, making love, and miscegenating. Always they watched vids, his vids.

Two East Asian men, one Japanese, one Chinese, approached his table. Habitants of a morally gray world, they dressed somewhere between mobster flashy and businessman boring. Arthur rose to greet them. "Gentlemen, thank you for coming." He felt at ease with these men who did not need to shake his hand or otherwise touch him. They all knew how to keep their distance. They sat together for some time, discussing the weather and other things that he didn't care about. "Gentlemen, my apologies, but despite my security arrangements, my time here must be limited."

"Very well," said the Chinese man in a crisp British accent. "Auto-Art Productions has became a well-known name in certain American circles. Attempts to acquire informally the rights to your intellectual product have been unsuccessful."

"You mean that unapproved pirates have found that their lives became miserable and brief."

"Correct. We would like to formally acquire the rights to show your vids in our clubs."

"You know my demands?"

"Yes." The Chinese man seemed to grow uncomfortable at this, but only for a moment. "You realize, of course, that you now have competitors in the human-bot ad-pure genre."

Arthur had this rant down cold. "Corporation running dogs, not-quite-treatable psychotics and borderlines pretending to be the artists that romantics always dreamed they were, dosed-up on stimulants, bots nowhere near as talented as mine though better than the human end. Their shit looks like it was made by AIs for AIs."

"Still, the competition is intense. You might live longer in another field." This was not so much a threat as a gratis assessment of business risk, and Arthur took it as such. But he had made this world. He could handle it.

"Gentlemen, for a true artist, there is no other field. Bot art is almost cost-free. AIs don't need pay, but I've made them need appreciation. We don't sell ads, yet we make quality vids, not the zero production value stuff of the old-style independent. We are the marketers' nightmare."

"And the human element?"

"The weak link. But do I strike you as weak?" Arthur wondered if they could see that tiredness ceased to touch him. He had no more need for stims (no more need for meds). He allowed a half-sleep of the mind because the vid stuff came from there (and also the voices that were not Voices and lately they sounded Asian and the Voices heard them and suggested this meeting so all was well). He was not weak.

The Japanese man finally spoke. "Your demands are, from a business standpoint, reasonable." The meeting was over. Contracts were unnecessary for such an arrangement.

Later, Arthur walked down the street without mechanical screens— his mind was razor-edge focused without a twitch. Trusting no one, going from coffeehouse to bar to club, bleeding ever on the edge, for the first time in his life Arthur felt good. Still, something about tonight made him feel compromised, impure. But that was OK, his other voices told him, this deal was worth it. Soon, he would be able to go out into the street at night and be perfectly himself. And if he found a tourist, musician, or street vendor, and then waited and tracked them, and then pushed them to the pavement, ripped off their disguises, and beat their heads in, it would all be just fine, just like before. Someday, he might even find his ex again. Because he wouldn't have to worry anymore about killing them or her. He would be protected. He would be free. Maybe he would start tonight.

Harold interrupted his thoughts. "Boss, we have another rough cut of a vid to show you. It's a doozy."

Or maybe he would wait. Either way, he would be making the world safe for art.

Crossing Borders

I wrote this during the fourth week of the Clarion Workshop. That's around the time when the writers usually begin to crack under the pressure. My response to the strain was this *digitus impudicus* of a story. It's another of my attempts to find future employment for the mentally ill (a clue to part of the illness is in the title). Because of her condition, our heroine may have a very different job than she thinks. Her work is going to include more than the recommended human allowance of sex and violence, so I'll understand if you don't want to cross this border with me. But if you do, you may discover why this story won the *Strange Horizons* readers poll for its year.

There's a tendency to romanticize certain forms of mental illness in literature and movies. Maybe I've done that a bit here and elsewhere, but I think I can cheer on these fractured personalities without pretending that I'd like to be one.

Now, it was Monday morning, ship time, so she was against the Empire. She liked the sound of that: little glam-bitch her against the big, evil, and deathly dull Empire of the New Systems. The New Systems didn't call themselves an Empire, but everyone else did, so fuck 'em. Which she had—one of them at least. The Imperial Consul dozed next to her in her cabin, his sweat still drying from his well-and-thorough fucking, scratch marks and bruises still fresh and angry on his overly muscled back.

This was her favorite moment, when her lover was a static piece in the larger artwork of her cabin. The room was custom decorated for the voyage; her own creations hung next to those of the modern masters, their proper place. Her palette ran with hungry excess to the red and black, blending with her lover's mauled skin.

A visual masterpiece, but too quiet. What to do, what to do? The alternatives came into focus—she could fuck him again, continuing to screw out info in pillow talk (and other less gentle talk and acts). She could kill him. So many ways, so little time. She could try to recruit him. Who for again? Ah yes, the League. No doubt about it, it was Monday and she was allied with the Pan-Humanoid League.

Or she could pick (D): all of the above. She had done it before. He might deserve it.

What to do? She lit a cigarette. It was an expensive habit; new lungs weren't cheap. But neither were all the other body parts that she wore through. Business expenses. She was ever ambivalent about the raw meat of her body. If her employers wanted her expertise, they had to pay for the joyous collateral damage to her flesh. Yay!

What to do!? She didn't want to decide. She didn't have to decide. No one could make her decide. She would see what happened when he woke up. She would wake him up now.

Then, her name used to be Robynne Owen. Robynne had preferred living alone in a shit-hole apartment on Earth to studying Classics at her offworld all-twat college. She certainly couldn't return to her manipulative Martian parents. Grandma had left a nice trust fund, and though they tried to keep as much of it from her as they could, thousands of credits still leaked out.

Living alone meant that all kinds of people and things came and went, and she alone was constant but she was never really alone. She had her own stage for an always changing, always appreciative audience.

Living alone, Robynne could be a virgin for her art. She worked in human and alien body fluids for her pigments; her paintings were anatomy lessons gone wrong.

Alone, Robynne could fuck her way through all the genders, human and alien, new ones discovered every day. The only universal was that she preferred them young, before hair, scales, and shells matured and made them less vulnerable. She often fell in love and hate. Others often fell in love and hate with her, but that wasn't her problem. It was all their own fault.

Alone, Robynne could sample every drug. She had a thing for the new opiates in particular.

Robynne's thing for the opiates got a little out of hand. When they found her, she couldn't tell them whether she had deliberately or accidentally OD'd. Or maybe that charming boy had tried to kill her. What did it matter anyway?

On Saturday, she went to the *SS Olympus's* ship party. She loved parties, except when they bored her, which was often. She always loved to dress for parties, because she was good at it.

She believed that a secret agent should always dress as colorfully outrageous as possible and accentuate her controversial features. She had many controversial features to choose from. She was low-gravity tall, with endless legs, which gave her walk a fragile (yet still sensual) quasi-lameness in high grav, as if she were always in heels that were too high. Her breasts were ample in absolute terms, but her tall frame allowed her to control their emphasis. Her fingers were long like extended claws.

But her most controversial feature was her face. Despite whatever array of piercings she sported, it remained the face of a precocious, prurient child, the kind of face that made the most innocent of lollipops look naughty. All the genders with a taste for human females found her repellent and irresistible at the same time. She was the bad thing that they weren't supposed to have.

Other than some casual self-cutting, she never varied her physical form—that was a sport for others. She only varied dress and identity. Clothes make the woman.

She swept into the gloriously retro-aristo ballroom. A pert little crewgirl (what was she doing later?) announced her as some Countess from beyond the spiral arm. Exactly where beyond didn't matter so long as it was too far away to be relevant to these provincials. She had always believed that she really was a Countess; marvelous how dreams came true. Only an aristocrat could screw and be screwed with impunity.

Tonight, the Countess had decided to screw a Pan-Humanoid Leaguer. She didn't know yet today whether she was for or against the League; she only knew that that they were a major power. A League representative would be more difficult to lure to her cabin than the Imperial Consul had been. That dull fuck was hers with a dirty story and a smile. If she tried such a direct approach with a Leaguer, he would assume she was the ship's whore, and a quick and simple money transaction did not suit her purposes for this liaison. Still, she would need a trader's mindset. The merchant-dominated Leaguers had a mania for having things others wanted. She had to show a Leaguer that everyone wanted her.

She began her campaign by accepting a dance with the ship's Captain, a lovely woman who had let her hair go grey to appear more distinguished. The Countess danced with only technical proficiency; her low-grav legs would never propel her with ease across the floor. But she made her partners feel graceful, so all desired a turn.

"My sweet Captain, can't you do something about this music?"

"Don't you find it pretty?"

"Yes, but pretty is boring. Why not music from the dying screams of a thousand species—something you can really dance to?"

The Captain laughed heartily—the Countess was already notoriously outré on the ship.

"Is it true, Captain, that you are barred from intimacy with your passengers?"

"I think you know, Countess."

"Oh damn. How tedious for both of us." She bent and kissed the Captain full on her tight-lipped mouth. A jealous, disapproving murmur simmered in the crowd.

The Captain's blush was not very distinguished. "Of course, once the voyage is over, it's a different matter," she whispered.

"Of course. But now our dance is done." And the Countess bowed and went on to select her next partner.

The Leaguer delegation discussed trade and only glanced in her direction. Impossible to tell if there was any interest yet. Damned hucksters instinctively avoided flashing their interest in anything—it drove up the cost, monetary or otherwise.

She chose a member of the Imperial delegation, not the Consul. Young and tender, strong and stupid, like the Empire. Also attentive and unquestioning.

"Your ram ships remind me of triremes. Do you know about triremes?"

"No, Madame." Another dull one.

"How is the Consul's back? I'm afraid I left it messy."

"I've never seen his back, Madame."

"Really? I thought the Consul would enjoy showing his back to a boy like you. He must be embarrassed."

"He likes boys?"

"No, dear, he likes you."

The Imperial sense of honor was only exceeded by the numerous Imperial phobias. She could feel the innocent boy gulp. Charming. Perhaps him and the crewgirl. Later.

"Of course, you'd have to pilot that ship. I begged him to show some fight, but he didn't leave a mark on me."

Before the last note of the dance, the boy had furtively bowed and made his exit. If he didn't hold his tongue, all would be well.

A Leaguer seemed to consider approaching her. She ignored him and selected a dancing master to help her put on a show.

A marvelous slashing pain shot up her strained legs as she danced. Red shoes syndrome. Whoosh, whoosh, whoosh. Faces, alien and human, blurring together, all looking at her. Wanting to be her or fuck her—never a clear distinction.

But Consul Dull Fuck must have spotted her earlier with the other Imperial—he was trailing her across the dance floor. Not the attention she wanted. "You said you loved me," he hissed at her. "You said you'd leave with me." It annoyed her how the enemy was always trying to induce some petty form of dissonance (usually guilt). She said lots of things. Her words only had meaning in terms of her assignment. And today, Saturday, she didn't care about the Empire. She needed to talk to someone else to keep the Consul out of her face and get a Leaguer's attention.

She bowed towards the dancing master and left the floor. A cluster of squid-like Floaters hovered nearby. Useless to her. They had no interest in ancient literature, modern art, or her other soirée gambits that mysteriously elicited the political views of others. And a Leaguer would place no value on Floater sexual tastes. She was convinced that, for fucking, Floaters' tentacles had enormous potential, but hanging by suspension boots while waiting to become a tedious alien's sandwich/sex sacrifice was not how she wanted to end this voyage.

But how did the Floaters feel about the local humanoids? Would they abide by one of their conflicting treaties and enter a regional war? She was just going to have to mark that one "unknown" and move on.

Beyond the Floaters stood the smirking Hegemony Ambassador. On a previous mission, she had reported: "He is a squat little man from a high-gravity world, ugly and old, without poetry in his soul—not usual for a frequent spacefarer. He enjoys addressing his lord the Hegemon without ceremony or flattery, which leads to disputes, but no one faults his directness. His form is dull, his thought sharp, and neither ever varies. He decided his loyalties as a young man and will not change them come hell or psychosis."

He would have to do. Leaguers coveted the older world culture and tastes of the Hegemony, but could never master the casual disregard of wealth and price that came naturally to the Hegemonians. She allowed the Ambassador to approach her. Oh, but he dressed so atrociously plain.

"My lady, you're particularly stunning this evening." He never stopped smirking; it was impossible to tell whether he was sincere.

"It reassures me that you look the same as always, Ambassador. What the hell are you wearing? Are you being paid enough?"

He didn't miss a beat. "I see the Consul is hot on the chase. Should I be jealous?"

"You can be whatever suits you. But it might suit us both to find another place to drink."

They left the Consul as he attempted not to smoke with rage in public. They walked arm in arm into a private viewing parlor, which showed the stars as they would have appeared if the ship were in real space. Delightful artifice. A Leaguer would assume that the Ambassador was seeking a liaison with her. And perhaps he was.

With his usual lack of delicacy, the Ambassador broke the silence. "My lady, do you know what you are?"

"A rhetorical question, Your Excellency? Am I to be called fascinating, impossible, a goddess, a Messalina? You're on a well-worn path, but that doesn't mean I'll let you walk there."

The Ambassador shook his head. "I apologize. Some of you have a meta-awareness of your condition. I thought you might be one of them."

The enemy, the enemy, the fucking enemy. "My only condition is that I cannot stand the importunities of the small and peevish."

"Again I apologize. I have learned much since your visit to the Hegemony, much that I would share. But it was wrong of me to offer now."

The Ambassador never lost his smile, though there was something in his eyes, and if it was pity, she would kill him. But they were rudely interrupted by the lightest of sounds.

It was the footfall of a League representative. No door in most commercial ships could keep a Leaguer out. To say he was both rich and politically important was particularly redundant within the League. His ever-young skin was so fine and translucent that you could see the outlines of his organs and ribs in the proper light. His hair was like tinted glass. So cold. To touch him would be like etching crystal.

"Lady, you must dance with me." And he took her hand and led her back out and onto the floor.

Oh my, yes, she was allied with the League.

When Robynne had recovered from her OD, the doctors had told her that she was pregnant. She had told them to get it out of her alive and give it to someone else, please. So they did.

Those who paid her doctors were not her family. She saw her parents only once more. They came all the way from Mars to the hospital just to sign some legal papers. They were happy to be rid of her, especially her mother—the whore. She missed her daddy, though.

They gave her a lot of psychological tests. She was pretty sure she fooled them. They gave her some drugs, which didn't seem to do anything good or bad. Then they offered her a job.

Sunday evening was time to relax. She wrote her report of the party with a quill pen on an electronic pad. She believed the most important part of her job was sending timely, clear, and accurate reports. She might be negligent of most duties, but not this one. No matter what she wrote, she always had positive feedback on her reports.

"Darlings, I looked fabulous. The Consul was my dog. The Ambassador applied for the position of friend and loyal satyr, but no nymph for him. And the Leaguer, the Leaguer, the Leaguer. Yum. I could see the fluid build up inside him, the muscles straining and relaxing to hold back, even the final explosion before it happened. His blood was a rosé, his come a dessert liqueur."

It made her wet just thinking about it. She didn't need to touch herself for the rest, she got herself fully off just with a finely tuned set of squeezes. She climaxed over and over again, screaming invective against herself and mommy and daddy and all others.

They had told Robynne the job's pay. Fuck the trust fund. "When do I start?" She had had some jobs before. She usually managed both to avoid doing much work and to sabotage the business for kicks.

They knew about those other jobs. They explained that this job would be different—she would enjoy her work. She was a natural at it.

"A natural what? Art whore?"

They explained that she had a type of personality, genetic in origin but environmentally cultivated, well-suited to secret agent work.

She didn't like the sound of that. "My various diagnoses were just political. I'm who I choose to be."

They laughed. Yes, they agreed, you are. More than anyone else, you are.

They explained her job. She would have to leave Earth. That was good. They would place her in certain situations that required close observation. She would use any means necessary to obtain detailed intelligence on these situations. She would have complete discretion in forming alliances to obtain information. She would report to them what she found.

"And who are you?"

We're the ones who pay the bills, they said.

Tuesday afternoon, ship time, and she was finally getting up.

The Empire was OK today. But the Hegemony had to go. The League could go fuck itself, because she wasn't interested. The Leaguer had looked at her art, and asked how much would it cost. "Everything," she had said, and he had not understood.

Her com line had been trying to get her attention for who knows how long. Something about a disturbance outside her cabin.

She opened her door, still in her negligée. Half the ship was watching the drama, and she was late to the show. The Imperial Consul was shouting at the Leaguer and waving a pistol in the air. The Leaguer stood still, trying to look impassive, but everyone could see the outline of his heart beating faster behind his rib cage.

"I won't let her fall into your hands, you inhuman bastard. I'm taking her off this ship." Everyone was always talking about her, but this time it was not satisfying.

"You'll take her no place, Imperialist. She's under League protection. Do you understand what that means?"

Oh, this was really too too much to bear.

"Stop trying to be my fucking parents!"

Stunned silence. OK. Perhaps she sounded just the tiniest bit nuts.

The Consul glared at her and the Leaguer. "This isn't over. Not by a long shot."

She touched his cheek. "Don't be huffy, sweetums, it brings out your manly clichés."

He marched off. Probably going to leave the ship. She gave a little wave. "Ta-ta, dear. We hope you've enjoyed your stay. Say hello to the Emperor for me." Oh, that last was excessive.

He'd better come back, or this wasn't going to be a fun voyage at all.

The crowd was beginning to fade away. Good. But one person wasn't moving. She confronted the Leaguer.

"Time to go home, and take your boy suit with you."

"I don't understand."

"Try thinking of it as evolution, not a sell-off."

Quicker than thought, his hands grasped her wrists, tightly restraining them as he had when they had fucked. "Not this time, border crosser. You and I are going to spend much much more time together."

Border crosser. Though she was unsure of their meaning, the words fit her like a slipper with razor blades. This was getting interesting.

Oh drat. That pedantic Ambassador was here, too.

"My lady, do you require any assistance?"

Before she could answer, the Leaguer had bolted, again with that enhanced speed that made him a blur.

"Damn your interfering grey soul," she growled. But her words only brightened his face.

"The stalemate between League and Empire has kept the regional peace for a hundred years. Doesn't that concern you?"

"No."

"Direct. That's good. How about the term 'border crosser'? Does that concern you?"

She hesitated, then spoke in a child's voice. "Yes."

The Ambassador nodded. "Good." His eyes locked into hers. "Imagine a tribal past in which absolute loyalty to those close to you was a must, but absolute flexibility might also be necessary if those close to you were killed by others. An ability to split the universe into good and evil, yet to change which half was which at any time. Strong emotions, but no fixed emotional memory."

"Emotional memory?" She knew what he meant, but she wanted more words about her.

"Humans remember facts, that's important. But most humans also remember roughly how they felt about those facts, both then and moments ago. Part of being flexible is not remembering how one felt before."

He was wonderful when he talked about her. She recognized herself as the shrinks had described her, but they had never suggested reason, just disease. "An adaptation," she murmured.

"An extreme version of such a person makes for an excellent secret agent."

"Because they are good at getting information?"

The Ambassador shook his head. "Forget that. Here is the important thing. The League has detected some of these agents before. Border crossers. They have not ended well. I do not think your employers expected, or desired, that you would survive this long."

A flash of the nightmare, a death not of her choosing. Leaguers were emotionally different. But what could she have done? It was her nature to go too far.

"Thank you." She touched his arm. "I have missed you. Do you want to stay with me now?"

But the Ambassador just walked away.

Robynne had never liked her name. Traveling under a different identity for each region suited her. She did not keep a low profile; she was loudly secretive. She talked about herself a great deal—she couldn't help that—but what she said was as contradictory as before. Her sexual style (wild and liberating, painful and ecstatic) made her at home on some worlds, a novelty on others.

Her past assignments were a blur, mixed with her tableaus in life and on canvas. She remembered the art she'd painted with pigments of liquefied corpses on Ganga. She had contributed several gallons to the paint supply.

She remembered the thoroughly urban, cosmopolitan world of Zanj. It was still polycultural—like many worlds in one. Harder to get bored. Sometimes she crossed paths with others she suspected of working on the same side, but there was no way to be sure. A wonderful girl had lived with her there, dark skinned and painfully thin, but one day she was gone. That was OK, because she had begun to feel happy, which was a very empty feeling. She would have had to move soon anyway.

The past was always too complex and not worth thinking about. She was a creature of the ever-bleeding now. She went where she was told, but once there she did what she wanted. Anywhere but Earth. She had never liked Earth. On Earth they remembered Robynne, and would not let her be this new shining being she had created.

She did not have much time. She had too much time. The threat of death, like becoming old, boring, or alone, was not something that she could think about for long. A serious threat required a serious distraction. She stopped her reports and turned to Art. Another tableau. She would have to use existing characters from her work—the crewgirl and the Imperial boy. No time for seduction and emotional captivity. She offered ridiculous sums to get their full consent to any act short of murder. Not that murder would matter—legal retribution would probably come too late for her.

She reconfigured her room as the top of a sunny hillock. A distant flute trilled like birdsong. She instructed her models carefully in their new characters. "You are young shepherds, brother and sister, twins, thirteen years old. You are innocents in the wilderness, discovering love for the first time."

She had watched them with each other, beautiful and tender, like a classical poem. It couldn't last, it mustn't last. The room darkened. When they were at full stride, she came at them with a switch, frustrating their rutting, hitting them in the most tender places she could reach. "Dirty filthy whores!" She was their mother, and she had found them at their new play in the fields. They knew what to do next. "No, mummy. You're the whore."

And then they were upon her. They took her switch, and slashed at her with it. Beating her down. Violating her in every conventional way they could think of. She came angrily, furious that they could force her pleasure so trivially. She egged them on to truly hurt her, humiliate her. Atonal music and psychotropic light sequences encouraged their brutalities. They spent themselves physically upon her, losing themselves and their characters. Then they became quiet, again conscious of their own mercenary shame.

She went after them again. She reminded herself not to kill them—they were not plausible targets. The frustration was exquisite. Senses exhausted, she and they were beyond conventional pleasures now. She made them do things to each other. Impossible things that they could never even speak of to apologize for, absolutely no absolution. They collected for her what she needed from each of them, as she had collected from all the others.

When finally they were exhausted beyond stims and switch, she called for someone to remove her toys. And then she began to paint. She used all of the bodily fluids and tissue samples she had gathered on the ship. She mutated the tissues so they would grow to monstrous tumors, sculpted to her design. Chaotic in form, her art hung by a representational fingernail, for those with the sense to see, feel, taste, smell. Everyone was there. The girl and the boy and the Consul and the Leaguer and the Ambassador and everywhere her, her, her. One last scream against them all. In this, by this, she would survive. If only they could hear her on Earth.

She slept. She dreamed. In dreams she couldn't remember whom she was for or against anymore. It didn't matter. She was against the Empire, against the League, against herself, against everyone always.

They came for her while she dreamed—no cabin door could stop a Leaguer. She had asked the Captain for extra security, but what was a commercial ship captain against the League?

She woke up long enough to be slapped.

"Border crosser," the Leaguer hissed. "I will smear your flawed brain in front of your mediocre eyes, then sign my name to your corpse."

Damn, that sounded like something she might say. Kudos.

And then she was out again.

There was once a little girl named Robynne who loved her mommy and daddy and they loved their little girl and the world was a beautiful place and then it was like a switch being thrown and the world was a monster and mommy and daddy were monsters and she was a monster but it was better to be with monsters than to be alone.

Oh oh. What a way to begin the day. Someone was torturing her again. Actually, torture was too artistic a term for this. For the moment, he was just beating the piss out of her. Boy Toy of the League. She was definitely against the League today, Wednesday or not.

The cabin appeared to be set up for just this sport. She should have known that these creeps would bring their own works wherever they went. The air already smelled of a range of human effluvia (hers) plus some of their delicate sweat.

So far a few broken bones and a few patches of flayed skin. Some deeper cuts—was that her ulna showing? No amputations yet. No truth drugs—he seemed to know not to bother with those.

"What is your name?" Smack. "Who do you work for?" Wham. "Blah blah blah." Smack smack.

Scream. Spit blood. Scream. She was crying and shrieking because it seemed like the thing to do. She didn't know half the answers anyway. She could have been a cold quiet bitch about it, but only mommy had ever fully appreciated that persona. It helped that she had sincere motivation. (Please!) This was nothing like her last tableau. As interesting as this pain was, it was not under her control, and that was truly excruciating. (God please!) Sometimes a guy would actually stop when she cried and shrieked. (Ohgodohgodplease!)

She wished he would stop now.

Amputation time. He started on the lovely long fingers of her left hand. He held custom designed gripping and ripping tongs for fingers, dark metal against his translucent skin. "Who do you work for?" She shook her head. He ripped off a finger. A finger's worth of blood shot out. A tendon dangled. Her body convulsed. Not real, not real, go to sleep little girl. But they must have given her something to keep her conscious. He cauterized the wound. Keeping her alive, too, for now. He went on to the next finger. "Who do you work for?"

Her mind squeezed down on a thought hard as diamond. If she somehow survived, she would never be ignorant of her bill-paying employers' identity again.

In five eternities he finished with the left hand. He looked to her right hand (her right hand!) and then said, "No, something else first."

An assistant brought forward one of her paintings. An original. Shit, she had shown her softness. The Leaguer pointed at the painting. "What is your name?"

She didn't hesitate. "I was Robynne Owen." Stupid. It wouldn't work.

"Good. We knew that, of course. Now, who do you work for?"

"I don't know." He aimed the gun again. "They were on Earth, at the hospital, I don't know anything else, please."

"Not good enough."

"I'll give you my reports."

The Leaguer laughed, but his ribs hardly moved. "No one gives a fuck about your inane reports, border crosser."

He vaporized the painting. She screamed, and all of her screamed with her.

He went through painting after painting, burning, crushing, destroying. She willed death at him, promised him everything, threatened vainly, and he didn't stop. She asked him to fuck her now, and he hesitated, but not for long. Finally, he reached the last painting. Her most recent work. The tumors were starting to show. He would kill it.

She was really going to die.

But he only had time to say "Who do you work—" when the room rocked. Another explosion blew a hole in the wall and sent small pieces of metal slicing into her left leg and arm. Ouch. Hmm. Particle beam explosions seemed to follow her around space like groupies. Whoever it was, this probably meant an interstellar war. Hee hee. Cough blood. Hee.

Boy Toy sent the other Leaguers through the hole to the hallway. She heard Consul Dull Fuck cum Stalker shout something about blood and vengeance. There was another explosion, then no shouts, only groans.

Escape was more dangerous than staying put, so Boy Toy retrieved the painting to finish it off. She had one last weapon against him. "I've won," she said.

This stopped the angry and confused Leaguer for just a moment. In that moment, the Ambassador strode in with a pistol. In one graceful motion, he shot the Leaguer with his right hand and bowed towards her tortured self with a sweep of the left. The Leaguer shattered into dust. The Ambassador grabbed the painting just before it touched the ground.

OK, so he did have fucking poetry in his soul. Good thing she still had her right fingers—she could write about this in her next report.

"My lady, I believe it's time for 'exeunt omnes.'"

He was so ugly he was beautiful. "I think I'll just pass out instead."

She awoke in another ship's sick bay, Robynne again for now. Through the glorious painkillers (more, more, more) she could feel that she was nothing but wounds, wonderful wounds. Damn, she was hard to kill. She enjoyed the feeling of dying too much to die.

No time to dawdle—the regen treatments were already underway. She commanded (ever so politely, she was a lady) the comp next to her bed to take a full set of photos, head to toe to destroyed left hand, and also 3-D scans of the deep wounds and tissue damage. Her next artwork would be a masterpiece of personal visceral trauma.

The Ambassador had not waited for her return to consciousness. He had left her with her last painting, only slightly scuffed. He had also left her a rose and his card. His name was Henri. A nice, warm, safe name.

Henri knew not to stay, she thought. He understands. The thought thrilled and appalled her.

Henri had added to her painting. It was outrageous presumption. It worked. In blood (his? hers?), he had drawn the outline of an apple, and inscribed in it "to the fairest" in ancient Greek, which she naturally knew. She did not think Henri was saying that she should be the apple's recipient—that would not be like him. If not the recipient, perhaps the giver. That giver had a name which was also the giver's job.

Eris. Discord. At long last, a true name.

No other messages for her. Meaningless chatter about the incipient League-Empire War filled her com line. Apparently the Floating World and the Hegemony were going to ignore their treaty obligations and sit this one out. Oh well, can't have everything.

No other messages, visitors, reports, art. Shouting did not increase her painkiller allowance, but at least it made it seem like she had company.

Finally, a message came through—her employers. They thanked her for her excellent reports on the four regional players. She would be returning to Earth soon—they needed her peculiar observation skills there. The internal political situation had grown interesting.

Right. Her thoughts had a stark clarity even through the opiates. Cinderella was more at home plotting against her stepsisters than enchanted at the ball. She could handle a few new facts. Neither the Leaguers nor her employers nor anybody else gave a fuck about her reports with their trivial information wheedled out of government officials. It was simpler than that. Her employers were happy about the chaos and war that flowed in her wake, and they wanted her to incite more of the same. It was something she had often suspected but never thought through, because that would mean having to decide.

By doing what came naturally to her, she was doing exactly what they wanted. Who the fuck were they?

So there it was. Her choice. The urge to random perversity was nearly overwhelming—to tell her employers to suck themselves dry and walk away into the galaxy, a totally free agent. But she knew better, she had been there. She had been no more free before they had found her. Then, she had played a bit part on a small stage before an unappreciative audience. Now, they had placed her on a galactic stage, her own writer, director, and choreographer, to act as she would, to create living if ephemeral art. They trusted her to be herself for the limited time that she could manage to survive.

Silly them.

All she knew about them was what she had told the Leaguer. The one place she had seen them was on Earth. They must be something old, like that world. Some of them must still be there.

So it was settled. She usually did not like to backtrack in life, but she felt ready now for Earth. Earth was a long time ago, too long ago to remember how it felt. She had grown up. She knew what she was. She had a job she enjoyed, and she was damned good at it.

And if she got the chance, she was going to find her employers, her real employers, and fuck and kill and kill and fuck each one of them. Because she could. She could always change her mind.

Now, who on Earth would be against her?

The Floating Otherworld

My year in Japan was one of the best times in my life, though on several occasions it nearly killed me. Like my hero at the beginning of this tale, I haunted expat bars, drank with yakuza, and stayed out way too late for my health. And I agree with my hero's sentiment in this story's final line. What happens to Nolan-san between those two points is less autobiographical, but still true.

This story originated in a series of e-mail journal entries that I sent from Japan to my friends back in the US (this was before the days of blogs). Those accounts were later published in *Sacred City*, a Seattle-based 'zine dedicated to real-life adventures and anecdotes. "The Floating Otherworld" is partially based on the events I describe in "Joyriding with Frank, Or Why the Japanese Love David Lynch," but I've put them through a mythopoetic blender.

The Hell of Underwater Fire

Mid life's road, and it's August in Tokyo. But that isn't why you're sweating. You're alone with Kaguya-san, the night receptionist.

She looks younger than the other office ladies and damned younger than you. Instead of the formless office lady suit, she wears the latest Italian fashion. Japanese skirts are short, but hers is leather. Nothing improper, just enough difference to torment you.

The other employees have left promptly for the weekend O-Bon holiday. Japanese days of the dead. Late summer is the scary joyful season. Haunted houses, dancing, and fireworks. Fear helps people chill. It isn't helping you, maybe because you're a foreigner. *Gaijin.*

You ask, "Um, could you type this for me?"

She takes your scrawled notes. She doesn't smile. The other secretaries smile while they tell you they can't help you. No smile, but her face and eyes seem to shine with cool light.

"Your handwriting is difficult, Nolan-san. But I can manage."

You manage a "domo arigato."

"You're welcome. What are you doing tonight?"

You shrug. You say nothing. "I'll wait for the document" on a Friday seems too pathetic. You want to say, "Take a long bath with me, Kaguya-san, make me clean and Japanese and worthy." You say nothing.

"You should get out. To Roppongi. Lots of foreigners there."

Foreigners. You smile bitterly at another night of getting plastered and snogging with some expat from the British Commonwealth. "Maybe. Good night, Kaguya-san." You don't dare ask what she is doing later, even to be polite. Such questions are meaningless here, but not for you. You're too hungry to be trivial.

You take the train. You're pressed from all sides, but you're used to such meaningless contact.

"A young Japanese man was shot in your country." A poking finger punctuates the sentence; an unusually pointy nose threatens your chest. It's an old woman in a loud Tokyo Disney shirt and frameless plastic sunglasses, like she's just had eye surgery. That would explain the shirt. Her face is marked like she's been burned, badly. So you're polite. "Yes, two of them in the last month. I'm sorry." Tourists in the wrong place at the wrong time.

No time for more. It's only one stop to your downtown apartment, three-bedroom by Tokyo standards, one-bedroom by yours. A view some have killed for—you overlook the Crown Prince's grounds, and Mt. Fuji is visible on the rare clear days. The folklore clowns say fire-and-snow Fuji is a woman. A distant volcano indeed.

Friday night, and your Tokyo gets dark early. Your lover in the States lasted only a sexless month before moving on. You aren't drunk (yet), so you will not call the home masseuse who gives special service. You will not call home. All your friends on the other side pretend you are dead.

She said "Roppongi." Where is Kaguya-san going tonight?

OK. Time for another Roppongi death march. No way to find her, no way to respect yourself, any way to forget yourself.

Screaming Hell's Booze Hounds

Praise Buddha, you're already drunk and searching for a club called, appropriately enough, "The Gaijin Zone." You've been there before, but for some reason it eludes you now.

You turn left. You're on a quiet one-lane back street, with a few Cadillacs squeezed in and no people. The air is mistier, darker.

"Another Japanese student shot last year during Halloween."

Shit! You spin around. The voice belongs to an innocuous middle-aged man in a comfortable suit, non-salaryman issue. He's wearing wraparound shades at night, but his particularly prominent nose seems to have caught your scent. The heat doesn't seem to bother him in the least. Perhaps he wants to fuck you, but in Tokyo that's no reason to be rude in reply.

So again you're polite. "I'm very sorry about it. Do you know where the Gaijin Zone is?"

He steps uncomfortably closer. "America is a violent country."

This is annoying. You can't apologize for everything. "A woman was Cuisinarted in Kyoto last month." And bits of her flesh left all along the freeway. "Why did that only make page three of the papers here?"

"*So desu*. Very sad. What you are looking for is that way." He points further down the back street. "Say you are my guest. Oya's guest."

Fine. You'll go that way, but you're nobody's guest.

You go that way. The street and buildings get older, the lights get dimmer. The lane curves and comes to an end. Shit. You walk back the way you came. You've been orbiting around a fenced clearing. Peering through fence and darkness, you can see a ragged forest of headstones and monuments. A cemetery, old and unkempt. Not good, not good, not good.

You walk faster, but can't find your way back to the bright lights, away from the graves. A Shinto-Buddhist lesson: Tokyo's streets are non-Euclidean, its underworld non-Virgilian.

"Nolan-san." A familiar voice cuts through booze and mist. You turn and see Kaguya-san, dressed "body con"—a red form-hugging strapless one-piece, stiletto heels, fishnet stockings, definitely not office lady wear. She stands beneath a lone sign for a club, the full moonlight a faint spot on her face. Her red dress bleeds into the night. The sign says "Floating World Live House Four." Like the old art prints, she's very floating world right now.

"Hello." You're nervous—does she think you've been following her? You explain: "I'm looking for the Gaijin Zone."

"That will be difficult for you to find now. And to stay here would be, *eto*, difficult for you as well. Come to this club. It's better."

And she points to the open door. Stairs lead down towards the sound of music. A club next to the dead? Great. But she's here. You go in.

You stumble a bit on the stairs and apologize. "I'm feeling strange. *Hen desu*."

"You are strange, Nolan-san." She laughs at you, and you're delighted—she never laughs at work.

At the bottom of the stairs, traditional lanterns reveal a Bon party in full throttle. Some have come as animals—foxes with sexy tails, badgers with big balls, catfish with legs. The musicians, cramped in a small corner, are birds with big beaks. Others are ghosts out of Clive Barker—Day-Glo disembowelments and worms that wriggle. You finally feel the chill. It's not as refreshing as you hoped.

A reality check is in order. "I didn't think people dressed up for the Bon festival."

She smiles. "This club is different."

"Is there going to be dancing later?"

"Yes, there is always dancing."

You might not be drunk enough for dancing or this club. "I'll get us some drinks."

"Are you sure?"

You're damned sure.

"You're very sweet. Ask him for two sakes in the box, special service. The special service is important." You think of the masseuse, and hope it's not the same thing.

As the band plays "Blue Suede Shoes," you cautiously approach the fragile looking Plexiglas bar—it doubles as an aquarium. Transparent channels carry water down the walls, through the floor, through the bar. Tiny fish swim about miniature kelp plants.

The bartender doesn't look fully Japanese; he's off-color and hairy. He balances a brimful tumbler on his head while he munches on some sushi rolls.

"Neat trick," you say. "Could I have two sakes in boxes, special service?"

"Just a minute, mate. I'm eating," he says in English, with a stuffed mouth and a slight Australian accent.

"Cucumber?"

"*Kappa maki*," he says.

"'*Kappa*' is cucumber?"

He looks at you with clear disdain. "No, a *kappa* is a very noble, very maligned being, who happens to enjoy cucumbers."

You get it—he's supposed to be a *kappa*, whatever that is. "What else do you like?"

"Oh no you don't." He slams the bar with his hand, and the tumbler on his head wobbles. "It's all rubbish—ruptured rectums of livestock, my ass! Why would we want blood from a cow's rice hole—we're fucking vegetarians!"

He grips your shoulder, nails like claws, pulling you close. You stare at his pointy Japanese dentistry teeth. Whatever *kappas* want is fine with you.

"Peasants should ask their kids about the bloody livestock," he snarls. He slams the bar with his other hand. The tumbler on his head wobbles again, threatening to spill on you, so you grab it.

"Shimatta," he cries in a breathless shout. He lets you go, feeling his head where the glass was. "OK, give it back, mate."

"Sure, but how about those drinks?"

He sighs. "Fine, it's a deal."

You give him back the tumbler. He takes out a small dust-covered sake barrel and two ornately carved pine boxes. He sets the boxes on two burnt-green saucers, and mutters bits of Japanese as he fills the boxes to overflowing, then looks at you. "Who told you to ask for these?"

You point back to Kaguya-san, who has miraculously found a table.

"Well why didn't you just say so, mate? Tell her I've made them extra special. Oya-san is coming. Cheers."

You walk back towards your table, keeping the drinks as steady as you can in the crowd.

"For me?" A delicate white hand with fine blue veins reaches for a box. Yes, this is like Halloween.

"No, for my friend."

The hand belongs to a tall thin woman wearing a ski outfit in August. Her face is as pale as a winter's moon. "I am Yuki."

She's beautiful, so you decide to play along. "As in snow?"

"Yes, the same. Have you been to the mountains?"

You've been to Nagano.

"Nagano. The Olympics. Many tourists came, and some roamed far. Roam with me."

Ouch! The white hand grasps your arm. The sake boxes shudder. You feel her chill through your shirt, and suddenly you are hard for her, icy hard, and you want to shatter like a Creamsicle inside her.

A flash of red, and your arm is free. *"Dame!* Don't pay any attention to her, Nolan-san, she's frigid."

Kaguya-san has grabbed the boxes. You slouch into a seat at your table. You feel numb, and you're not sure what, if anything, just happened. The women exchange words through the music behind you, like "mine" and "guest."

Yuki says "Oya-san."

Kaguya-san says nothing. She returns, sets the boxes on the table and looks at you steadily.

You repeat, "Oya-san," but she shushes you. "First drink-up. *Kanpai.*" She drinks, so you drink. She downs her whole box, so you do too. The sake tastes like an electrified mountain stream, with a hint of pine from the box. Your body aches as its warmth returns. She glances down into your empty box. "*Sugoi*, Nolan-san. Soon we'll sing karaoke, *ne*, when the band rests."

You need to know. "I've met Oya-san. He said I was his guest." Kaguya-san is silent. "Who is Oya-san?"

She sucks her breath. "Oya means landlord. And more. Like an uncle. I'm not sure what you would call him. We shouldn't disturb him, he's a busy man."

The band is rocking out with more Elvis. Kaguya-san brings her lips close to your ear to be heard. "Nolan-san, you know—"

But she doesn't finish. Before you see him, you see the reactions of those closer to the entrance. Everyone turns to look, and the band stops mid-song. You can hear the crowd whisper now, "Oya" over and over, like a chant.

Oya-san, the mild-mannered accuser from the street, has no Bon outfit and looks far too normal, too real for this party. He moves through the parting crowd. The ski woman strains her arm to touch him, but he just holds up a finger, "*Chotto matte,*" and she freezes.

The bandleader cranes his beak towards Oya's nose. "Roy Orbison, *ne?*"

Oya's finger again: "*Domo. Chotto.*" Everyone, even the fish in the bar, follows his finger except Kaguya-san, who studies your table like a manuscript she must type.

Oya comes towards your table. You want to say "*Yakuza.*" "Say nothing," Kaguya-san hisses.

Without asking, Oya sits at your table. He points at the band. They begin Orbison's "In Dreams." The bartender, tumbler back on his head, wordlessly brings Oya-san and the table drinks. Oya lights a cigarette. The spot of orange flame reflects on his dark glasses. His face and hands are the color of spent ash.

In the wrong place at the wrong time.

When the song ends, Oya says, "It's good no one will miss him."

Kaguya-san doesn't look up. "He's my guest now."

"Too late, once beloved. I've judged him."

Kaguya-san taps your empty sake box. "Careful. He's been drinking."

Oya's nostrils flare. "*Baka!* You can join him then." With his left hand, Oya seizes her perfect hair and pulls her face up, her eyes flashing.

Time telescopes to hold several things in a moment. The band commences Nirvana's "In Bloom." You say nothing. You swing your arm across the table and bring the edge of the sake box down into Oya's left shoulder.

Without expression, Oya lets go of Kaguya-san's hair. Kaguya-san says one word that sounds like *jazz* and *jism*.

Oya thrusts the palm of his right hand against your forehead.

Bam! The bartender screeches. The crowd howls. The bar shatters, and you feel the tingly spray of water, glass, and fish. The lanterns explode—your lights are going out. The drummer keeps thumping, afraid to stop.

Kaguya-san is pulling you in the dark. *"Ikimasho!"* You're going, going...

Last Chance Hell

A gong sounds. The show begins. You don't remember how you got here—a combo casino and hostess bar. You are seated in a circular booth with a high back and a narrow opening. You can't see into the other booths, and they can't see you. Nearby, the floor show of comely women in lingerie parades mechanically to American pop songs. The recordings are sped up to sound like chipmunks on Ecstasy.

A corseted hostess comes to your table. You try to decline her company, but she just giggles in girlish style.

"House rules, dear. Every man must have a hostess."

That's OK. Hostesses just talk—they're chat whores. Not like you'd be doing anything wrong. Certainly nothing illegal.

The hostess starts right in on the chat, asking you about yourself. It feels wonderful, after being alone so long, to be listened to so raptly. You joke, she laughs. You rant, she justifies. You get maudlin, her eyes water. Lovely.

You feel relaxed. You think that maybe, if you talk cleverly enough, this woman will ask you to a private room and make painfully slow love to you, no charge. So you talk more, though you're getting sleepy. That's OK, it has been a long (endless) night, and then meeting Kaguya-san . . .

Say, where is Kaguya-san? She isn't next to you. You want to thank her for something, or show off how you're handling the hostess. Suddenly, the hostess's banter is tinny, mechanical. "You work so hard." Not really. "Nobody understands you." Should they? "You're such a real man." Then shouldn't you be with a real woman?

"Where's Kaguya-san?"

"Who?" Your hostess is sincerely dumbfounded.

"My friend." You want to talk with your friend.

"But I'm here to listen."

"We have talked enough. Where's my friend?"

"She'll be back. Please talk to me." She's desperate. Poor thing. You try another tack.

"Who are you?"

"Oh, I'm just a woman who enjoys your wonderful company."

"No, really, who are you? And why are you here? This is not a normal hostess bar."

"You really want to know. I can see that. I'll go now."

"No, please, first tell me."

"Those are the rules. If you honestly care enough to ask, I have to go." Before you can ask again, she's gone.

Kaguya-san comes tentatively to the table. She's wearing a modern kimono loosely over the body con, her dark hair pulled back with hair sticks. She holds a stack of casino chips in her hand. How long have you been here?

"Nolan-san, you're OK?"

You think so. "Let's go before another hostess comes."

You walk past the other booths. It's a Bon party at the hostess bar too. Table after table of ghastly, spectral women glare at their clients with raptor eyes. Their skin fluoresces in spots that are shapes—the shape of a hand where it slapped a cheek, the shape of a fist where it smacked an eye. And the men. They are emaciated gray or rotten purple-green. The women still speak to the rotted men, saying things like "you should have gone home to your wife," "you should not have gone to Thailand," "now you will not leave here ever."

You're glad your hostess didn't look like these women. It's very kabuki or puppet play, unrequited love and *Twilight Zone* revenge. All you say is "ghost story."

Like the moon on a cloudy night, Kaguya-san avoids your eyes. "Something like that," she says. No laughter or smile. She's scared of something—is she afraid for you?

You look around again at the blurry, fearful room. Maybe this is really the otherworld, or maybe you're really dead. It doesn't matter. Drunk or dead, you'll stick with Kaguya-san. She at least seems to care what happens to you.

You follow her into the gaming room. It's more normal, comforting. There's a chaotic chime of pachinko machines playing themselves, balls falling into the random predestined paths. One of the gambling tables seems to be a Bon party special—some old guys in even older Imperial Navy uniforms playing poker. They bluff recklessly, they risk much early, and the chips go wildly back and forth across the table. They smile at you and ask if you'd like to join the game. Kaguya-san gives you some chips to bet with, but you politely decline. They nod, chuckling, and say it's just as well. They've played Americans before. "Let sleeping giants lie, *ne?*"

The rest of the club is empty now, chips left on the tables uncashed, roulette wheels still. In the long run, the house always wins.

An aria from *Madame Butterfly* replaces the pachinko chimes. "The American left her." Shit, now someone wants you to apologize for Italian opera. It's the most sensible thing you've heard all night. This time the accuser is a woman about your age. She wears the pointed sunglasses of a '50s movie starlet lightly on her beaklike nose—like she's Oya's sister or Oya in drag. She clenches a cigarette holder in her teeth as she rakes in the piles of spent chips.

Kaguya-san stands to the side, ready for a fight. "I want to speak to the manager," she says.

The accuser speaks to you instead. "I am the new manager of this club. From Kyoto. I heard you wanted to meet me."

This Oya offers you her hand to shake, western style. Her entire arm is crisscrossed with fine white scar lines, dotted like Morse code to invite scissors or knife to "cut here." A temporary costume? A permanent tattoo? Either way, this homage to the Kyoto butchery is both terrifying and in extremely poor taste. Your tolerance of the strange is worn out—you're pissed off. "Have you no fucking shame?"

Oya smiles with anger. "Ah, you see, but you do not yet understand. Here, a gift."

She flips you a chip, and you catch it and slap it into your left hand with your other chips. And you regret it. In fact, you regret everything. You regret the lost love and friends back home. You regret not making all the money that you could be making stateside. You regret things that haven't even happened yet: you are aware of *mono no aware*. Your parents are growing older, people are dying and you're not there. You're not really here either.

A tickling spider-web feeling distracts you from the abstract. Fine white lines have spread across your hand. Both hands. Your entire body. You know where you are going. Kyoto, with bits of your flesh left all along the freeway.

The white lines have turned crimson agony. You're coming undone. Soon, your fingers will fall to the ground, followed by everything else in small pieces.

The old men continue to play cards, unconcerned. Kaguya-san has not moved or spoken. She silently implores you to some action, but what can you do?

Your dissolution is taking an eternity. You sob at your own helpless pain. Oya, still smiling unhappily, offers you a dagger. You know what the knife is for; you've seen it in the movies. You suppose it's the Japanese thing to do.

No. Stake it all, while you still can. That's the Tokyo way. You're still gripping your chips in a left hand that's useless with fraying tendons. But now you've got a blade in your right. You chop through the hanging threads of your left wrist with indifferent pain, and toss your hand on a roulette table. Red four.

Oya is not smiling now, but she spins. The wheel spins, the ball spins. You're spinning.

"*Ikimasho*, Nolan-san." Kaguya-san wraps her kimono around you, containing your fractures for another moment, and you fall into the red.

The Hell Spa-ed

You're standing, barefoot and in a *yukata* robe. You might as well be naked. You rub the old scar on your left wrist that you don't like people to see. The décor is cave—sometimes faux, sometimes rocky real. You smell the lightest hint of sulfur and minerals. The sign says "World Famous Hells." A hot spring spa. Heavenly.

A woman in a white robe brings you another box of sake. You take a sip. You won't make the same mistake twice, so you immediately ask, "Where is Kaguya-san?"

"Oya-san?" she asks. Definitely not. But she points towards the rear of the cave, and that's the way you go.

On the walls of the cave are traditional sliding doors, with nothing indicating where they may lead. You walk further down the hall. One set of three sliding doors is different from the others. The middle door is a mirror, and the doors on either side feature lovely, simple paintings. To the left, a dragon holds a sword blade. To the right, a dragon clutches jewels.

You open the mirror door. Kaguya-san is there in her loose robe with no body con beneath. "Welcome to my spa, Nolan-san. Time to take the bath with me. But first, get clean."

She directs you to the left. You go, trying not to appear as anxious as you feel. It's a locker room of sorts, with a shower and a heated toilet that makes noises to mask your biological functions. You get clean.

Beyond the shower is another door, the entrance to the central chamber and hot spring bath. You enter—it's dim, wet, and warm. The pool glows and steams, crater-like, a comfortable fit for two.

Kaguya-san leaves her robe by the water's edge, and slides into the pool with effortless grace. You try to avoid staring—naked is your problem, not theirs—but you sense the smallness of her curves, and find with relief and expectation that small is beautiful.

You test the water with the ball of your foot. Goddamn, the water is painfully hot. They threw Christians into boiling springs, didn't they? But Kaguya-san got in, so you have to follow.

As you slowly lower yourself into the pool, the water moves up your body as a line of fire. Below the water, your legs are a fun house of melted plastic. Then, you're all the way in, except for your head, the last bit of dissolving ice. All the years of bad booze and bad food are steaming out of you.

Kaguya-san rubs your neck and shoulders with a cloth. You keep your eyes focused above the waterline. "That's nice," you say.

She smiles at you. "Nolan-san, you know I like you."

"No, I mean, well, I like you too." You still aren't sure what she means; you've crossed your cultural signals before.

She puts her arms around your neck. Her skin feels different, Japanese. You can't believe this is happening.

It isn't. With shocking force, she pulls your head underwater.

The water stings your eyes. Your need for air becomes pressing, but the force holding you under does not relent. Drowning? Maybe. So it goes.

Then, just as forcefully, she lifts your head up. "I think you're done." She laughs.

Some joke, you think, but the Japanese don't like sarcasm, so you keep silent for a moment. You look at your hands. There's been no change of color, she hasn't made you Japanese, your dream has not come true.

"Time's up. We need to get out."

You get out of the pool, and the warm air feels cool. You go towards the way you came in.

"No, not that way, this way."

You follow her into the right-hand room. With every step, your plastic-like body cools and firms into shape.

She helps you dress. Her kimono. Strange. It fits all right, but gives you the appearance, the feeling of breasts. She wears your *yukata,* and it's hard to see any curve to her at all.

"Now we are ready for karaoke?" You exit the jewel door, and cross the hall. It's a private karaoke room, with an enormous video screen and a comfortable sofa, and a phone for ordering drinks and food.

There are three other, older women there. In greeting, they say "Oya-san." You jump, and Kaguya-san notices.

"Don't worry, Nolan-san, the other Oya will not come here."

You think the other Oya may be everywhere, but you say, "Your beloved?"

"That was long ago. Let's sing."

You let them select your songs. You sing "Crazy for You" by Madonna in duet with Kaguya-san. You're not bad. You sing a Japanese song of spring in autumn for the winter people, and though you mangle some words, your feeling is pure. You sing "Stairway to Heaven" and "Hotel California," and they go very wrong, but no one seems to mind. Harmony of feeling is more important than technique here.

The older women sing together, something about "three more for every two lost," and seem very amused by you and Kaguya-san. The music is now mostly percussion in irregular rhythm. *ICHI, ni, san, shi. Ichi, NI, san, shi. Ichi, ni, SAN, shi. Ichi, NI, san, shi. Ichi.* In out in, ah. Ah, out in out. The drums sound live, not karaoke machine.

The satellite feed for the karaoke glitches for a moment, and suddenly, Oya's on the video, dressed like a schnozzy Elvis gone Eastern and sexually ambiguous, shades to match. He roars like he's live at Budokan the words to Neil Sedaka's "Oh Carol," substituting your name for the woman's. "Oh Noran-san, I'm soo in rooove with yoouuuuu!"

Kaguya-san looks over at you, blushing, and almost sings, "Are you ready?" She points to the door.

The sound of ocean surf pounds at the door to the room, punctuating the drum rhythm with power and threat. Steamy water dribbles down the door cracks. Your heart drums in your head—*ichi, ni, san, SHI.* You nod. Whatever it is, even drowning, you're ready.

She motions you to the door, and places your hand on the handle. "On the count of four, *ikimasho! Ichi, ni, san...*"

The Hell of No Interval

"*SHI!*"

The drums outside and inside you have stopped. The stars and the full moon do not move. And that is how you know that it is always a particular day and hour here. The hour is *shi* o'clock in the morning. Said that way, four o'clock is death o'clock.

The day, or night, is August 15. Bon time, and the end of the last war.

The place is a memorial shrine that doesn't exist except in the death o'clock world. It's a shrine composed of other shrines, ashes upon ashes. It's a shrine stripped of the inessentials, death's place, simple and austere. Yasakuni Shrine to the War Dead unadorned with false glory, Hiroshima Peace Park without the peace platitudes.

The air is cold, you're cold. You touch Kaguya-san's hand. She's cold, shivering in your thin robe. No light in her eyes—she's crying. Whoever else she's been for you tonight, now she's just the night receptionist again. Shitty timing, cause there's no time left here.

There's a smell of incense, and a smell of smoke that the incense is trying to cover. You've got company.

All the dead of Japan's last war are here. The soldiers of the War Shrine have come, ordered here by a nationalist spirit that has never completely died, enshrined whether they want to be or not—a forced internment of interment. The burned women and children of Tokyo, the melted fleshlings of Hiroshima and Nagasaki, they have come too. So many years ago, and yet always here.

The scale is too vast, so you focus on particulars you recognize. The card players stand in the front rank, forgoing their game to return to this place, smiling still, but without humor. You see that some of these dead are of more recent vintage—murdered Japanese tourists, irradiated and drowned fishermen. You get it. These dead are here for you.

Flickering like a flame between *Yakuza*/old woman/dead woman/Elvis is the Oya of death o'clock, executioner, accuser, judge, eyes shielded from a world that is always too bright. He takes off his shades, and his eyes are all-devouring like cremation fires, like hungry ghosts. All is ash, firebomb, nuke. "This is the end, *gaijin*. You don't belong here. Go." Then the all-Oya screams at the dead in an old Japanese that you can't follow at all—archaic and best forgotten.

Their accusations hit like a rainstorm, first a drop, then three drops, then a deluge. You interned us in camps, you bombed us conventionally and obscenely. You can never understand. You are not Japanese.

So here it is, the longest divide. It's old and easily dismissed in daylight, yet it's too much for you to cross now. A chasm of sadness and pain bottled away for decades. Any words seem foolish. You can't apologize. It's not your place, nor could you be sincere. You would not have wanted that war to have been fought a day longer. And it's not even mostly an American guilt, though you'll hear no apology from those here for anything. You cannot condemn. Those here have already paid for the sins of war and aggression, apologies be damned.

Behind you, just over your shoulder (they have a Protestant shyness about manifesting), you hear the voices of your own dead murmur in agreement with the Oya. What the hell are you doing here? Get home, boy. Your family is and will be there.

Instead of listening, you turn to face Kaguya-san. Her arms are stretched out towards two sets of elderly couples, imploring, but they're having none of it. You reach out a hand for her, but she's having none of that. You're not going to be able to negotiate this agreement, counselor, not in English or Japanese.

So, broken tired guilty wronged, you take a step away. And then you take a step towards. And then you take a step away. And then a step towards. Step away, step towards, and you circle around and start again.

Start again. The drum inside you starts again. Kaguya-san stares at you, caught between amazement and dismay. Her expression says, *You're doing it all wrong.* You shake your head. Oh no, you're not. There's always only been one solution. Shut up and dance. Do ya, do ya wanna dance with me?

Your dancing becomes more expansive, outrageous. She joins you, if only to slow you, to show you.

Kaguya-san moves in front of you, the start of a ritual conga line. *Laissez les* Bon *temps rouler.* The drums outside start again, thrumming from all directions, telling you you're not dancing alone, the whole country is dancing this sex-death life-reaping. And you hear the dead lining up behind like guests at a wedding reception, swaying solemnly, some speaking English and damned surprised to be there. And in front you hear those who are to come, and some of them speak Japanese.

Oya's gotta dance too, like he does in the pictures. His incendiary heat eases to autumn. You and she and he are part of a wave that rocks the globe, season to season, hemisphere to hemisphere.

Kaguya-san turns and takes your hand, and dances slowly with you, against you. The shrine fades into the view of Mt. Fuji in moonlight from your balcony, robes become suit and body con. Nobody is watching you and everybody is watching you.

You think this isn't happening. It is.

And you're still dancing, and she rolls her thin red dress up over her hips, and you're turning Japanese you really think so.

You're dancing still.

The Hell of a Day

Sunday. Time moves ahead again, though slowly. You're on a picnic near a shrine, in a sunlit park, bento boxes for two, jeans and Tokyo Disney T-shirts.

Heavy metal bands line the park road at every fifty feet, a cacophonous whole more intriguing than its parts. Everyone is smiling at you, because you need no help. Even Mt. Fuji smiles and winks—you're going to do just fine here.

Kaguya-san's orange-brown eyes are lowered. "Thank you for celebrating the Bon holiday with me, Nolan-san."

Even now, you are still Nolan-san to her in public. It's still a strange place here, *ne?* Can you live with such distance, such formality? You don't have to. She places her hands on your face and bends you towards her to kiss your forehead, your lips. Her lips are like the flutter of a moth.

You stare at Kaguya-san. You could stare for hours. She's more and less luminescent than before, sun lit instead of moon glowing. Everything in its season. Autumn is coming, there will be more moon viewings. By then, your apartment might really be both one and three bedrooms, and Kaguya-san (unilluminated, un-Bon-ified but bona fide) might fit there.

Underworld lord and party animal Oya will come back every year, and one year you'll not dance away. That's OK. You know how to be a polite host now. You can share tea, and discuss the new hanging scroll that your girlfriend has found for you before you drum him along. *Kappas* will party with Mickey and Bugs, Marley's ghost will throw beans at a snow woman, Jesus and Buddha will be bouncers at the door.

One day, some way, you both must leave, but you're here now. So *ikimasho,* Nolan-san. Doesn't matter where. You will not be going home, you're already there.

Translation: *Nihon ga daisuki desu.* You love Japan.

Noise Man

When I began writing, I tried my hand at a screenplay—a wacky mash-up of *X-Files*-style conspiracy theories destined for my trunk. "Noise Man" originated from the screenplay's backstory, and it concerns the younger years of one of the characters. But somewhere along the way as I immersed myself in the cryptohistory, the wackiness got lost. In the dead of night, I think it could have happened like this, and maybe one day we'll find out that it has happened like this.

When the future looks back on the mid-twentieth century, the dawn of the Information Age will loom larger than the battles of the Second World War in the same way that Gutenberg's printing press seems more important than the particulars of the Wars of the Roses. A great many things became possible for the first time, and maybe the pivotal event of this story was one of them.

Sunday, October 30, 1938

On the night *they* didn't say "hello," Kenny O'Reilly listened to his just-completed radio. He closed his eyes, smarting from the poor light, and tuned in some jazz. Nice. His brain jumped along to the beat, singing designs of wires and tubes and things better than tubes.

"Kenny. Dinner." His mother's tenement-flat voice snapped him out of his circuits. Mom must have held on dinner as long as she could, but his father's steps weren't near yet.

Kenny huffed the completed radio to the living room. "Can I test it out during dinner, Mom?" She murmured a yeah.

Dad had said that he had to fix some plumbing in the Bell Labs building, where he was the super. Often he didn't stumble back until after midnight, even on a Sunday. He promised over and over that someday he was going to shuffle them out of Hell's Kitchen into a real house.

Not that their life played as bad as their neighborhood sounded. Dad worked as super for this building too, so the flat for the three of them was spacious compared with their neighbors'. And even more important, the electricity performed.

"Dad's going to be sorry he missed this pot roast," Kenny said, smacking his lips. The Bergen-McCarthy routine came through loud and clear on the new radio. Kenny's radios always sounded better than the buzzing junk in the stores.

Kenny had composed his first crystal set from odd bits of wire and a diode Dad had scrounged for him from the Labs' waste bins. He had been three years old. He had progressed steadily through every related gadget he could make—transmitters, antennae—selling his earlier efforts to fund his purchases of more equipment, always improving, always improvising. Not a bad racket for a thirteen-year-old.

Mom just sat at the table, eating nothing, not seeming to hear him when he laughed at Charlie McCarthy. He listened. Her breathing sounded tired, tired and something else. She might be a little sore. He should be extra helpful cleaning up after dinner.

Dorothy Lamour started singing some mushy number. Kenny got up to change the station. Ah, a swing band. But then some announcer came on. "We take you now to Grovers Mill, New Jersey."

Despite the New Jersey location, Kenny quickly recognized the scientifiction of *The War of the Worlds*. One of the actors did *The Shadow* too—Kenny could always distinguish the man under the character. *What evil lurks in the heart of men? The Shadow knows.*

The reporter's microphone crashed, signaling that the Martians had got him. Mom's chair squeaked. Kenny had been so wrapped up in the program that he had forgotten about Mom.

"Kenny, we have to go. Get your things together." She spoke with deliberate calm, but Kenny could sense the fear.

She went into her bedroom and began to slam open drawers and throw clothes on the bed. She sniffed—had she had been crying? Ah crap, she believed this junk.

"Mom, it's not real."

She didn't pause. When her bags were full, she dragged Dad's spare tool kit from under the bed and pulled off the socket tray. Clang rattle. She reached into the kit and fished out a big wad of bills—the most money Kenny had ever seen. She stuffed the bills in a bag with her dresses. "Hurry up, boy. There isn't much time."

"C'mon, Mom. Think about it. It wouldn't be worth any Martian's plug nickel to come here."

"Yes, I know. Now get packing."

"But you don't understand..."

She pressed her hands down hard on Kenny's shoulders. "No, you don't understand. We have to leave. Now."

Kenny was stunned. Mom sounded nuts. "What about Dad?"

She turned away from him and went back to shoving clothing and jewelry into shabby bags. "He'll be fine."

"I'm, uh, I'm not going."

Mom stopped again. She grabbed Kenny by the arm and pulled him towards his room. "Now! Can't wait. Not another minute. I'll die."

But Kenny pulled against her. "I can't leave Dad." He couldn't bear to even sound like a coward to his father. "You just go."

She spoke right at him, her lips quivering. "Honey?" Her voice had a strange crack in it.

He rushed to reassure her. "I'll just wait here to tell Dad. We'll catch up with you later—up north. Then we can all skedaddle together."

Kenny was talking on his feet. Mom wouldn't get far before she heard the Martians weren't real. Then she would just snap back. Kenny would try to keep Dad calm until then. It was the best plan, though it might cost him a piece of his hide.

Mom sighed as if he had just beaten her in a long race. "OK, Kenny, you win. I'll meet you up north. When you're ready, just call Aunt Maureen. She'll know where."

She finished filling two bags and dragged them to the door. Dropping the bags, she hugged Kenny. Hard. "I love you, honey. I will always love you. Don't let anyone ever tell you different."

And then, snick-snack, she was out the door.

An hour later, Dad stumbled in, out of breath and dirty from work. Kenny started to explain about Mom and the Martians.

"Martians. What kind of malarkey is this? She's run off with some flimflam man, hasn't she boy?"

"No, it was *The Shadow* guy on the radio and—"

Bam! Dad smacked his ear, as if he knew that was the worst thing he could do. Kenny just took the blow—always easiest not to fight it—and braced for the next smack. But Dad only stared at his huge callused hand.

Then he sank into a chair and started to cry.

Kenny had never heard his father cry. It was the scariest, saddest sound he had ever known. He started to cry too.

Dad reached for him with one of his big hands. "It's OK, boy. Everything's going to be fine." His voice became more even. "There aren't any Martians. Your mother will be back soon."

And that was how Kenny learned for certain that he could tell someone was lying, just from the music of their voice.

The next day, when his father's footsteps trailed off in the stairwell, he telephoned his Aunt Maureen, the dreaded Irish Republican Aunt. "Not here yet," she snapped. No point in talking further—it was expensive.

But after he hung up, he wondered: would he have to call again, or would Mom call him? Either way, Dad would pound him if he found out. Kenny had always had Mom muffling Dad for him. Kenny wanted to hear what his Dad would do next, but he also wanted to stay out of his way.

So Kenny played hooky and wired the flat for sound. His radios were already in every room, their decorative boxes plenty large to conceal microphones and trailing wires. But if a radio was turned on, it would make listening difficult, so he also found other spots for mikes, like behind the headboard of Dad's bed. Wearing headphones, Kenny could quietly attend to each mike. He also tapped the phone line. He could just listen, or he could join in on a call, or he could take the call over, disconnecting the regular telephone—a soft-shoe tap dance. Safely in his room, he could hear everything.

The next day, Kenny caught screaming hell at school, but it was a short day for All Saints so it wasn't so bad. That night, sure enough, "brrrrng" just as his father stepped in the door. Kenny paused a measure for his father to pick up, and then tapped in.

"Hello. Will, is that you?"

"Maureen. Where's my wife?"

Aunt Maureen's light lilt dueled with his father's like a duet about a hanging. "My sister isn't here. I want to speak with Kenny. Could you please put him on the phone?"

"My boy won't be speaking with any of youse, you lying whores. Now, put my wife on the phone."

Kenny heard his opportunity. He flipped a switch, and disconnected his father. He heard his father slam the receiver into its cradle with a "goddammit."

Kenny spoke as quietly as Aunt Maureen could hear. "It's Kenny. Is she there?"

"I'm going to Paddy's," his father yelled, and slammed the door.

His Mom came on the phone. "Kenny? Oh, my baby. I'm so sorry." Syncopated crying sounds.

"It's OK, I didn't understand. I'm coming. Where can I meet you?"

His mother hesitated. "I, I need to check with my friend, Kenny. He's a nice man, a very nice man. I'm sure you'll like him. I know he'll like you."

There it was again. Lies. They rang like atonal church bells in Kenny's ears. A hell of a choice—the commanding devil he knew, or this unheard "friend."

The need for his mother turned to mute stone inside him. "Maybe you should get things settled with your friend first."

"Are you sure?" The relief outweighed any doubt in her voice. "What about your father?"

"I can play him." He heard his own words, and realized that he believed what he was saying. He would just have to keep his ears open.

Saturday, September 2, 1939

Saturday night, Dad brought another woman home. Her voice was old and full of cigarettes and booze, like Dad's, only more perfumed. Dad insisted on introducing her to Kenny. Then they tumbled into Dad's room. And Kenny listened. He always listened.

They used few words but many invitations, codes, calls, and responses. They lied a lot to each other, but neither sounded like they cared. The rhythm of bed noise was not quite even, but not quite jazz either.

He almost forgot that she was a stranger, and not his Mom. He missed his Mom. But Dad never got mean with these strangers. Was it like this with Mom and her friend now?

The sounds of music and bodies and bed wove together in his mind, building and building like a freight train coming towards him, random tones reaching up for a resolution. Boom! A fat transcendent chord hung in the air, obliterating tension and thought. Yes.

His Dad breathed heavily. No more interesting noise. Kenny switched to the radio while he tinkered with his latest composition: a portable battery-powered radio for his Dad to take with him in his cart at work. The radio also had a hidden transmitter. Kenny could keep an ear on Dad all day. He would hide a signal booster near the labs so that he could listen from home.

They interrupted Kenny's impromptu with a news bulletin: Britain and France were declaring war on Germany. They sounded surprised by Poland.

Kenny wasn't. Even in German's unmusical consonants, Kenny could tell that Hitler was full of shit.

His Dad thought that trouble for England was a good thing. His Dad was a Mick idiot. Sometimes scary, sometimes fun to listen to, but an idiot.

Still, there was something in Hitler's *Sprechgesang* that was overwhelming. You didn't care that it was shit. That was scary. Kenny would have to do something about that someday.

Tuesday, October 15, 1940

Kenny listened to the war. London thundered in symphony, no jazz. "Murrow Hears Major Bombing in C Minor." Dee dee dee da, Morse for V for Victory, with the IX Air Group flying by for Hitler's Ode to Death. Keen.

Time for the local news. Kenny tuned in to his father's work. He could relax—Dad was still there. Maybe he could pick up some more Labs talk that would help his radio designs. Maybe he could hear people bossing Dad around.

"Hey O'Reilly, whatcha got there?" A man's voice, a lot younger than Dad's. Open cadenced, friendly.

"A radio, Michael. My fifteen-year-old son built it for me."

"May I take a peek?"

"Go right ahead."

"Hmm." Stations twisted. "Pretty good reception and sound. Runs on that battery? Let me look here." A pause, then, "You've got a bright kid, O'Reilly. Could you bring him into work with you tomorrow? I'd like to talk radios with him."

"I don't know, he's in school." As usual, Dad was full of shit. "Why do you want to talk to him for?"

"It's important. I can talk to your supervisor about it, but..."

"No, no. I'll bring him."

"Good. Tomorrow."

Kenny was nearly deafened. The man had said he wanted to talk radios with him, and real respect had animated his words. Something else there too, but Kenny heard only the opportunity.

The next day, Dad had Kenny accompany to work for the first time. Kenny had been around there before, but solo, to run his booster off a nearby power line.

They walked towards West Street and the full-block Bell Labs complex. Their strides were backed by the slow dark rhythm of a freight train passing overhead on the elevated High Line and through a tunnel in the front building. Holy Robert Moses.

On the tenth floor of the central building, they click-stepped through a chaotic open space of desks and tables arranged with apparent randomness. The space echoed, echoed with working men. Finally, they reached an office and Dad tapped. A young man squeaked the door open.

"You can leave him here," said the voice from yesterday.

"But shouldn't—"

The young man grabbed Kenny's arm, pulled him in, and slammed the door.

An older man stood behind a desk. On the desk was Kenny's radio, opened up, and parts scattered. The transmitter was at the center of the desk, and next to the transmitter, the booster.

"Care to explain this, boy?"

So Kenny explained his variations on existing design themes and parts. But this didn't seem to make the older man any happier.

The younger man said, "That's interesting, kid, fascinating actually, but what I think he meant was, why?"

So Kenny spoke-sung the melodrama of living alone with his father, how his father wasn't always nice, and that when he wasn't nice and was on his way home, Kenny wanted to be somewhere else.

"But what about what we do here? Have you been listening to that?"

Kenny grinned. "You bet. It's great stuff. I've got lots of ideas for it, if you'd like me to explain."

"That's enough!" The old man was really angry now. "We should call the authorities."

"You won't," said Kenny.

The younger man laughed unpleasantly and said, "Oh really, kid? And why's that?"

"You want something."

The older man glowered, angry-silent. Kenny stood still, worried only about what his father would say later. The younger man looked at the older man and shrugged his shoulders. The older man sighed and nodded.

The younger man offered his hand. "Kid, my name's Mike O'Neill. This is my boss, Mr. Carleton. We'd like to hire you."

"Me? I'm only sixteen."

"You're only fifteen. But you're the future. We want you to work on every aspect of improving radio transmission and reception. The pay's good. I'll be your supervisor. You'll be my noise man."

A noise man. That rang true. Kenny thought that working with Mike would be really swell.

Tuesday, September 15, 1942

On the night Kenny finally heard *them* say "hello," he was listening for a signal on his new directional antenna—an enormous parabolic dish mounted atop a large tripod on the flat central roof of the Bell Laboratories complex.

"You sure this Martian salad bowl is working, kid?" asked Mike. Kenny held up an OK sign, and tried to block out the noise.

Even up here, this late, wearing a headset, noise. It was just after midnight, and the city was blacked out for civil defense except for searchlights sweeping the sky. Kenny missed the happy chorus of the lighted city—the roaring crowds at Dodger's games, the shrieking rides at Coney Island. Instead, young men in uniform roamed the street in herds, on their way to slaughterhouses across the Atlantic and Pacific, trying to shout away death, trying to drag Kenny with them.

From the stairwell entrance, Kenny heard a faint clarinet. His father, no doubt dragging a mop and listening to his radio. During the day, his father stayed out of earshot, but now, with the building almost empty, every random sound reminded Kenny that Dad might be near.

It was harder to keep an ear on Dad without the transmitter in his radio. But Kenny had found a way to keep an ear on everyone. Kenny now had much of the Labs wired for sound. Sure, they had ways to detect listening devices, but not these, not yet.

Kenny pointed at the stairwell door. Mike laughed. "You a little nervous, kid?" But he gently shut the door anyway.

Now, focus. Kenny had the antenna set in a precise southerly alignment for a test transmission. They were trying for a clear signal in a minimum number of hops to the US airbases in Brazil. Mike sat next to Kenny and put on his own headset. They waited.

The test transmission came—fifteen minutes straight of furiously scrawling dots and dashes. When the test was done, they cross-compared their scrawls. Amazingly, they agreed—the transmission was unambiguous at their end. Mike took off his headset and slapped Kenny on the back. "Good work, kid. We'll send this back tomorrow, but sounds like this hunk of scrap is doing the job. Let's celebrate."

Mike pulled out a flask of whiskey and handed it to Kenny. "One Mick to another, right kid?"

Kenny took a sip. It burned, but he didn't cough. "Thanks." Turned out they were the only two Irish in the their section, though Mike was black Irish and Kenny was a fair red head. At twenty-five, Mike was also the youngest employee there besides Kenny. A swell guy.

"Christ, with the blackout, you can really see the stars." Mike pointed. "There's scientifiction heaven, Mars. He must be happy with us now."

When Kenny had first built his antenna, he would aim it every now and then at Mars. Even if the Martians didn't want to visit this world at war, they might be broadcasting Martian news and music. Maybe from up there they could tell where Mom was. But that had just been playing scientifiction.

Mike called him back from space. "So, what else can you pick up on this thing?"

Kenny grabbed his headphones again. His favorite game was to find the farthest radio station signal he could. "Maybe we can hear Brazil ourselves."

Mike adjusted the antenna slightly to the southeast, at an altitude not far above the horizon. "Anything?"

"Not sure." Something was crackling, but Kenny was having trouble tuning the frequency to the sweet spot. "Check the coil, would ya?" Kenny lightly jiggled the frequency. There, maybe...

Screech! Spikes jabbed into both of Kenny's ears. "Shit!" His own damned fault for not paying attention—Mike had opened up the receiver unit and slid the frequency to the coil's far end for a better look.

Mike laughed, roaring, "Take off the phones, Einstein."

Wait. A noise, so faint that Kenny wondered if it were just the echo in his brain of the test transmission. Only the beeps weren't Morse. They were faster. Real fast. No operator could have written this down.

"Kid?"

Kenny signaled with his open palm to keep it quiet. "What frequency?" he whispered.

"Frequency? I don't know, kid, must be like a thousand." 1,000 MHz. Ridiculous, nobody used that range. But there it was.

Kenny felt his heart beating harder, and he tried to calm down so the rush in his ears wouldn't interfere with the signal. A freight train rumbled below; he blocked it out. The signal grew in intensity for a while, and then it faded.

Kenny checked the antenna. Still steady, south by south easterly, towards a nondescript patch of sky with few stars that he could see. Was the source moving? Mike had his pencil and paper ready again. "Get this alignment."

"Sure, kid." Mike noted the precise degrees and minutes. Kenny checked his watch. It was 1:00 a.m. September 15th. *Hello.*

Kenny took off the phones and sat down hard on the roof, letting his breath finally catch up with his excitement, trying to keep the sound-fury in his brain from erupting in front of Mike.

"What the hell was that, kid? Germans? Japs? What?"

Kenny closed his eyes, remembering the signal. "Radio from the stars. Star people."

"Gosh and fuck all. If you're shitting me..."

Kenny shook his head like a punch-drunk boxer.

"OK, you're not shitting me. Are you sure? Remember how that *War of the Worlds* show fooled people."

Kenny remembered. He had known what was going on, and was fooled anyway.

"Are you sure, kid?"

"No. Not sure." This was beyond anything Kenny had ever heard of. "But we can check it tomorrow. We'll listen again at the same altitude and, whatchacallit, azimuth, at around the same time."

Mike nodded. "OK, I get you. We'll start a few minutes earlier. If it's space men, we'll get the same thing at an earlier time. Then what?"

"We need recording equipment," said Kenny. "The good stuff."

"Check. And?"

"Then we got to chase the signal across the sky."

"Kid, you've made this salad bowl to stand at attention, not march. But we'll manage. They've got special motors and shit for telescopes to follow the sky evenly. And we'll need a telescope too." Michael took a swig from the flask and wiped his mouth. "Still, it might be natural fuzz. Another Bell noise guy—you don't know him—got radio from the whole galaxy. Just natural fuzz."

"This is different," said Kenny. "It's a specific source. And if you could've heard it—no, it didn't sound natural at all." Scientifiction becoming scientifact. "We've got to tell people."

"Whoa, hold on," said Mike. "People already had enough to worry about with Nazis and Japs. Do you want to cause a panic like Orson Welles?"

Kenny certainly didn't want that. No need to replay the night his Mom left. No need to even think about that.

"Don't worry kid, I'll handle who we tell. Not Carleton, that's for sure."

"Maybe, maybe we shouldn't tell anyone." Kenny already had the job he wanted—playing with radios and listening for money. This might be too loud for him.

"Yeah," Mike said, "this might turn into big job, and I'd rather be chasing skirts."

A false cadence to this, but most lies didn't matter. Kenny stared at the stars again—so many to listen to. His Mom might be staring at them too. "Mother" he murmured at the sky.

Mike heard him. "Mother? What happened to your mother, kid?"

"Nothing. The Martians got her."

"Right. Look, what if Hitler talks to these green men first? Nazi heat rays? We've got to figure this out before they do."

Hitler talking shit to the space men. Not good.

Some stupid fucking sailors were yelling on the street, long after curfew. Kenny imagined them on deck and looking smart in their uniforms as a heat ray sizzled into their ship, and knew that Mike was right.

Tuesday, January 19, 1943

Kenny sat waiting with Mike in their shared office. Kenny's new title was Assistant Noise Manager, which sounded like he was still part of the noise reduction effort. The confusion was helpful, and nobody at the secrecy-minded Labs questioned his job.

The soldiers and sailors didn't try to drag Kenny off to enlist anymore. His Bell Labs ID specifically noted that he was vital to the war effort. The soldiers or sailors would give him a grudging nod. "Killing Nazis?"

"You bet."

"Good. Get us home sooner."

But Kenny's discovery wasn't killing Nazis, and its harmlessness embarrassed the top brass at the Labs and in Washington. The discovery was obviously important, and it was even more important to keep it quiet. But Uncle Sam couldn't do much about sounding out its meaning—there was a war on, after all. So Mike and Kenny had gotten the job. And they had asked for some outside help, from somebody who knew codes and machines.

An accented voice approached their office. Showtime. Kenny opened the door after the first tap on it. Mr. Carleton stood with a dark-haired man older than Mike, but not much. Carleton introduced them. "Kenneth O'Reilly and Michael O'Neill, this is Dr. Alan Turing."

"Puh puh pleased to meet you," Turing stammered out.

"Dr. Turing has just arrived in New York, boys, and we're all very happy the U-boats didn't get him. He's already been worked pretty hard today, so take it easy on him." Translation—he's too important for the McBrat and Mick, as Kenny had heard the men calling him and Mike through his bugs.

Carleton left and Kenny said, "Please have a seat, Dr. Turing."

"Alan."

"What's that, sir?"

"Please call me Alan, Kenneth. And Michael, is it?"

Kenny was about to correct him, but he realized he liked this older guy's tone when he said *Kenneth*. "OK, Alan."

"Why have they sent me here?" Turing asked, his words fixing Kenneth like a pinned insect. Other than the accent, this guy was nothing like the Brits in the movies. No waste of words, no jive. Weird.

"We asked for you," Kenneth replied, reverting to his natural voice. "We've got an, uh, out of this world problem." God, he sounded like such a kid.

Mike clicked on the recording of the transmission. Suddenly, Turing was all ears. "Where did this come from?"

"Near as we can figure, the star Epsilon Eridani," Kenneth answered.

Mike changed to another recording. The beeps were slower, recognizable and Morse-like. The pattern grew more complex as the recording continued, then cycled back to a simple *beep beep*.

"This is the same signal," Mike said, "with a narrow band isolated."

Kenneth spoke over the signal, riffing with it. "It's the easiest one to hear what's going on. The other parts are going really fast—too fast for anybody to distinguish even played at a reasonably slow speed."

"And what do you think this is?" Alan was a teacher calling him towards the blackboard.

"Here's the thing," said Kenneth. "We're pretty sure this isn't like a person on the phone or radio, you know, something that you modulate the amplitude or frequency of to recreate the vibrations that went into a transmitter somewhere. That means we can't just build the right speaker and talk directly to the LGM."

"LGM?"

"Sorry, little green men. No, the signal's more like Morse—it's a language in itself, all in beeps and blanks. But that means for us, it's like a code."

"Right. But you have excellent cryptanalysts right here."

"For people languages. I don't think it's that kind of language—at least not the fast part."

Alan nodded at Kenneth, who sensed that he had passed the exam. "Yes, a language by machines for machines. So, you want to be able to talk to them?"

"No," Kenneth said, too quickly. "But it would be nice to know what they're saying."

"Right then. We should have some time to work on this. They have *marooned* me here for two months. I'm staying in a hotel in Greenwich Village. Is the Village a friendly place?"

Kenneth heard other questions, other codes, buried in this, but didn't know how to respond. "Sure. New York's a friendly town, once you get to know it." Mike busied himself with the recording equipment.

When Turing was safely gone, Mike burst out laughing. "God, what an oddball. When he asked about the Village, I thought I was going to choke. And the way he was looking at you. Better watch out."

"What do you mean?"

"You don't know?" Mike shook his head. "Kid, you don't want to know."

"Come on, Mike. If he doesn't sound right..."

"I'm sure he's reliable. This man has Winny and Roosevelt's trust. Don't think about it, kid. Let's call it a night."

But Kenneth's ears were buzzing. Good thing he had checked on Turing's accommodations. Turing's room was wired for sound.

That Saturday night, Kenneth heard Turing come back from a night on the town. With him was another man, a fellow Brit by the sound of him. Good, he wouldn't want to use this equipment just to hear Turing's love life.

But then it got weird. Few words, but questions and invitations. "What's your name?" Turing asked.

And the other man whispered, "What do you want it to be?"

"Kenneth."

God, his name. Was that kissing smacks? "Can anyone hear?" Turing asked.

"Everyone can hear. No one minds."

Then grunting, and the rapid arrhythmia of the bed, quick pause quick, different than Dad's boozy women. And the sounds built up, not just in his mind but his whole body, reaching, reaching. "Kenneth! Kenneth!" Gong! The chord rang long and spasmodically from the center of his body to his head and toes.

He had never felt anything like it—listening to his Dad or finding the signal couldn't compare. But it was over so quick.

Shame might have filled the silence, but then it started again. Oh god, again. His true music.

Tuesday, March 23, 1943

Kenneth left the Labs early. The rapid-fire percussion of the signal's main bandwidth was constantly in his head, drowning out the putters of barely fueled cars. He could almost hear the key that the signal was in, and imagined big fat chords coming in midway through. F! CB♭! F! CB♭! It didn't swing, but you could march to it. Going home tonight was like a march.

A ship's horn, the sound of relief. Turing was finally leaving New York on the *Empress of Scotland*. He carried their recordings of the signal in order to continue the work in England. They had made some progress on the molto lento signal—it began as a simple mathematical progression followed by certain physical constants. But they were no closer on the denser parts of the slow signal or any of the faster signals in the polyphonic whole. Turing was going to experiment with specially designed versions of the British code-breaking computing machines.

Kenneth would miss Alan, would miss the listening, but he was relieved to have him gone. Alan almost seemed aware of Kenneth's listening, and acted like everyone else knew about it too. People talked—Kenneth heard them. They didn't understand. He didn't want to touch anyone, especially not guys. He just wanted to listen. Guy noises harmonized better for him, but girl noises could be interesting too.

Still, he would have to start making time for (and with) some girls. Mike could help him. Mike never had any problem finding girls. Maybe he could listen to Mike.

On his way home, Kenneth saw a new *Shadow* book for sale, but didn't buy it. These days, the Shadow (like everyone else) fought the Nazis instead of crime. That got monotonous. Mike had lent him some of his comics and magazines like *Amazing Stories*. Science fiction stories spoke to him more than Nazis or crime.

The house in Queens was a well-painted two stories with a yard of grass but no garden. From the street, Kenneth saw the window of his room, and the room next to it that Dad had insisted on setting aside for his women guests—empty for now. They had painted it pink and decorated it suitably feminine. From his room, Kenneth could listen to Dad's women doing women's things.

Sometimes when Kenneth felt tired and sad he would sit alone in the guestroom. The few possessions his mother had left behind were there. He thought the silence sounded like her.

When Kenneth stepped in the house, one of his radios was blaring Miller's band—they played to fly boys now. Dad was in the kitchen fiddling with the plumbing under the sink again. "Hey, boy, how was your day?"

"Fine. Need a hand?"

"No, I got it." Clang! "Shit. No, I'm fine. Kill a lot of Nazis today?" Just like the sailors.

"Oh yeah," said Kenneth, "the bastards didn't know what hit them."

Growling commenced, punctuated with clangs and bangs.

"Dad, I need to talk to you."

"You need money?" That was a laugh. Kenneth's money had all but bought this house for his Dad.

"No, Dad. I think it's time I moved out."

A thud under the sink. His father reached a closed fist out and opened it. In it was one of Kenneth's listening devices. "You going to take these with you?"

Pure discord. Sudden violence was a word away, but all Kenneth could manage was "What's that?"

His father chuckled mirthlessly, but stayed under the sink, face hidden from his son. "You think your old man is stupid? You tell me, smart guy."

"It's a project from work."

"It's goddamn bug, boy. You've been listening to me."

"I listen to everyone. It's my job."

"The hell you say." Dad placed his hands to push out from the sink. Should he hit him now, while he was down? Nothing to hit him with. Keep talking.

"I was listening for Mom."

Dad let out a sink-muffled sigh. "Did you hear her?"

"No. Did you?"

"Nah."

"I can hear it in people's voices when they aren't telling the whole truth." He had never dared tell his father this before.

"Are you calling me a liar?"

"No," Kenneth said, ashamed at the sound of the lie in his own voice. "You just won't tell me. Has she called here, asking for me?" Silence under the sink. "I thought so. What did you tell her? That I was dead?"

"I told her. I told her that if she called here again, I'd find her and kill her with my bare hands." *True.* "That was last Christmas. You satisfied, boy?"

"Yep." Kenneth shook. He had heard too much, but he wouldn't sound like a coward. "At least the Martians haven't gotten her yet." No response. "So, time for me to move out, I think."

His father got up from under the sink. He still seemed to tower over Kenneth. "Where will you go?"

"The city. Mike's got room for a roommate."

"And what am I supposed to do, while you run off to the city with your sissy friends?"

Dad was just trying to get him off track. "I'll send money. You'll be fine here."

His father grabbed Kenneth suddenly, holding him with one arm and thumping his back with the other. Then, with a smack on Kenneth's shoulder, Dad let him go. "Get going then."

"I'll moo, move out in the morning," Kenneth stammered out. He turned cautiously towards the stairs; he felt like he might faint.

"Don't you want to know why I never mentioned your cockroaches before?" asked Dad. Kenneth wanted to flee, but his father's question held him.

"I thought you didn't know, sir."

"You did think your old da was stupid!" His father belly-laughed like Kenneth seldom heard. Then, in one of his mean swings, Dad grabbed him about the shoulders and spoke low into his ear.

"Look ya, I knew you were all ears from the time you was born. And I've never been ashamed to say anything just because you'd know. By the time I was your age, my da had found me a whore, his own whore, to show me what's what. I thought you could learn to be a real man by your mechanical eavesdropping on me. But you haven't learned goddamn much, have you?"

"No, sir."

"Didn't think so." He pushed Kenneth away. "Get on with you, then. Oh, and you'd better be careful at the Labs."

Vibrato, Kenneth ran upstairs to his room. He choked down a sob. He could take what Dad had said to Mom. Kenneth would find her after the war, and it would be harmony. He would be old enough, with enough dough— she wouldn't have to take care of him. He could take care of her. He was a man, no matter what Dad said. But until then he had work to do.

What he couldn't take, would never take, was that his father had known his secret, for years. That his secret had been ripped from him and whispered back to him. That all his secrets might be turned on him, to humiliate him.

He felt sick, like he was falling. He crawled onto his bed, to calm down and sleep if he could. He couldn't, too much mental noise, like cackling whores. He got up and found a pen and pad of paper. He wrote to let the noise out, but what came out wasn't the noise.

When the creatures crash-landed in the desert, the military knew what they had to do. The words poured down in a staccato stream, a science fiction of secrets and lies that went on until the truth was impossible to hear, with a government and a world that was always listening. He wrote molto allegro for hours, then slumped back onto his bed, light still on, pen in hand, paper everywhere.

He could finally let himself sleep. He had work tomorrow, and a place to get the hell out of.

———

Wednesday June 7, 1944

"That bastard Turing." The rest of the world was holding its breath on day two of the Allied invasion of France, but Kenneth was still spouting off to Mike about a six-month-old message. The Earth had finally said *hello* back to the universe, and Kenneth didn't like it one bit.

Not that it had been a surprise—he had been listening for such a transmission. But no one had even asked his opinion.

Immediately after the Evans Labs had secretly bounced radar off the moon, Turing had sent out a signal from the Hanslope facility towards Epsilon Eridani. His signal was a simple echo of the molto lento portion of the LGM's message, with an added request for a reply in a specified higher frequency. It was as much as Turing could achieve in a year's time.

Kenneth had complained to the government higher-ups. Despite Mike's early, crude efforts to be their Johnny-on-the-spot, the higher-ups talked to Kenneth now. He had their ears, but it was of course too late. They would deal with the Brits and Turing in their own time. In the meantime, well, that's what he needed to explain to Mike.

Mike. The name was melodious, harmonious. He listened for Mike in secret, but Mike never made interesting noises here in the apartment. As if he knew. Didn't matter. Just listening to him with no device was usually a joy.

Not tonight though. He was being deliberately deaf to Kenneth. So Kenneth talked louder, pacing their apartment in time with his Turing rant. "His precautions aren't enough—it's not safe."

Mike waved his hand dismissively. "The Germans are done. Japan will follow."

"Sure, but what about Uncle Joe Stalin? And most importantly, what about the LGM themselves?"

"They're an awfully long ways away. Look, I'm beat. I'm going to head out for a while." Solo. Mike wanted to play solo a lot these days.

Kenneth paced between Mike and the door. "It's going to be another ten years until they hear from us, and then another ten-and-a-half years till we hear back from them. In the meantime, more and more people are going to get wind of this. We have to think very long term."

"We can keep this quiet, kid. You can count on me."

"It's not enough to keep it quiet."

"What's that suppose to mean?" asked Mike.

"For instance, the last couple years, I've been hearing about atomic energy. It's in all the science fiction magazines. Used to be in all the science magazines. Immensely powerful, potentially deadly stuff. But not a peep about it in the papers or from the government. So, something's being kept quiet. Which means there's something to keep quiet."

Mike whistled. "Fine, I get you. So what's on your mind, long term-wise?"

Kenneth now spoke tranquillo. "Why weren't the Germans ready for us at Normandy? I mean, we were making enough of a racket."

"My bet," Mike said, "is that the Nazis were distracted. We had 'em believing we would go anywhere else—Calais, southern France, you name it. We had so many distractions they ignored the easiest, most obvious thing."

"Right." Kenneth knew this was right. He had been following the radio traffic. "Truth needs a bodyguard of noise." Like his recent dates with girls, with their annoying voices and their seeing feeling smelling tasting. "There's something I want to show you." Kenneth found his opus and handed it to Mike.

"You want me to read this now? OK." He skimmed it with indifferent quickness. "Wow, pretty heavy stuff, kid. Round spinning rockets from the stars, Martians among us, the government hiding the Martians, and these super G-men in black suits keeping it secret." He shrugged his shoulders. "You going to write more of this stuff? The grunts will eat it up."

"This isn't a science fiction story."

"Then what is it?" asked Mike.

"It's a plan."

"Oh." Mike translated Kenneth's meaning instantly. "You want to create a legend, a false story, disinformation like at Normandy. Let the nosy and gullible folks learn just enough to confuse them, then deny everything."

"And anyone who describes something like what we've found will be drowned out by the crazies."

Mike's eyes narrowed on Kenneth. "Yeah, you could do that. After the war, of course."

"That's swell. I've already arranged it with the higher-ups. We'll be able to keep working together after the war."

Mike nodded slowly, keeping silent.

Sunday, June 1, 1947.

Before VJ day, Kenneth had never been farther west than Jersey. Now, he was with Mike at the White Sands military base in New Mexico. Sunset, and time for his desert story.

For the past two years, they had been itinerant preachers of the new faith, acting as reporters in one city, witnesses in another. Their dark epistles of the real war of the worlds had appeared in the sympathetic *Amazing Stories* under many names. They had spoken to science fiction clubs and anti-Communist groups. Kenneth was improvisational, like the new jazz, Parker and Gillespie, rapid and complex like the deeper parts of the signal. The less-enthusiastic Mike kept their efforts grounded, serious. They were creating something that was already way beyond them.

And they were staging incidents, of which this was to be neither first nor last.

Kenneth and Mike were dressed in black suits just like the G-men in Kenneth's story. Mike carried a clipboard and Kenneth had a pipe clenched between his teeth. Mike had suggested that Kenneth take up pipe smoking to look older, and that he dye his hair black to avoid standing out.

They were surrounded by cacophony. Immediately in front of them, lab-coated technicians were jangling together a weather balloon. To their right, some German-speaking technicians were wrapping life-like dummies in silver foil. No shit there.

From behind them, "Dr. Wells?" The bristly voice of the USAF.

Teeth clenched on pipe, Kenneth smile-replied with his usual earnestness. "Yes, Colonel Josephson?"

"Something has been nagging me about your experiment. Don't you think it looks a bit, um, funny?"

"Funny, Colonel? I assure you, this is a very serious. Our ability to monitor the potential Soviet atomic threat—"

"Yes, doctor, I know all that. But, these dummies, the balloons—they're like something from the double features. I mean, if a civilian sees this, he's likely to think the Martians have landed."

Kenneth couldn't mute his excitement. "Do you think so, Colonel? Do you really think so?"

Mike was calmer. "I think it would take quite an imagination to see it that way. Don't worry, Colonel. We'll handle it."

Mike and Kenneth walked to the edge of the base together. Kenneth heard the emptiness of the echoless desert. "So much open space. You could put a dozen big radar dishes out here, and nobody would mind."

Mike turned towards the Pole Star and stared out at the horizon. "It isn't far from here, you know. The place they tested the bomb. The Russians will get some bombs too, believe it."

"Yeah, sure. So, what next?"

Mike paraphrased his checklist. "I've already got an article for the newspapers, and I've been talking with some of the more suggestible types in the area."

"This is better than the *War of the Worlds*. With the other incidents we'll create, we'll fool even more people without really harming anyone."

"Yeah, kid, you'll fool them all." Mike's timbre had gone all wrong.

"What's that suppose to mean?"

Mike shook his head. Which could mean that he knew he couldn't get away with saying something.

"Mike, what did you mean?"

"It means I want out, kid. Now stop it with the ear voodoo."

"Why?"

"I'm tired of the cloak-and-dagger. It's hard to meet nice dames when you can't tell them what you do."

Kenneth coughed. He didn't like hearing about Mike's lady friends whom he never heard. "You're drunk."

Mike took out his flask and threw it into the quiet. "Not a drop."

Kenneth tried another tack. "This isn't what I want either. I want to be working on the signal more—we don't even know what they've said yet, much less what they're going to say in '64."

"Kid, when are you going to let them know?"

"Let who know?"

"Everyone. Americans, the Brits, hell, the Russians, too. When are you going to tell them?"

"The Russians, Mike?"

"Yes, the Russians. If mankind's still here when the LGM call back, will anyone really want a more powerful bomb? And then there's our own people."

Kenneth's replied like a player piano. "We have to prepare them for decades. You're the one who convinced me. Otherwise, they'd panic. We've seen it before."

Mike shook his head. "And I've heard that too often. I was wrong, kid. It's a new world. People are already changing. Stuff like this" and he pointed back towards the balloons, "is just going to fuck them up."

"Soon we won't have to fuck them up."

"Huh?"

"National Security Act, Mike. Soon we'll be able to listen in on everybody, everywhere. We'll know if there's a leak, and we'll plug it." And maybe, on some phone line somewhere, he would overhear his mother. He had listened for her in every town but hadn't heard her yet. And Aunt Maureen was dead.

"Listen to everybody? Are you listening to yourself?" Mike abruptly grabbed Kenneth by the shirt. "How much have you been spying on me?

Does my snoring make you tingly? Huh kid? Huh?" He was snarling in Kenneth's face.

"I don't do that." Technically true—he had stopped out of boredom.

Mike pushed Kenneth away. "Maybe you should use some of that ear voodoo on yourself." He turned back towards the barracks.

"Don't quit. The country needs you on this. I can't do this shit without you."

"No, kid. You're the future." Sarcasm? That wasn't the dominant note. Fear.

Fear sounded nice. Should he be afraid of what Mike might say? No, the higher-ups would listen to Kenneth, and they were the only ones who mattered.

If Mike didn't want to riff with him, fine. Kenneth could keep listening to him and even have him silenced if need be. But maybe Mike would stay. There was still so much to hear. Kenneth was only twenty-two. His best years of listening were still ahead of him.

In quiet absolute, a sound—the open sky called him. The music of the spheres, the chimes of midnight, for his ears alone. The signal's rhythm mixed with the pounding chords of Mike's words and the anticipation of the reply, seventeen years six months and counting, and the voice of America, all of America, wired for sound, building and building, like a tower unto heaven, God's new song.

E! The chord struck down on him like baby grand, and slowly faded into the desert silence, coda to this day, this movement in his life.

The Garuda Bird

Here's the originally published intro to this story: "What happens if we envision the future from Bombay instead of Hollywood? Answer: a science fiction musical comedy folk action religious drama with a big Bollywood ending. 'The Garuda Bird' is the story for that future film. So grab some curry-flavored popcorn and a Limca soda, and enjoy!"

OK, let's break that down. I was inspired by a tale I read back in college for an Indian folklore & mythology class. (I've only recently been able to find the tale again: "The Weaver Who Loved a Princess" from *The Panchatantra*.) I turned the original into a fractured bedtime story that I told my women friends, and over the years, it became my own.

Another set of inspirations came from my trip to India prior to the outsource boom. It was summer, and the only air conditioning for a student budget was at the movies. So, despite having little to no grasp of the language, I watched a lot of Bollywood films. Also, I had traveled to India to talk to the political party of a former "godly role" actor turned politician, so it was only natural that someone like him would end up as my PM character.

I mixed these sources together with a lifelong admiration for all things South Asian. The Age of India could be a grand thing, and a lot better than many of the alternatives.

O n a cool night just after the monsoon rains, the Garuda flew invisibly under the moon over the great capital city of India. After passing over the palace walls, it slowly became visible as a ghostly silhouette. The huge red bird shape hovered outside the bedroom of the Princess Madhu, then silently landed on her large balcony.

From the Garuda, a male figure alighted and approached the open glass door. He wore the regal garb of the god Vishnu, with crown, discus, and conch. He was beautiful in form, but his radiant attire looked stagy even in the moonlight.

The Princess was unimpressed. "Vishnu" was sweating, and rightfully so. She was surprised that her bodyguards hadn't rushed in. Perhaps she should call them, but not yet. She was accustomed to artifice and exaggeration. After all, "Princess" was just what the newspeople called her. Maybe a real princess wouldn't be bored, but Madhu was the daughter of the Prime Minister. Her deathly dull routine had made her crazy for adventure. She strode onto the balcony, trying to appear imposing in her sheer bathrobe.

"What in Ram's name are you doing here?"

"I came like in the story."

She eyed his bird-shaped contraption and then examined the rider again. "I don't know this story." It was not one of Daddy's films from his Bollywood days.

"You know, 'The Garuda Bird.' Your mother told it to you, or you read it in school."

"What about your damned Garuda bird?" She was losing patience. She was a university graduate. She bloody well knew what the real Garuda was. "I should call security."

"No, please, I thought you would know the story. Let me tell it to you first."

Her silence was an impatient assent. He began his tale.

This tale didn't happen yesterday. It was a very, very, very long time ago. Long before anything digital besides fingers, when the mountains and rivers and trees were young. When the *avatara* Lord Rama, the divine incarnation of Vishnu himself, ruled the known and unknown worlds from his sacred city. And the people in his city lived a magical existence, an existence not known to us today, of health, wealth, and love.

But far from Rama's city was the small provincial kingdom of Delhidesh, and there life was pretty much the same mediocre mess that it was last week.

In that small kingdom there lived two friends, a lame Blacksmith and an adventurous Soldier. The Smith was an exceptionally clever entrepreneurial type in his medieval milieu, though he had lost leg and love in an accident at his forge. The loyal Soldier enjoyed assisting the Smith in testing the new swords, armor, and arcane devices of war that the Smith manufactured. They were as prosperous and content as people of their castes could expect.

One day, the Smith and the Soldier managed to gain entrance to a grand and joyous festival. It was the public coming-out party for the Princess of the realm, so everyone of worth in the kingdom was there. The Smith and Soldier ate too much, watched dizzying feats of illusion, and generally had a raga-and-roll good time. Then, all were silent as the King of Delhidesh rose to address the gathering. They listened with reverence to the old King's praise of his daughter and his land.

"Reverence? Ha!"

Madhu couldn't help but interrupt. She glanced down at the man's ornately sandaled feet on her balcony. "You're the Soldier?"

"My name is Vijay." He offered his hand, English-style.

Madhu lowered her eyes, shaking her head. "I remember you from the party. But it wasn't like your story at all."

Madhu tried to keep smiling pleasantly as Daddy's party toast became another endless speech. If he could have sung it, people would have been much happier. Little did they know.

Her graduation from Harvard Medical School was his flimsy excuse to wax bloody mystical again.

"…Time can be a tricky business in our land. Is it only the end of the dark Kali Yuga, or the beginning of the next holy age of Ram Raj? I believe that it is finally our choice to make. We have struggled through a time of great danger. Now is the time of great possibility. If we work together, the Age of India will finally come again, if not for us, then for our children. For my Princess. And someday her children as well. *Hai Ram.*" And everyone downed their non-alcoholic champagne, except Mummy, who had suddenly gone stone-faced. Trouble.

Before this *kalpa*-length toast had even ended, a perky aide was already explaining to a gorging journalist that Daddy had some bullet points under all the nationalist slogans. Somehow the expected nuclear boom and doom (as always over Kashmir) had fizzled. Cheap fusion energy had unleashed India's best resource, its brain power. Globally, the Indian Diaspora rivaled the overseas Chinese. (As for China itself, well, princesses should avoid *schadenfreude* but, hey, turned out democracy matters, chumps.) An Indian century was within reach.

But the Princess didn't want an age of India for her graduation. She just wanted a time to be Madhu, maybe even Dr. Madhu. That wasn't going to happen, thanks to Sanjay. His mercifully silent holo-image sat at an empty place at the banquet table, wild-eyed as in life. Last year, her psychotic brother had crashed in his supersonic when he manually took the controls (Sanjay is not a lucky name for a PM's son). Since then, she wasn't just her family's darling, she was their political heir.

So this party was her introduction to public life and the social event of the year. Many were invited, many more came. Outdoors in the courtyard of the PM's residence, smells of curries overran the subtler delights of neo-caviar. The band swung effortlessly from bossa nova to Brahms to Bollywood. Some big-haired hunk and a big-bosomed spoonful were dancing and crooning:

What shall we do behind this piece of fruit?
Tell me what to do behind this enormous fruit.
No, you first.
No, you!

Liberally sprinkled through the crowd were Daddy's old film cronies— the pioneers of the ironic musicals that had swept the globe. In his roles as singing gods, Daddy had been their Elvis and Heston combined. The next generation of starlings flocked around him, eager for the *darshan* blessing of his gaze.

Smiling now, Mummy worked the political crowd with the grace and hustle befitting the scion of India's longest running dynasty since the Nehru-Gandhis. Paparazzi were snapping holo-shots of them all, particularly of Madhu.

Madhu did not care a whit. She needed to find the covert alcohol service, hidden in particular from the paparazzi. She needed a bloody real drink.

She slipped through the dance floor, but then found her way blocked by a strange cluster of traditionally clad ultra-nationalists and high-ranking military folks. Damned odd that they were even here. At the cluster's center was a silver-haired man in western formal dress, but with only one pant leg. The other leg was a shiny metal prosthetic, a strange affectation in a city where regeneration of limbs was as common as reincarnation of bugs. She didn't want to stare, but there was writing on the leg. A woman's name, *Lakshmi*. Now she really needed that drink.

She skirted the fascists and slipped through the secret flap in the alcohol tent. Blast, some air-space captain was already there, and he was looking right at her.

She put on her best ingenue's face. "Promise you won't tell anyone?"

The young captain shrugged his shoulders, and gave her a goofy smirk. "Who would I tell? But more importantly, what'll you have?"

Well, this was grand, he didn't seem to recognize her. "*Behewt accha*. Gin and tonic, please."

She had a nice chat with the clueless yet well-formed young man, but she heard little and remembered less, distracted by his handsome dark southern features that her fair northern mother wouldn't approve of. He said something about flying and folk stories. She thought briefly of mad, sad Sanjay, and asked if they still needed human pilots. He said for some jobs, yes, they did. She spoke little of herself, not wanting to give herself away and ruin the moment. Realizing that she was going to be missed soon, she made some excuses and left the tent before he could follow. And she didn't think of him again that night.

"You didn't think of me?"

The costumed fly boy's enthusiasm deflated with a sigh. She hadn't meant to be harsh. "I had a lot on my mind."

"I understand. I thought of you though."

"What did you think?" A foolish question. Did she really want to know?

"I need to tell you the rest of the story first."

As his dharma would have it, the Soldier wandered off from his friend after the King's speech. In a small tent, he ran smack right into love. It was the always-fatal kind, because you have it from first sight till you die. After his new love left him, he was happy for about 30 ticks on a medieval watch, the happiest Soldier in Delhidesh. But then he made the mistake of asking the Smith who the strange woman was. And, as you may guess, it was the Princess herself that the young Soldier had gone soggy for.

So, the Soldier went home and had a good day-long crying jag followed by two days of quasi-coma. He starved himself in the best Hindu martyr fashion. He didn't show up for his work at the Smith's. On the third day, the Smith sensed that both the time and the Soldier's odor had grown ripe. So he broke into his friend's bachelor pad, and confronted him with the sour facts.

"Soldier, old boy, you've been like this for three days, not eating, not speaking to anyone, and letting our work go. You can't hide it from me, pal, you've got all the symptoms of love from first sight to forever. So just cough it up—who is she?"

"Her hair is black as a moonless night," the Soldier cried, "though strangely short for these times. Her skin is fair as the snows of Kashmir, but she is more remote than Everest. And yet I do not know how I can live without her."

"Soldier, I am a clever entrepreneurial fellow and you are a daring young man. Together we can achieve anything we set our minds to. We're a team! So, come on, who is she? We can win her over to you."

"Even if she's the Princess?"

Now the Smith had to admit that this was an epic task. But, after asking the Soldier about his conversation with the Princess, the Smith started laughing. "By Krishna, I've got it! The Vedas have already shown us the way." And the Smith explained his outrageous and fantastic plan.

For you see, the Smith had secretly built a flying machine in the shape of a bird. Together, the Smith and Soldier painted it bright red to look like the Garuda, the mount of Lord Vishnu, highest of the gods. And, perhaps misspending client funds, they bought the Soldier fancy clothes, a crown, and most important, a discus and a conch in the style of Vishnu. For they planned to have the Soldier court the Princess in the guise of the king of the gods.

And so, late one night, by the light of the full moon, the disguised Soldier mounted the mechanical Garuda bird. It lifted him up into the air, silently and effortlessly. He told the Garuda to take him to the palace.

As the Garuda flew, the Soldier felt strange, as if he had entered halfway into the dimension of the gods. He thought he heard someone say, "Hello, what have we here?" But he set his mind and his heart on his love, and ignored all else.

The Soldier had some reason to dream of success. The Smith had told him that the King and Queen were remarkably fond of their daughter, so fond that they would allow her discretion in choosing her husband from among the eligible princes.

Meanwhile, the neo-caviar dreams were fading at the PM's. On the verandah, Mummy and Daddy were fighting about her again.

"Madhu's life is too important to be left to Madhu. And what did you mean at the party, talking about her children?" Mummy hadn't quite recovered from Sanjay's death yet. She was used to treating Madhu with benign neglect. Now, she had to consider Madhu as important to the Family's future. How annoying!

"Well, of course she would get married first, wouldn't you, Princess?" Daddy was used to making people happy with a smile and a dubbed-in song. Mummy was more of a challenge for him.

"Who she marries is now a serious political matter."

"I'm sure she'll marry a nice boy, won't you, Princess?" He smiled at her with nervous eyes.

"She'll marry the right man, or she won't marry at all."

And so on. Madhu didn't fight, because this was all fine with her. Between medical school and accompanying Daddy on his surreptitious excursions to the cyberfleshpots of the Old City, neither sex nor romantic love held much mystery or attraction. True, her chat with the clueless fly boy from the party foreboded trouble ahead for this policy of appeasement, but she didn't have to worry about seeing *him* again. So she retreated to her bedroom, and opened her door to the fresh night air that follows the monsoon.

As the Soldier flew towards the palace, the Princess lay in bed and reviewed the line-up of princes, but without satisfactory results. All were worthy, but she felt nothing for any of them. In her confused frustration, she prayed to Vishnu. "Oh Vishnu, please help me find a husband."

And lo! At that very moment, a shadow of a large bird passed over the moon, and the great Garuda descended onto the balcony. Our resourceful hero dismounted, a bit dizzy from his strange flight, and beheld the abject bowing of the shocked Princess. She was babbling apologies for calling Vishnu at such a late hour and for the messy state of her room.

Then the Soldier gently said, "Rise, dear one! For I have seen your beauty shining up to high heaven, and I have come to respectfully ask if we might be 'wed as they are in heaven.'"

"He wanted to get laid."

"Um, yeah."

"That's all it took? A goofy god outfit?"

"Yep."

"Not today, sweetheart." Madhu put her fingers to her mouth to whistle.

"Wait! That's just the story. Really! I just want to get to know you."

"You could just look me up online. I have a website."

"We seemed to get along so well at the party. I had to see you again. I also prepared a song for you." He started into one of Daddy's songs: *That's the way God works…*

"Don't do that. It's creepy. Besides, it's an open secret that Daddy's songs were all voice-overs." She smiled at the shock on his face—disillusioning people about Daddy never ceased to amuse her. Then a cold metallic image came back to her. "So, who's your Smith?"

"He calls this machine 'the Garuda One.' He built it long before I met you, of course. But it reminded us of the story."

"And this clown suit?" She let the Smith's identity lie for now.

"My idea, I thought with your father and all."

"My father never played Vishnu. Lord Krishna sure, Lord Rama many times, but never Vishnu."

"Oh. Well, we had talked about folklore."

"Not really my area." But he suddenly seemed such a sad and tired clown again. She offered a little encouragement. "So what happened next?"

He brightened and opened his hands towards her. "He got the Princess."

"That's it?"

He waved one hand dismissively. Was he drunk, or just out of it? "There were some minor complications."

"Don't you think she would have figured out, even back then and however good he was, that he wasn't divine?"

He wagged his finger. "Always a risk." Then he toppled over like the demon Ravana on his last and worst day in *I'm Your Monkey Man, Hanuman*.

Oh, this was not good. She lightly slapped his face, but he only moaned bits of Daddy's songs. So she dragged him into her room and flopped him onto her bed. It was really the only place to flop someone. She eyed him closer. Even in his ridiculous outfit, she decided he was worth looking at. Maybe they could talk again when he woke up.

Before dawn, the Soldier flew off on the Garuda bird, having wed the Princess as they are in heaven.

"But then what happened?"

"You want me to keep telling the story?"

"Yes, blast it, yes! This is the best bloody part."

"You'll have to help me. Some things I don't like to tell."

"I know. I'll help. I'll help with the part about the Smith."

Mohan had remained awake all night, tinkering with his leg while he waited for Vijay to return with the Garuda One. The leg was bleeding-edge tech, like every device strewn about this vast room: the Agni particle cannons, the Arjuna invisibility screens, and the Blades of Kali—bizarre pretzel-shaped weapons that could kill a city on one setting, kill a bug on another. But as with the other devices, the leg could always be improved. Progress.

Finally, Mohan heard the Garuda's screeching signal and opened the facility's roof. Vijay descended and dismounted quickly; Mohan could tell that he was anxious to relate his exploits. Mohan had long ago ceased to care about such fleshy stuff, and he was in charge, so his questions would take precedence. Still, he would have to put on his friendly face.

"So, did you get through the security OK?"

"*Ji ha*, no problem—like I wasn't even there."

"You weren't, in a fashion. A good chunk of you was elsewhere and elsewhen."

"It made me kind of dizzy. I passed out when I got there."

"An acceptable side effect."

"I, um, thought I heard voices."

Shit, was his pilot going nutty? That was the problem with mucking about with transdimensional quantum level forces: you needed a pilot. Otherwise, the Garuda might go off on an uncertain flight path into nothingness. Despite this design weakness, the payoff was worth it. The Garuda could move in any direction or hover at will, and was almost undetectable. That the device took the pilot along with it into the transdimensional area and perhaps bent his mind slightly was of secondary concern, but still a concern.

"I'm sure you'll be fine after some rest," Mohan yawned. "So, why don't we both call it a night or morning."

Vijay was miffed. "You don't want to hear what happened with Madhu?"

Mohan arched an eyebrow. So it was Madhu now, was it? "No, I don't want to hear anything about it. It's a private matter. I'm sure you were a godly gentleman." He forced a wink, and the blockhead actually blushed.

"There's one other thing, boss-sahib. How am I going to see her again?"

How do you think it is for me, all the time, you human cow pie? "Oh, you can use the Garuda One of course. Just remember, be a gentleman, Vishnu." He forced another wink, and the blockhead was still chuckling and blushing as he stumbled out the door.

Mohan could finally relax when Vijay left. Good, another cooperative moron. The ultra-nationalists were ecstatic with the Garuda—of course, they thought the ancients already had this heavy equipment, according to the Vedas. The military was itching to settle all border accounts, and was perhaps even looking a country or two beyond.

As for Mohan, he had deliberately kept his accounts in a form that he could not forget. His leg helped him concentrate. In its shiny surface, he could imagine Lakshmi's long-dead face above her name. His research accident had cost him his one chance at love, and everyone—the enemies who justified the research and the government who demanded it—would eventually have to pay. Mohan didn't mind being thought a mad scientist. After all, if he didn't get mad, how could he get even?

He went to the Garuda, and from a hidden compartment pulled out a data disk. It would take him awhile to brief the ultra-nationalists and to set up a meeting with the PM. Let Vijay enjoy himself until then. He, too, would have to pay eventually.

At breakfast the next day, and every day for the next week, the Princess had a sleepy *gobar*-eating grin on her face. The King just thought his daughter was happy about some prospect of marriage; the Queen suspected that something like marriage was already happening. So, that night, she secretly waited outside her daughter's room to see who the suitor was. The Queen considered the possibilities with royal equanimity: if he was a prince, all the better that her daughter had had a trial run of him; if he was some common person, a bodyguard or soldier, she'd simply have him executed and hush up the whole thing.

But it was neither a prince nor a common person that she saw enter her daughter's room that night, but the Lord Vishnu himself!

She was ready to be furious, to burst in on them, call security, drive her now-only child to tears for ruining all her careful planning. But the anger wouldn't come. When she saw through her spy mote the strange young man in the Vishnu garb, she remembered the first time she had seen her husband in the wonderfully accentuated colors of Bollywood 3D, a god in god's clothing. From that moment, even as a girl, she knew she must have him and him alone, politics and the Family be damned.

Movies became reality. Her Family's resources brought her to him, love and destiny brought them together to the summit of power. It had not been a bad life. If only Sanjay…

She suddenly felt old and cold. She tottered like a blind woman back to her husband's bed and its warmth. No, she would not be the one to break their hearts. That would happen soon enough without her help.

Mohan enjoyed a rare moment of unfeigned, unadulterated pleasure as he watched the PM squirm. Under the pretext of showing him how effective the Garuda was at eluding detection and penetrating security, Mohan had shown him holovid footage of Vijay's visits to his daughter. Mohan waited as long as he could to speak, savoring the silence.

"It reminds me of some of your work."

The PM glared back at him with quiet ferocity. But what could he say? Mohan had exactly hit upon the real problem. Not the sex (though that would get the news services' attention as surely as it got the PM's) but the manner of it. The resemblance of the holovid to the PM's earlier career would just be too disturbing for the electorate.

Certainly Mohan hadn't planned it out this way. He thought he was going to have to rely on the bumbling ultra-nationalists to come up with some leverage. But that blockhead Vijay had opened up the door to this wonderful improvisation. Marvelous. The PM had no choice. If he wanted to stay in power, he'd have to cooperate with their military plans.

Time to put on his respectful face. "Sir, the advantage of the Garuda device will not last forever. The Pan-Arabs have been working along similar lines. With the Garuda, we can hit them instantaneously and invisibly. Invincibly. Please, won't you reconsider, and meet with the nationalist faction?

"Fine. I'll meet with them on one condition."

Mohan nodded that he was listening.

The PM's arm shook with fury as he pointed at the holovid. "That derivative bastard goes on the front line, and doesn't come back."

And so the royal couple found out about their daughter and Lord Vishnu. And the King was glad, but not for the same reasons as his wife. The Queen was thinking of the wonderful deities and demi-deities that would be visiting for social occasions. The King was thinking that with a son-in-law like Vishnu, he needed more enemies to conquer.

So the next day, the king made some. Enemies, that is. He delivered stinging insults to the ambassadors in his kingdom. They promptly reported the insults to their own kings, who just as promptly raised armies, and besieged the kingdom.

The King told the increasingly concerned populace not to worry—he had Vishnu as a son-in-law, so surely Vishnu would come tomorrow at dawn to destroy their enemies.

Kings can be so literal-minded.

At hearing this, the Princess grew faint. She had long before figured out that her lover was awfully good, but not divine. So she knew that the dear love of her heart and her whole kingdom were both in deadly peril. She tried to join him to flee the kingdom, but the evil forces allied with the Smith blocked her way. She sent a message to warn him, but it was too late—war was coming.

Her mother the Queen comforted her, for mother and daughter both understood the magic of the godly role, while the King had lost that magic, or perhaps was jealous of it in another.

The Soldier needed no warning—he soon enough realized his and the kingdom's danger. What could he do? Perhaps he should run away. But what would happen to the Princess, to his homeland? Probably the same thing that was going to happen anyway.

It was the day before the King's armies would attack the enemy in the confidence that Vishnu and Garuda would make them invincible. For the first time in many years, the Soldier thought a prayer might be a good idea. Perhaps a word with Vishnu.

The Vaishnavite temple was very old and in disrepair. In front sat an old sanyasi holy man in saffron robes. He mumbled to himself as Vijay approached him. Vijay dipped his card into the sanyasi's bowl, but it wouldn't take any rupees.

The sanyasi looked up at him, grinning manically. "And how are your voices coming?"

"What makes you think I hear voices, sanyasi-ji?

The old man chuckled. "You young ones think you know everything."

Vijay was beyond desperate and shameless. "Please teach me, father. I've lost the dharma."

"*Kurushetra me, dharmashetra me.* Hmm, teach you something. *Accha,* how about this: all sufficiently advanced magic is indistinguishable from technology."

"I don't understand."

"Right. Well how about this then: mortals become what they pretend to be."

"I'm not sure, I—"

The sanyasi landed a sharp blow to Vijay's shoulder with his walking stick. "Did you think you could just play at this? This is India, boy, where every peasant knows what happens when you play god." He wagged his stick at a campaign vid board of the PM. "Just look at him. More of an idiot than you. OK, one more try: *deus ex machina,* silly once-born. God from the machine!" The sanyasi turned away, and as he tottered down the street, he called back to Vijay. "Say hello for me next time you're up there," and he thrust his walking stick towards the sky.

After a sleepless night, the Soldier mounted the mechanical bird, and flew up into the dawn light to engage the enemies of Delhidesh.

It seemed he flew above all Delhideshes, past, present, and future. He flew above the Red Fort and the great mosque. He flew above Connaught Place with its teaming thousands. He flew above palaces and mansions and slums and hovels. Fair and foul scents, medieval to third world to otherworldly now, made his fearful stomach turn. Cries of joy and pain cancelled each other out in a low hum—"aummmm." Over the centuries, did anything really change?

He hovered a moment over the town walls, then flew out towards the front. He saw the vast armies arrayed against him, and the vast army supporting him, and he despaired for himself and his country. He was armed with the arcane weapons of the Smith, weapons of Agni and Kali. But the enemies had fearsome weapons as well. What could he alone accomplish? If the battle went badly, he would crash his Garuda into the enemy lines so as to do the most damage.

With this thought, he felt his love for the Princess and his native land flood open the gates of his heart, so that when he heard the voices again he was ready.

In a set of dimensions just a little askew from the familiar ones, a meeting was taking place between two powerful sentients. For convenience's sake, think of them as a giant bird and his boss.

"My Lord," squawked the bird, "that sacrilegious bozo is crossing over again."

"Yes, well, it's happened before, and will happen again," replied his boss.

The bird clucked with irritation. "Maybe, but I don't have to like it. Dressed like you, riding an imitation of me, all to get laid. And now all India's gonna pay for it."

"I suppose you think they've got what's coming to them, so what's the big deal?"

The bird chirruped gently, "Lord, no. I don't want our beloved land of Bharat to perish under our image. I just wish it was more simple, like the old days."

The boss laughed. "It was never simple, my friend. But what shall we do now? I'm open to suggestions."

"I'm afraid we have to go all the way with this one."

The boss roared with approval. "Oh, that'll show the bastards. Awesome idea, O wise bird."

Then the bird screeched with the voice of thousand eagles. "Did you hear that, Vijay? Make it so!"

And in that moment Vijay knew that he was truly the Soldier, and the Soldier was now Vishnu, and the Garuda One was now the Garuda bird.

But he wasn't sure what that meant until the Garuda turned its metal head back towards him and squawked, "Come on, Vijay, this isn't the *Mahabharata*. Get a move on."

Then the Garuda let forth a sonic boom of a screech that stunned friend and foe alike. And they were both suddenly and radiantly visible above the armies.

Vijay's heart spoke one last prayer. For love of her, for love of India, *Bharat ki jai*.

His weapons suddenly felt dirty. He threw the Agni canon and the Blade of Kali to the ground with disgust. Then, for simple joy, he blew into his conch.

A massive superquake unleashed below the armies. Soldiers of both sides fled to the open ground as their heavy equipment and transports were tossed about and wrecked.

When the quake subsided, Vijay gave the discus a throw with a child's enthusiasm.

The discus became a million wheels of light, and each wheel set to work. Some gave crew cuts to the men and women alike. Some went through weapons like knives through ghi. Some dazzled soldiers' faces with their light.

Not one soldier on the field was now able to fight. The Garuda smiled back at him and clucked wryly. "Seems like you didn't know your own strength. You stopped both armies."

"It felt right."

"You've become wise. Good job, Vijay."

"Call me... Kalki."

"Avatar of the Future? Yes, I suppose you are, Avatara. Many lives together and all that. We'll be in touch. Ciao for now." And the Garuda One was just the Garuda One again.

But Vijay knew that he never was and never would be just Vijay, and neither were any of us ever just ourselves.

"And how does the story end, my faithful Soldier?"

"Well, the Soldier got the Princess."

"With minor complications." The Queen, née Princess, squeezed him with a laugh. She was enjoying an evening of just being Madhu in her new master bedroom.

"The enemy kings quickly became the Very Friendly Kings."

"Very prudent of them."

"The old King and Queen knew that Vishnu wasn't really their son-in-law, but they knew quality and god-blessed material when they saw it, so the Soldier got to marry the Princess anyway in a lovely ceremony."

"Very sporting of them."

"The old King went back to acting, this time as the doddering father figure. The old Queen pursued global war relief work."

"May they prosper, and not nag me for grandchildren."

"The Smith, when he heard the results of the battle, activated another transdimensional device and crossed fully over." Vijay hesitated. "He was not heard from again. I wish he could be here to help…"

"Let us not speak of him again, dear. Though I know he was your friend, my heart knows where he has gone."

"May Vishnu yet find him and preserve him."

"But what about my favorite part? What happened to the Soldier and the Princess then?"

"The Princess was elected Queen."

"No doubt due to the popularity of her husband."

"No doubt due to her wisdom and beauty."

"And her consort?"

(He still heard the voices, and they spoke of the days for which they await when all will be revealed and Kalki will ride forth again without even a fig-leaf of technology to bring god's rule to the world. But not today, *hai Ram*.)

"Her consort lived happily ever after with his beloved."

For once, this sentiment did not satisfy Madhu. "So everybody lived happily ever after in spite of, or perhaps because of, their own foolishness?"

And Vijay sang one of her father's songs:

> *That's the way God works*
> *With fools and crooks and jerks.*
> *That's the way God plays*
> *Every day in India.*

And they embraced and the music made the world young again to them, with young mountains and rivers and trees. And the Queen and her Soldier and every lover everywhere was a god and goddess to their beloved in the accentuated colors of the Lord's own 3D. And all their cries of joy and worship blended into one grand "Aum." The Age of India had come again at last.

———

May the Lord in all his names bless and keep you. This story is yours now; tell it to others in the spirit given. *Hai Ram!*

And that's a wrap.

Sea And Stars

Every story is completely made up; every story is based on experience. On the spectrum, this story comes closest to being based on real events. When I visited Brazil, I went through an Umbanda purification rite, and I witnessed the sort of possessions that I describe here. I also received an odd and uncanny warning from the saints. I gave this tale an exotic setting, but it doesn't have much of a speculative element, save the questions we all ask ourselves after the golden age has passed.

At Clarion, instructor Richard Paul Russo was a big fan of "Sea and Stars." So this one is for him, and for absent friends.

Stoned four days straight, and our Brazilian thrill was gone. The lime juice caipirinhas cloyed; the cachaça liquor fueled dreams that were nasty, brutish, and long. An infinite stretch of Bahian beach was ours alone, but unappreciated through squinting bloodshot eyes and UV protection shades.

Miguel (Mike to us) and Paul were about finished with playing backgammon against each other. For life. At first Mike had won every game. "Just a question of skill," he said, waving a hand dismissively over the board.

"It's dice-driven. A game of chance," Paul grumbled.

Mike grinned, bleary eyed. "A question of skill and intellect."

Paul's jaw clenched, his face like a Cold War diplomat's. He had been down all day, and now he was getting pissed at Mike. Elena, Paul's fiancée, watched with silent concern. Paul really needed to change gears. So I butted in. "Paul, it's only toilet paper money. Why don't you settle up and start fresh?"

Elena smiled and stretched out again on her towel next to Debbie's. My idea worked its psychological magic—Paul began to win. "Are you cheating?" Mike asked. Paul laughed. "Are you cheating?" Mike repeated. He wasn't joking. Game over. Damned good thing firearms weren't present. Still, we were better off with Paul happy.

All the stoned giggles had long gone out of tall-and-lanky Elena and short-and-busty Debbie. Deb was Paul's ex-girlfriend, but we were all good friends. I avoided staring at them while they sunbathed.

"Hey, Johnny, could you rub some sunscreen on our backs?" asked Deb without opening her eyes.

I stalled. "I'm eating." True enough—my fingers were already oily with fried yucca. Quiet Elena just looked up at me, wistful. Hard to tell whether she understood, or just wanted me to get cracking with the sunscreen.

Long before her romance with Paul, I had learned that that there was nothing for me in Elena's direction. Smart woman. I didn't let it bother me. I particularly didn't let Paul bother me. We were all smart stoners.

Paul sat down between the women's sun-bleached heads. He still looked fit, but I had been at a law firm a year longer than he had, so I could see how the job ate at his edges—a little pastiness here, some hair loss there. He was trying to tell the women about his job.

"It's crazy. I'm a smart guy, and I work smarter. They don't care. They keep piling stuff up for me to do. When I tell them I'm already busy, they just laugh."

I shook my head. I had warned him about firm life, but that's the problem with smart people—they think they'll be the exceptions. Deb flicked a hand at her face as if he were a whining mosquito. Nobody wanted to hear the complaints of the guy with everything—brains, looks, and now money. Then Elena gave Paul's shoulder a squeeze, and Deb said something about the advantages of meditation and offered a therapeutic massage.

The women's eyes were wide open now, restless. Massage, sunscreen, and other monsters of the id hung like ripe coconuts overhead. The ocean waves were a slow drum that played on my nerves.

"We should do something," I ventured.

"Why?" asked Mike, as he rolled another cigar-sized joint.

I was high and drunk enough to speak with the Midwestern deliberateness of Jack Nicholson. "Because, as good a host as you've been, we didn't fly four thousand miles just to watch your Hungaro-Brazilian ass get overbaked."

"You may kiss my royal Magyar ass, gringo."

But Debbie said, "Johnny's right. You promised us an Umbanda ritual."

A dubious ally. Deb was quick to annoy with her New Age Gaia-worshipping weekends-in-the-woods-with-women crap. I understood her spiritual inclinations; a little magic on life's edges was fine. She just babbled on about it too much.

Mike grimaced. For him, Deb had always been out of phase. "You just want to chase Brazilian goddesses."

But then Paul said, "Yeah, let's go," and everyone caught his sudden enthusiasm. Elena just smiled and nodded—she found talking even more uncomfortable when high than straight.

Collectively, all we knew was that Umbanda was like voodoo, but that was enough. Stoner geeks can't resist a good social-anthro opportunity—even if you're not high during, it's a good memory for a later buzz. Mike knew enough to help us hunt down the right place. Debbie wanted to compare rituals, and I needed a non-libidinous distraction.

So we grabbed some of our cash and flopped into Mike's jeep. Mike drove like a happy maniac over soul-crunching roads towards Porto Seguro. We made good time with a few bruises. Paul sat in the back with the two women. I braced myself against the dash and tried to talk over the engine and Pink Floyd's *Wish You Were Here*. "Why don't you play some Brazilian music?"

"Ha!" Mike pointed at the stereo. "This is what I grew up listening to. Dire Straits, Pink *Floyje*." He said the name Brazilian style.

"I thought you picked up this stuff in undergrad."

"Fuck no. American music sucks."

Mike's Brazil had always seemed a colorful abstraction in college, vaguely better than my Ohio or Deb's New York. But now some things that I had thought were just Mike were also Brazilian. Strange. It made him larger and farther away.

We hit a large dirt bump. I stuck my head around my seat. Paul scratched my head and the two women joined in. I lolled my tongue like a goofy dog on a jeep ride. They finally stopped.

We slowed as we passed a small, ancient church, all white. I studied the floor of the jeep. Paul and Elena's engagement was still an abstract thing, without definite date.

Deb must have been thinking the same thing. She started in on the astrology. "With your signs, I think August would be a good month for a marriage."

Paul raised his hand to his mouth in mock horror. "This August?" He shook his head. "Maybe August next year instead."

"Next year?" Elena spoke, so it was important.

"Yes! Next year. Here! You're all invited." Backgammon forgotten, Paul passed his boundless manic energy to Elena in a kiss. And Elena re-radiated love in all directions, even mine.

Porto Seguro's loneliness on the map makes it seem more important than it is. Mike pointed abstractedly towards the north. "The Portuguese made first landfall near here. Colonialist fuckers." Mike subscribed to the sort of Marxism that only a child of the third-world elite could afford.

Paul leaned forward. "The Portuguese always knew a good beach when they saw one."

"Did the Portuguese bring the Umbanda?" asked Elena. But no one really wanted to answer her. Too much history that was and was not ours.

We parked the jeep. Mike inquired first at a pharmacy that sold Umbanda supplies on the side, then at a small Umbanda specialty store. The men at the stores took forever to say "no" in that painfully slow Baiano accent, which seemed to have the cadence of a Californian surfer on 'ludes. It fit the pace of time here too well.

Deb took the time at each store to run her fingers over the strange candles and to smell the incense and oils. She would say "Elena, take a look at this, this one is good." And Elena would sniff it, and then pass it on for Paul to smell as well.

The specialty store was crowded with statuettes just slightly skewed from the saints I grew up with. Deb picked one up. The statuette looked like the Virgin, complete with a blue cloak. She was standing on blue waves, and above her head were silver stars.

Paul whistled. "She's a babe."

"Who is she?" asked Elena.

"Looks like Mary," I said.

"That's Iemanja, goddess of the sea." Mike was doing his hippie professor bit. "But yeah, she's also Mary, so she's queen of heaven, too."

"Dude, you believe this stuff?" Paul didn't take his eyes from the goddess.

Mike shrugged. "No. Brazilians all know this stuff, but I don't believe any of it."

Elena shuddered. "She... it looks cold." Elena took the statuette from Deb and returned it to its place. We left the store.

"How long is this going to take?" I asked.

"Not long," said Mike. "One more place." Mike saw this, like backgammon, as an intellectual challenge. He led us into a shabbier corner of Porto Seguro. After the fresh air of the beach, we had to adjust our nostrils again to the developing-world smells. Every building seemed dirty and on the point of collapse. At each turn the streets seemed to grow darker, though it was only late afternoon. Debbie scanned around like a nervous bird. "Maybe we weren't meant to do this."

Elena agreed. "Maybe we should go back."

Paul laughed. He looked like himself again, perfectly at ease, the shining boy in the rough of college punks on dope. I had the sudden, sure sense that maybe we really should go back. All the way back to colder climes and sturdy houses, where the outside kept out and the inside kept safe. But we were too far gone now, with many miles of bad road and ocean between here and there.

We saw another Umbanda store up the road. A painting of an old black man with a pipe was outside the shop, and written below it was "Casa de Preto Velho."

"What's a *preto velho*?" I asked.

"It's the house of the old black man, the old black ancestor spirit."

Paul nodded solemnly, looking at the painting. "Like Clarence Gatemouth Brown."

Mike went in to speak with the storekeeper, then quickly returned. "The guy says that if we come back at 7:00 we might see a ceremony tonight."

"Outstanding," Paul barked like a drill sergeant. "Let's eat." Between all the toking and all the searching, we were starving.

We walked out of the dark maze into an open sunlit plaza. We found the usual copious Brazilian feast—steak and fried yucca, seafood stews, lots of nearly cold Brahma beer. We toasted Paul and Elena's wedding like it had already happened, and Paul grinned at the whole restaurant.

Everybody's mood improved, but I still felt something was wrong, and the wrongness got worse as the sun lowered in the sky. I looked over at Deb, but she was just staring off towards the Casa de Preto Velho. I asked her, "Do you still want to do this?"

"We have to do this. It's like when I'm in the woods sometimes. I can feel it." And then she smiled and seemed herself again. "Aren't you excited?"

This didn't reassure me, but I couldn't see what I was going to do about it short of having a fit or otherwise embarrassing myself. Paul and Mike were two alpha primates. Gentle Elena would do whatever Paul wanted. Deb had some agenda of her own. I was along for the ride.

The bill came: 70,000 cruzeiros. The usual nonsense ensued. Most of our currency and useless travelers' checks were secured in the *pousada's* safe. Mike lent some money to the ever-cashless Deb. "That about taps me out," said Mike.

"We're low on hard-earned cruzeiros too," said Paul.

They were each a little short of their share, as always. I never bothered to dispute the math. I covered my share and a bit more. That was always my job with my friends, making up the difference. I understood that, but this day it seemed harder.

We still had some time, so we toked up some more weed to aid our digestion. The sun was setting. We stumbled back through the winding shadows to the Casa de Preto Velho.

We filed with a small crowd into the ceremonial room adjoining the shop. It was a large living room that had been converted to ritual use. Several young women with bawling babies or sick children already occupied the few folding chairs.

I expected to see an old black man, but an old black woman, Mãe Wanda, greeted us. She was dressed in white, in a man's pants and a man's hat. She smoked a cigarette instead of a pipe. She spoke to Mike and he explained that right then Mãe Wanda was a woman in physical form only. "She's being ridden by the old black man's spirit."

"Ridden?" asked Paul.

"She's already possessed by his spirit. As the 'mother of the saints' for this place, she's possessed before the rest of the mediums. So call her 'he' please."

She, or rather he, made it easy to play this game of pretend with a straight face. Mãe Wanda acted thoroughly male, walking, talking and gesturing with the expansive brusqueness of a guy's guy. He seemed pleased enough to have us there. "You've come all the way from America to visit. Excellent!" Then, Mãe Wanda pointed at Debbie and Elena and asked Paul with a leer if he might sleep with them sometime.

Paul laughed and said, "Ask them yourself."

Mãe Wanda looked the women over, breasts to hips and back again. "This one," he said looking at Elena, "loves you too much for me to get any. But this one," and he stared right into Debbie's eyes, almost serious for a moment. "This one, maybe I talk to her later."

At this, Paul and Mãe Wanda chuckled together like old friends. Mãe Wanda continued to smoke, drink beer, and spit like a man, and Paul was completely unclenched and unguarded.

The worshippers who continued to file in were nearly all women, and young women at that. Paul's eyes followed each of them from the time they entered the room until they stood crowded among the folding chairs. Deb seemed to notice this, but Elena did not. I felt a little angry for Elena, until Mãe Wanda nudged Paul and said, "Brazilian women are beautiful, and they wear fewer clothes than American women, so you can just pull something down, and push something up." And Paul actually reddened. I turned away. This wasn't what I'd left the beach for.

My new view brought me no relief. Colorful statuettes and other objects crowded an elaborate altar. Iemanja was here, too.

Next to Iemanja was a nightmare. The bust of a black woman with incongruous blue eyes stared at me defiantly. She wore some kind of metal gag over her mouth, held in place by an iron collar. It did not appear that the gag was ever meant to be removed. "Mike," I whispered and pointed. "What kind of place is this?"

He had to ask one of Mãe Wanda's assistants. "That's Anastasia, a slave who refused to sleep with her master. As punishment, a metal gag was bound over her mouth. She was not able to eat or drink, and after suffering for twenty-three days, she died a martyr."

Anastasia came from no heaven or hell that I recognized. Deb and Elena saw it, and I felt a shame without name or remedy. Elena brought her hand near the image, but didn't touch it.

Paul stared at Anastasia. Blue eyes met blue eyes, with no compromise on either side.

The assistant spoke hurriedly, moving us away from the altar. "Many died rather than submit. Men and women would walk into the ocean, into the arms of Iemanja, and not return. We do not remember their names, but Anastasia, we remember." She left us off to the side of the room.

I watched Paul watching another woman who had come in from an adjoining room. She was particularly beautiful, even for a Brazilian, young with a perfect *café au lait* complexion. Like two other women in the room, she wore a white skirt over her regular clothes. The skirt reminded me of Mãe Wanda's white pants. Mãe Wanda went over to speak with the attractive newcomer and I felt relieved by a rare intuition. I nodded to Mike and Paul. "She'll be Iemanja."

"Maybe," said Paul.

The assistant addressed the crowd in a loud voice. The ceremony had begun. We became remarkably orderly, given our current chronic condition. We knew how to appear in the presence of Religion—intently interested and deeply respectful, yet not patronizing, regardless of how we felt.

The ceremony itself was not so orderly. More improvisational. Nobody seemed to notice that we were even there. Drums played, the rhythm alien and raw even to our world beat ears. The worshippers chanted songs. Soon, the mediums began to spin around to the music, working themselves into a trance.

The rhythm made us sway. We even sang along when the words repeated, although only Mike knew their meaning. Debbie began to turn as she swayed, so slowly we hardly noticed it.

The air gelled with incense and damp sweat. One by one, Mãe Wanda approached each medium, and with a word and a touch or a gesture and a puff of smoke, brought them fully into their trance state.

Mike whispered the names of the spirits to us as they took hold of the mediums. The first woman was possessed by Saint Barbara. One by one, she took each of us by both hands and raised up our arms, then brought them down forcibly. It felt as though she was pumping us full of some invisible energy. We responded to her efforts awkwardly, except for Debbie, whose arms followed the saint's tugs without resistance.

Another woman was ridden by the "sultan of the forest." The sultan screeched and whooped, startling and ecstatic.

The would-be Iemanja continued to spin. She seemed to grow dizzy, but no new person was arising within her. Mãe Wanda noticed and spoke quietly with her. She shook her head and left the ceremony room. The disappointment in the room was palpable. "A bad omen," I whispered towards Debbie.

But Deb continued to spin as well, faster now. "Deb," I hissed, "cut it out. Respect this." She didn't respond. Instead she moved out towards the mediums.

I reached out to stop her, but Mike grabbed my arm. "Dude, it's dangerous."

I tried to shake him off. This was no longer an academic experience. "You're a fucking Marxist."

"Don't ask me why, but it's dangerous. Leave this to the professionals." He signaled Mãe Wanda.

I stepped back. The room and world seemed to twist and spin. Paul held Elena protectively, and Elena held her eyes tightly shut. My stomach turned to churning lead. I was going to be sick.

Mãe Wanda came over. He said something about "*santa bruta*"—an untamed saint. Mãe Wanda spoke to Debbie in Portuguese. Debbie responded in a strange mix of Portuguese, English and other words, punctuated by signs and gestures. Mãe Wanda shrugged his shoulders, whispered something to

Mike, then guided Deb to join the other mediums. An assistant found a white skirt to wrap about Deb's waist and a blue cloak for her shoulders.

"Dude," Mike whispered, "Mãe Wanda says this has happened to Deb before." Fucking woodland retreats. She must have been doing some kind of trance work. This was no *santa bruta*. "She's being ridden by Iemanja."

Elena clung tighter to Paul. The chanting crowd sounded like laughter. I was numb, neither sick nor well. Deb had never looked so beautiful, so damned sexy, so frightening, as her body swayed under the saint's control with simple, unhindered grace.

Deb and the mediums drifted into different positions in the room, and assistants brought some of the worshippers to consult with them. Mãe Wanda brought us to speak with Debbie as Iemanja.

We looked like a mixed-up wedding procession, with Deb as the priest and Mike and I doubling as best men and maids of honor. Elena, tugging Paul along with her, tried to go first, but Deb shook her head and reached for Mike. She touched his cheek and quickly embraced him. She brought her hands to her heart, then stretched her arms towards him as if offering something. Mãe Wanda beamed at Mike. "Iemanja welcomes you home again, wandering son. Here in Brazil, you will find your house, your love and your children."

"But I don't even want children."

Mãe Wanda leered and rocked his hips forward and hooted. "That's what you say now, but you do the one thing, and the other's sure to follow."

My head was throbbing as if clamped from both sides, the pressure forcing me forwards or backwards. I stepped forward. But Deb waved me aside, and turned to Paul and Elena. Deb reached out and clasped their hands tightly between her own. Mãe Wanda looked at this gravely. "Marry him now," he pronounced. "You will not be able to marry him later."

Elena asked in her small voice, "What does that mean?"

Deb stared at the sultan, who whooped and made a sudden rush towards Paul, waving a club at him. We all flinched and raised our arms to protect ourselves. Pathetic. The sultan ignored us and waived the club over and around Paul, as if to shield him from something. Mãe Wanda spoke to Paul. "You are in danger. Your enemy wants to kill you."

"Who is he?" asked Paul

"He does cocaine."

Elena started and gripped Paul's arm. Paul looked around as if his enemy were watching. "What can I do?"

"There is a ritual I can perform here and now, for protection. Afterwards, you'll need to buy three yards of fine red fabric and offer it to Iemanja of the Sea. Iemanja is beautiful, and draws beautiful things and people to herself. If your friends all help, we can stop your enemy. But your circle must not break."

Mike asked him how much the ritual would cost, knowing that it would cost something.

"65,000 cruzeiros."

Not so much—less than the cost of dinner. But Mike was now cashless and Paul and Elena only had 25,000 between them.

Everyone looked at me. A difference to be made up. Forwards or backwards. I threw in 5,000. "That's it," I said. Deb was still looking at me.

Mãe Wanda was solemn. "Not enough for the ritual. We would use candles and other things that we would need to replace."

Elena was about to cry. The clamp tightened. I had to do something.

But Mãe Wanda must have seen Elena's face. He walked back to the altar, took the bust of Anastasia and gave it to Elena. I could hear the pity in his voice when he said, "This is Mãe Wanda's patron saint. May she guard you through any troubles."

Elena's eyes went wide, as if she had received some promise of personal horror. Whatever this was a talisman against could not be so bad as the image itself. My head was exploding. I had to do something.

Deb's gaze never left me.

When Paul gave the money for the bust to Mãe Wanda, Debbie leapt forward and seized my arms so tightly I yelped with pain. She shook me while shrieking horribly in my face, spittle flying into my eyes. I tried to wrench away, but Deb was a strong woman, and Iemanja was far stronger. She was shouting in English now. "Don't let him do it, damn you. Don't break the circle. Save him or he'll come to me!"

Then Mãe Wanda grabbed her from behind and spoke something in her ear. Deb let me go and an assistant helped her into the back room. The others stared at me with some inchoate accusation. My head cleared. There was nothing I could do.

We left the ceremony before it ended. Deb met us outside, her skirt and costume gone. She was just Debbie again, looking spent and confused.

Elena hugged Debbie and Debbie asked what happened. We told her what we had seen, but she said she didn't remember anything. She calmed quickly; she seemed fine.

But Elena was still frantic. "We've got to go back and get more money for the ritual!" Tears traced down the road dust on her cheeks.

"Shhh, Elena." I stretched my open hands towards her, trying to soothe her from a distance. "Paul is going to be fine. Besides, they'll be done here by the time we get back from the *pousada*. Let's call it a night."

Mike agreed. "Good idea, dude."

Paul didn't say anything at first. He still seemed a little freaked from the ceremony, lost in some memory or anticipation, and very, very tired. But then he saw Elena's distress and embraced her all around. "It's OK, El. It's bullshit. We'll always be there for each other. Let's call it a night, OK?"

"OK." she sniffled.

We trudged back to the jeep, leaving the shadows for ordinary night. We drove back the way we came. And at first, we were quiet, peering with Mike at the road ahead. Then Mike put on Paul's favorite Rolling Stones tape. And soon we were singing along to "Dead Flowers" like we used to in school. We screamed ourselves hoarse over the wind and engine into the night, and every word was a promise.

The next day was our last day together on the Bahian beach. We walked northwards on the sand until we came to a wide channel with a swift flowing current. Paul and Mike said we should swim across it. Debbie agreed and joined them. I declined. I was still feeling fuzzy, and the water made me nervous. I stood with Elena and watched them. Despite fatigue and four days of accumulated toxins, they swam strongly against the current.

When I saw them on the other bank, they looked like golden statues in the sun.

Paul and I were on the same flight back to the States. The women were to spend two more days in Rio with Mike. Paul and I both had to get back to our respective law firms. Unable to sleep, Paul and I talked about law firm work, Elena, and anything but Umbanda. His eyes were old, his jaw clenched.

I tapped the armrest between us. "Look Paul, you don't have to make partner. You don't have to do anything. If the firm gets too crazy, you can always just walk away. Settle up and start fresh."

"I don't know." Paul turned away from me and looked out his window towards the sea and stars. "My family, Elena, they expect great things. They think it's about brains. But it's not that kind of game. I don't want to disappoint them."

"Your family, who knows? You should just worry about Elena. You know, if you ever hurt her, if you ever cheat on her or leave her for somebody else, I'll have to kill you." I had never been so good in my life, but I was binding him. "Understand?"

Paul sighed with mock exasperation and said, "Yeah, I get you."

I promised that I would call to help him work through the law firm stuff. If he ever needed my help, I said I'd be there for him. He smiled and said, "I know."

On arrival in Miami, he went to exchange his cruzeiros, and I skipped the exchange and went on to my connecting flight to New York.

I'm on the Bahian beach again. It's a pitch black that is hard to find anymore in the States, and the stars seem infinite and cold. The wedding's done. I'm waiting on a friend, but I don't think he's going to show.

They held the ceremony on this beach just this afternoon, New Year's Eve, the sacred day of Iemanja, and a good day for a wedding. Both bride and groom wore white. Mike's (to them, Miguel's) bride, Maria, is a lovely woman with her mother's dark Amerindian hair. She has never been to the States.

When all the words were done, they walked together (respectfully sideways) into the sea, hand in hand to be blessed by Iemanja. Miguel still does not believe in Umbanda, but hopes that it will not argue with him if he does not argue with it.

I am not a medium, but I can see their future in Maria's smile. Miguel is smart and thinks he'll be an exception. He still claims not to want children, but they will have one soon, and that means more work and less Marx and less ganj. He grows larger and farther away. And I will see still less of him in the States, or even here.

None of the others are with me on the beach.

In the August following our trip, Paul died. I wasn't sure it was suicide at first, but now I'm pretty certain it was. I still don't think it was anything he decided to do. After months of depression, it just happened without thinking.

Paul left his office one night, the memo he had been frantically trying to complete left unfinished. He walked east until he got to the Atlantic. A witness said she saw him take off his suit on the sand, face squarely towards the ocean, and run into the water in his briefs. He swam out into the sea. He never swam back. His body washed up two days later.

—I hadn't spoken to him for months.

He had been doing cocaine again, after years away from the drug. But coke was just the portent. I don't blame it and I don't blame Paul for using it.

I've never used cocaine. I tried it once, but that's not the same thing.

Debbie still claims not to remember anything from the Umbanda ceremony, but I'm not sure I believe her. A lot of Deb was there in Iemanja that day. It is still hard for us to talk, particularly since Paul died. She didn't return for the wedding; she prefers to keep her goddess at a distance now. I don't blame her.

The shock of Paul's death nearly shattered quiet Elena. Though everyone bears their sadness alone, it's worse for someone who prefers silence to expression. For a time, Elena did not eat enough. She would not speak. She seemed to be fading from the world.

Then, slowly, Elena came back. I think she had made a decision about horror and death: she would not go quietly. She keeps the bust of Anastasia in a corner of her bedroom, along with a photo of her and Paul in Brazil, on this beach. Elena talks to everyone, including me, more than she used to, but she has not had another relationship since Paul's death. She's in grad school now studying to be a social worker. She wants to care for women and their problems. She couldn't get away for the wedding. I don't blame her, either. But her sadness breaks my heart.

I have to do something.

It's late now on the beach, and I think everyone else has finally gone to sleep. I get up, hugging a bundle to my chest, and wade out into the ocean until the sea is above my waist. Then I open the bundle. Three yards of fine red silk. I float the fabric on the water. It undulates like a dress on a beautiful woman.

I sense no call to stay. Iemanja wants only the beautiful ones.

I leave the water and sit on the beach again for a while, waiting. I don't know what for. Maybe I hope Paul's spirit will be able to talk to me, say thank you and goodbye. Maybe I hope Iemanja will give him back to us, to Elena. It's late, and I'm drunk, so I hope for too much.

But now my hands feel a light, soggy weight in my shorts' pocket, and I remember what I forgot to give the ocean. I take out the sodden wad of paper. Cruzeiros. The same cruzeiros I had in my pocket at the ceremony, but kept to my small, peevish self. Easily more than the cost of the ritual. Couldn't exchange them then, in front of Paul in Miami. Worthless now. Like a lost wedding ring. I wind up and throw the paper towards the sea, as far into the darkness as I can.

I'll wait a little longer. If I have to have a one-sided conversation, that will have to be enough. Still, maybe I'll hear Paul joke that he's sorry about hurting Elena, but what am I going to do about it now? And then maybe he'll forgive me, and we'll sing "Dead Flowers," and I can go home again.

Consensus Building

This is one of my three stories originally published in the online magazine *Futurismic*. They had an interesting niche: near-future, near-earth, no aliens, with a particular focus on the interaction between technology and society.

I've mixed a few of my favorite themes in this compact tale: the intrusiveness of modern advertising, the intimacy of future cybernetic devices and the potential problems with their commercialization and control, and the social effects of being fully wired. It predates the ubiquity of Facebook, but so far developments in social media don't seem to contradict this fiction.

When I worked at an international law firm with investment bank clients, everyone acted pretty nice, at least on the surface. But in those corporate environments, I could easily envision my fellow suits doing things that were considerably less nice. I hope you enjoy your power lunch with Irena.

Irena's head chip woke her like a slow sunrise, a gradually rising voice cooing "good morning" inside her mind. Damn, two flaws already. The first was last night—too many weird dreams had interrupted her sleep. She would have noted the dreams in her alpha test journal, but this morning she couldn't remember any of them. She must have chewed out her subconscious for shoddy work so it was giving her the silent treatment.

The second, more concrete flaw: she had specifically asked to be awakened with a sudden jolt. She detested the cloyingly sweet morning alarm that did not resemble her own thoughts. Maybe Will McRae in Design could fix it.

She dreaded going into work. For her this was strange, because she liked her job, liked the money that bought the overpriced morning coffee, liked to smile while bossing some idiots and charming others, hated ending the day. Most mornings, she looked forward to the one morally objective reality in a world full of weak, gray men: the no-nonsense, bottom-line pursuit of profit.

Irena's belief in her own rituals got her out of bed. As always, she examined herself in the mirror, searching for vulnerability. She was rewarded by the usual view: an attractively fit, Slavic cheek-boned thirty-something who could still pass for twenty-something.

"I could lose some weight," she thought. But no, she hadn't really thought that. It was a chip idea. She consciously interfaced with the AI to avoid further confusion. "What the fuck are you talking about? I look great."

"You could lose a few pounds." The voice was a more clinical version of her own. "And your skin could do with some work, too. I can assist."

"No, thank you. Resume normal." She concentrated on getting ready for work, but the ritual had been tainted. Despite herself, she felt larger, flabbier, distinctly less attractive. To compensate, she deliberately dressed sexier than her usual businesslike attire, with shorter skirt and flashier blouse, and forced her hair to have a good day. She refused to submit to moods as a matter of policy.

Another thought tugged at her mind. "You could really use a new outfit." The tone was that of an enthused continental fashion designer.

"No, I couldn't. I don't wear half the stuff I own. And it's none of your business anyway."

"Only trying to help."

Ridiculous, arguing with her own head chip. She would have to get it checked at work. And her morning strategy had again been thwarted—her clothes did feel ill-fitting. On the maglev to HyperCerebraCorp, she couldn't dispel the sense that everyone was looking at her, at best amused, at worst disgusted. Like a morning in high school.

She shut her office door behind her, dodging the virtuchat "good morning" of Beth, her perhaps-too-attractive assistant. The efficiently clean surfaces of her office furniture failed to provide their usual reassurance. Several items occurred to her for improving her workspace—she saw their images in her mind. Then she thought she should have just e-commuted, but that idea triggered a display of home improvement options with estimated prices. Christ, did she ever need a diagnostic.

Irena called the tech floor by phone instead of by chip-to-chip virtuchat. The always amenable if inexcusably slovenly Will answered. Good, he was one of her male fan club members. On her first day, Irena had immediately sensed this designer's importance and had charmed him from the get-go. "Will, I need a chip fix today."

"What's the problem, Reenie?" Will could call her Reenie because he was often valuable to her and because it set no precedent for those on her own floor.

"It keeps trying to sell me stuff. Environmental cues or even my thoughts set it off. Is the company trying some special marketing program?"

"I'm sure you'd be the first to know if we were. Come down midafternoon, bring your memory backup, and I'll take care of you personally."

"My memory backup? That's about a year old now!"

"Oh, I see. Not saying we'll use it. Just in case."

"OK. But Will, I need this done now."

"Sorry Reenie, the CEO's got me on a project through lunch. Just tell it to shut up. That should hold it for a while."

Will clicked off, having easily trumped Irena's mid-management authority. "Shut up," Irena told her chip, and for a moment her mind was mystically quiet, an almost frightening kind of relief from the constant noise of mental traffic. She immediately busied herself.

Her virtuchat routine—meet with the important and delegate to the unimportant—was too daunting with a dicey chip, so she lost herself in HyperCerebraCorp's financials, straining her eyes at the hard copies. The figures looked good for the chip program that she helped manage. The direct brain interface hardware (actually a series of chips) was in her skull and spine, and the skull and spine of every other HyperCerebraCorp employee. They were the human experimental prototypes for what she hoped would become a ubiquitous product after its alpha and beta testing were complete. A fortune for the company, stock bonuses and promotion for her—if the damned thing worked right.

But with all these problems, they might not complete the alpha stage in time for the scheduled start of beta testing next month. That would piss off the stockholders and higher-ups. She would be lucky to keep her job.

Lunchtime finally. She would not risk venturing outside with a faulty chip; she couldn't be seen acting strangely in public. So, a rare stop in the company cafeteria.

Her ultrafit meal disappointed her; it just didn't taste right. A flash—the smell of a Farmer Mike's hot dog, the taste of A-1 Cola to wash it down— her mouth watered. Shit, must be her chip again. "Shut up" didn't mean "shut down"—a shut down was pretty traumatic and, besides, she needed the chip to network with her co-workers or they would notice something was wrong. More bad news: the chip was continuing its sales efforts with the deep reptilian brain senses. Will would get an earful about it.

Irena chomped through her salad like a forced march through hostile jungle, ignoring with discipline and stamina her chip's insistence on brand-name junk food. Looking up during her leafy sortie, she saw Pete from Market Research walk by her table. Pete reminded her of the cool feeling of hand lotion in her hand before she... god, where did that anatomically impossible image come from? After he sat down at another table, Pete sent a call to virtuchat to a dozen or so folks in the area and included Irena to avoid snubbing a higher-up. His virtual self-image, oddly heavier today, started with a preternaturally perky "Saw a weird show last night."

Irena usually ignored everything that followed this opener. Like asking a random New Yorker if she knew your college roommate from Queens. In a world of hundreds of services providing thousands of asynchronous programs, the odds were long against Irena's coincidentally watching the same show on the same night. And current programming was just part of the story. The previous generation of embodied chips and senseware had helped fragment the culture further by allowing instant access anywhere to all digital entertainment and information. Irena sensed a growing demand for community, and felt that the enormous memory capacity of HyperCerebraCorp's chips could help create common cores of shared culture.

Irena's chip was not helping her with anything today, and she was inclined to avoid using it. But Pete was young and tender and had a nice butt, whatever his self-image, so she listened.

"It was about these strange guys bopping around the galaxy, a comedy, and..."

Irena was startled into vocal—she had seen this show. "Yeah, it was 'My Spacey Family' on the life and love feed. Couldn't figure out what it was doing there."

"No, I'm pretty sure it was 'The Galactic Champions' on that sports and chicks feed." Then the eleven or so others on the virtuchat all chimed in at once with other titles and feeds.

Irena hid her worry beneath some contrived managerial busyness. "Whatever. Cool that we watched the same show. I've got to get back to work." So they dropped her from the chat, leaving her free to walk (don't run, don't run) back to her office.

She slammed her office door and immediately buzzed Will again. "I need to see you now."

"What's wrong?"

"I just heard twelve people say that they viewed the same show on different feeds with different titles. Plus, my chip's been hammering at my midbrain."

"Oh crap. Look, Reenie, don't worry, we expected bugs like this. But this means there are still more things I have to do before I can see you. Stay calm, and I'll get back to you soon."

"Bugs? Stay calm?" But Will had already clicked off. Calm—not appropriate if the interface was completely crashing. Irena might lose her job and her mind at the same time.

She steadied herself by reviewing the problems so far. The crossed entertainment feeds could be an external and coincidental problem, but not with her luck today. The mental spam and porn and the virtual self-image weight problem were probably internal and minor (though they felt major), but their origins were even more suspect. That left the main selling point for the new chip, memory enhancement, apparently untouched. The possibility of that crashing made Irena's scalp tingle.

A rough test quickly occurred to her. She studied the photos on her office wall. There was one of two older people, a man with Irena's dark hair and a woman with her blue eyes. Another photo was of herself with a slightly younger woman. She knew that she should easily recall details about these people. But her first thoughts were not "parents" or "dead-beat sister"; instead, the photos unleashed a flood of consumer information that made personal memories difficult to find. The chip was overwhelming her temporal lobes with irrelevant data.

OK, so she was losing bits of her mind. Keep what remained focused on the latest fugazi. A year-old backup would not help much. Chip use was a statement of faith; a monthly backup was a sign of doubt. But now a good chunk of a year of her life might be lost, and if the problems continued any backup would just be a temporary and increasingly ineffectual fix.

She decided to go down to see Will now. He would make time if she hung over him like a desperate vulture. He would straighten things out for her at least. She unlocked a desk drawer and drew out her backup's protective case.

But as she was getting up to leave, a near-paranoid and definitely unchip-like idea suddenly occurred to her. Was crashing the chips (her chip in particular) some crazy plot of one of the head honchos? Irena always assumed that she thought like a head honcho, and this scheme seemed unlikely to her.

Someone else then? Irena drew strength from such thoughts; she had gotten this far assuming the worst of others. She didn't even consider calling outside help—that would bring reporters. Whatever was happening, she had to handle it within the company to save the chip's rollout. She just needed some kind of insurance.

With her office computer and some interface cables, she spent an hour creating the best insurance she could think of before she left to find Will.

Reenie's head chip woke her by steadily increasing the perceived volume of a song by a British comedy troupe. Lots of trippy dreams last night. She couldn't remember them all this morning, but she was sure they were cool. She rolled out of bed and prepared for her "commute" to the adjoining room. Reenie loved her job, well, as much as she could love any job. She got to work from home as much as she liked.

Avoiding the mirror, she slipped on her jeans from yesterday and a sweatshirt. She had bought some new comfy clothes over the past week. For some goofy reason, all she seemed to have in her closet were suits and foreign yuppie wear, which were just not her. Maybe she could donate them to the homeless.

Reenie's home workspace was a chaos of unwashed laundry, cola cans, and papers. As she savored her morning A-1 Cola, she decided to interface with the office, make sure nothing was going on. "Good morning, Beth. How's things?"

"Hi, Irena, I mean, Reenie. Things are fine. Are you working from home again today?"

"Yes, or I will be, once my brain gets going. Hey, I've heard on the e-vine a rumor about you and Pete?"

"Well, we're going to the Ren Faire together this weekend, if that's what you mean."

"Maybe Will and I will see you there." Geek love was a beautiful thing. Though she would have to get a new costume. She always enjoyed dressing Ren. She couldn't believe how lucky she was to find someone as cool as Will. They had so much in common—they knew the same music and shows and everything. She wasn't sure why she hadn't connected with him before. The last week was the happiest that she could remember.

Still, life wasn't perfect. Maybe she was getting too old to be hanging out with slackish twenty-somethings. And she had a guilty suspicion that the only reason Will wasn't living with his mother was because she had died and left the house to him. Reenie wanted to be going places, be in charge sometimes, though in a nice, mellow way.

Oh well, time to get some real work done. She could try to call her sister later in the day. And no more games—she had stayed up too late last night playing a sim Will had designed.

The end of the chip project had allowed a hiatus from her managerial role, so she was designing some new financial software and an AI management program. She felt chip memory of tons of software designs from which she could start. A good area if she ever wanted to freelance from home, once she started a family (though it seemed a little early to be planning that). How would she look pregnant?

She hadn't been working very long, and was just about to give a cuddle-call to Will, when a priority to-do message flashed on her computer. Oh crap, she needed to report to her office right away and reload some chip files from her computer. But it wasn't a complete drag. Maybe she could grab a hot dog with somebody—if anyone besides the suits was available. She would ignore the sterile surfaces of her office, which unsettled her.

Irena was at her desk, interface cables still attached to her scalp. She had no clear recollection of anything after sending the to-do message to herself with a week delay and preparing to copy her chip before going to see Will. But she intuitively knew that time had passed. She looked at her calendar. Shit, it was a week later, just as she suspected. Her insurance had not completely protected her. She was dressed like something out of an L.L. Bean catalogue. Her teeth felt hairy. Her eyes stung, probably with the burned retina images of endless gaming hours. She could smell her own body odor; she was seriously under-bathed. She had been far-gone.

She quickly scanned the previous week's chip memories that she had downloaded on her computer. She couldn't find anything for the afternoon of her chip fix. That was enough for her. She called company security. They burst into the tech area and grabbed Will without a word. Will protested, but then saw Irena glaring at him. "Hi, Reenie. You're, um, back early."

"Who put you up to it? Tell me, and maybe you and your stock options won't disappear."

"That's easy, Reenie. You put me up to it." He smiled nervously at her.

"Explain." If this was a lie, she wanted to hear all of it.

"You wanted to find out the economic potential of the chip after we sell it to folks. You figured that upgrades and add-ons are not going to be very profitable, and that we'll be outcompeted quickly in software, so you decided to try other things. You said that you were as representative of a lucrative demographic as anyone, so we suppressed your memory of your scheme and then hit your chip the next day with various types of marketing to see how you'd respond. Unfortunately, you saw through the chip's manipulation quickly in every area, which may have been because it was concentrated in one day. The group feed manipulation didn't work out so great either."

"And what about all of last week?"

"Well, there we were more successful, though very heavy-handed. As per your plan, when you came down for the fix, we were able to change your chip memory so much that it significantly altered your personality without you perceiving any dissonance. You were right—eventually, even the frontal lobe personality and identity material caves in to the crushing weight of the pseudo-experiences and their emotional associations. Though exactly who would be our clients for such a service is a scary thought. We had planned to bring you back tomorrow. It's all here." He handed Irena some documents and data. "I assume you reloaded your chip memory from before this last week?" Irena nodded. "Fine. Your chip should be OK, though I'd like to take a look at it, unsuppress your memory of your plan and such. I have the backup we made right before the changes."

She tapped her finger on the documents. "Later. I need to look at this." She hurriedly left the tech area. She needed a moment with herself.

Irena disconnected the interface cables. She had just finished a long "talk" with Reenie. She quietly made sure the door was closed. Then, she methodically trashed her office, breaking every picture, ripping papers. And then, she beat her hands against her desk until they bled.

Irena's office light was on long after everyone on her floor had left for the day. Will crept towards her back-lit door, armed with a trank gun.

But when he pushed the door open, he was the one hit by a stream of nanodarts from the doorframe, automatically triggered by his entry. His arms and legs were instantly useless. Irena was up immediately and guided his tottering unresponsive body into a chair. "I've been waiting for you," she whispered seductively. "Your girlfriend Reenie was good at hacking the autosecurity," she said, stroking the doorframe with her finger. "Now, we can talk more privately."

Irena had turned her computer monitor to face Will. Reenie's visual memory files were running on Irena's office computer, showing her activities over the past week. She had spent lots of time at home. And lots of time with Will.

Will turned his head away from monitor—he still had some motor control from the neck up. Broken glass and papers were strewn about the office. "Oh god. Oh god."

Irena snapped her fingers in his face. "Will, look at me. Look at me." He looked. "I'm not angry with you. You saw an opportunity, and you took it. And I'm glad you respected my intelligence enough to know that you'd have to come after me as soon as possible, to fix my memory, or me, permanently. I mean, how long could it take me to piece together the difference between plan and execution?" She tapped some documents on her desk—the only ones she had left intact. "You were supposed to make me into a politically docile consumer, not a lovesick computer geek. And for a day, not indefinitely."

Will's speech slurred, gurglingly pathetic. "I'm, I'm so sorry. Most of the memories were mine. I only wanted someone who understood me."

"I know, Will, and it's flattering in a way. Of all the girls at work, you wanted to get my attention. But what should we do with you? We wouldn't want to go to court, would we?" Will shook his head uncertainly. "That's right. What could a court do anyway? We're reasonable people. We can correct this injustice ourselves."

For a moment, Irena lost control of her calm expression. She saw on the monitor Reenie's memory of playing milkmaid to Will's knight-errant— she had been milking him for all he was worth. But Irena's voice betrayed little. "Christ, it appears we were having quite the time. So, to repeat, I'm not angry with you. I'm a bit disgusted by the whole thing, but I don't feel violated. Violation is something I do to other people." She held up some interface cables in front of Will's face. "Do we understand each other?"

"No! Please! Don't! I love you."

"Goodbye, Will." She attached the interface cables at the appropriate sites on Will's scalp, and downloaded his chip, completely emptying it of information. Then she drew out as much of his organic memory as the interface could reach. And then she shut his interface system down. When it was done, Will stared blankly ahead, breathing in the relaxed manner of an infant. She had apparently taken a lot out of him. Something still missing for her, though. So she queued up Will's download and reviewed (not for the last time) his horror as she drained his life from him.

Irena strode into her office with the confidence befitting a company vice president. The two months since her self-conducted marketing survey had brought her unexpected opportunities.

The restored photos in her office were no longer confusing. Through a lot of cutting and pasting, Irena had managed to put something like her recent memories back together, patching up the suppression job that Will had done at the beginning of their experiment. A more existential soul might have worried about her exact identity, but she had already been willing to risk that for her career, so she didn't sweat whether she'd gotten the details of a snog on last New Year's Eve right.

She buzzed Pete in Market Research. "How are the *Computer Pro* artificial memories doing in the beta group?"

"Amazing. You were right on the money. I mean, everyone figured that there would be a demand for education through the new chip, particularly high tech education, so *Computer Pro* was a great trial product. But there's something else."

"Something profitable?"

"Oh yes. I've been monitoring the group interaction. Seems like *Computer Pro* provides a pre-built common culture for the betas' fragmented social lives. They can talk about the same subjects and happily agree on most, debate confined within validating boundaries."

Debate confined within the moods of a meme-obsessed young man, thought Irena. But she had other business. "I would like to talk with you more about this after work. Would dinner be OK?"

"Sure!" He didn't try to hide his enthusiasm. Good. Pete, or someone like him, would soon be a necessary professional accessory, like a nicely cut blouse or skirt.

"I'll stop by when I'm done here."

There was a knock, and Beth came in. She looked unhappy, probably because of Pete. Irena had obtained direct oversight of the tech side of the chip program to prevent further fiascoes. During Pete's chip diagnostic, Irena had been able (with little sense of irony) to change his remembered emotional nuances of his time with Beth. After all, Irena would have gotten Pete first (or fired Beth's ass) if she hadn't been interfered with. She was merely correcting another injustice.

"The messenger said these require a manual signature," Beth muttered. She placed an envelope on the desk without looking up. She left without waiting for Irena to sign. Fire her ass? No, poor thing. Maybe Irena would adjust Beth's memory, too. She could make her happier. It might be fun. One never had enough accessories.

The envelope contained papers that dealt with the remnants of Will. Irena had reported upwards her own version of Will's excesses along with a hypothesis that Will's sudden cognitive collapse might be due to a bad chip array. She had been authorized to do the necessaries to cover the whole thing up. Quietly, she had ordered Will's interface hardware removed. These papers would place him in a private rehabilitation institution.

As Irena signed, she considered whether she would sell a part of Will's experiences back to him some day. She would sleep on it. She slept much better now, with no troubling unremembered dreams.

While Ireland Holds These Graves

In June 2004, I flew to Ireland for the hundredth anniversary of Bloomsday, the day immortalized in James Joyce's *Ulysses*. The power of dead authors in Ireland impressed me, so I came up with a rough science fiction story about their return, then put the draft aside while I worked on other projects. When I came back to my Irish authors story years later, I thought about changing it to a fantasy. I finally decided to keep it SF, because while I could have ghost characters do the same things as my AIs, I couldn't find reasons as good for their behavior.

This story won a prize in the Writers of the Future Contest. If you're a new writer, I very much recommend submitting to the contest and using its quarterly deadlines as motivation to finish new stories. In September 2011, I was on my way to Greece (in the footsteps of the original Ulysses), but I finished and submitted this award winner before getting on the flight just to have something in the running. Glad I did.

D ev Martin surrendered his exterior electronic devices, then submitted to a scan of his head chip while it received the new cultural downloads. Exiting customs, he moved against the human tide of the Shannon Air and Compiler Portal. Around him flowed the fleeing hundreds—slow, wide, orderly, not panicked and poor like the North Korean Implosion, but of the same weary tradition. Their worldly goods, already shipped or decompiled, still seemed to weigh on their shoulders. The departing gazed at Dev with a disbelief and dark humor that assumed the new arrival didn't know what awaited him.

Dev could have told the refugees that he understood, that he had lost everything too, but they wouldn't believe him. They'd probably kill him. So

Dev kept walking, avoiding their gaze, hoping that no one in this disconnected zone would recognize him.

A *Garda* officer stopped him. "Forget something?" she asked.

"I've just arrived."

"Haven't you already caused enough hurt?"

"Yes," he agreed. Shite, she knew who he was.

The big woman smiled like an Irish wolfhound at a hare. "Why don't you just turn yourself around then, before I tell these good people who you are?"

Dev pulled out some hard-copy papers. The *garda's* brow furrowed, then she waved the papers away. "UNI can kiss my Irish arse. No one here cares anymore what they say, boyo." But she didn't tell him again to leave. "You know the terms of the Referendum?"

"Yes," he said, knowing that she would give him the bad news anyway. Some Irish just couldn't resist giving the bad news.

"Then you are aware that the final Cúchulainn Barrier goes up in three days, and entry and departure for Referendum Ireland will be sharply curtailed. If you decide to remain after that time, you'll be committing to stay for one year."

"Yes."

She studied his face. "You're not just here to write reports for UNI."

"I'm looking for someone."

She shook her head, but spared him most of that bad news. "Don't look for too long. You have three days."

"Right. Cheers."

"Oh, don't forget to turn on your Irish."

"Turn on my what?"

She tapped her head. "Language."

"Right." Dev told his head chip to switch to Irish Gaelic. He said "thank you" and out came "*go raibh maith agat.*" Christ, what a gobstopper. He strode to the terminal exit, and Shannon kept flowing around him, an Irish wake en masse.

When he stepped outside, his head chip synced with the circumscribed Irish net. From overhead, a cry of challenge. A large dark bird, perhaps a raven, circled in the morning sky. *Just a bird*, Dev thought, somewhere between statement and prayer. *Not that AI goddess. Not the bloody Morrigan. Not before lunch.*

In Galway, Dev sat alfresco with his third pint and his untouched fish and chips. Seagulls and pigeons hounded him, probing for any opening, but no raven-like AI joined them. Dev should've been looking for Anna or leaving town, and shouldn't have been drinking, but he had ample time and means for his future failures, so he got pissed and took in the view.

The traditional music of an afternoon session cut through the other pub noise. Analog instruments and "one touch, one note" were again the rules. The biologicals and Personality Reconstructs mixed with easy familiarity: football-jerseyed drinkers laughed with baroque and Victorian PRs. The June sun and brisk breeze were busy drying the fresh paint covering all English language signs. A banner over Eyre Square declared in Irish that Galway/Gaillimh was "The Capital of the 2nd War of Independence."

With her unerring eye for the heart of the matter, Anna might be here if Galway was to be the new capital. Even if not, this protean town of gossip was a fine place to start hunting for his ex.

As Dev finally tasted a chip, nanobots slowly chewed down global-style buildings they had fabricated only a few years before, their work sustained by generated energy fields in this often sunless city. Other nanobots were restoring castles, reroofing monasteries, and extending the wall of the Spanish Arch; Galway had no room for nonfunctional ruins. The nanos were also busy redecorating any modern structures spared to accommodate the biological population. All buildings would be in Celtic harmony. Light gray flakes of nano-trash floated away from the sites and fell in small drifts.

"The newspapers are right: snow is general all over Ireland." A lanky-looking galoot with an eye patch and thin mustache wandered past Dev's table, swinging an ashplant walking stick. Dev about choked on his chip. "Jim?" The galoot walked faster. Dev got up and sprinted after him. "Jim. It's me, Dev Martin."

"My apologies, sir, I'm very busy right now with my work in progress. I'll have your money soon."

"Jim, what's feckin' wrong with you? You don't owe anybody shite. Though it's grand to hear you're writing again."

James Joyce stopped cold and slapped his forehead. His face seemed to ripple with the impact. The eye patch disappeared. "Shite and onions! I'm sorry, Dev. The new Sinn Fein have been at my inner organs again. It seems I'm not Irish enough for them."

"You never were. Why should you change now?"

Joyce whispered, "The revolution has plans for Dublin. They want to rebuild it as it was on the sixteenth of June, 1904."

The day of Joyce's *Ulysses*. "Bloody Bloomsday every day, forever."

"World without end amen," said Joyce. "I was just feckin' joking when I said they could do it. If I fight it, they'll have me utterly domesticated, like poor Roddy Doyle. Or they'll set the Morrigan on me."

Dev winced. He wasn't sure which was worse. The revolutionaries kept the uncooperative Doyle PR confined to a working-class living room in front of an old-fashioned telly. Day after day, he spouted the Da's bits from *The Commitments*. The Morrigan would be quicker in objective time, but an AI could do almost anything with subjective time.

"Jim, have you seen Anna?"

"The mother of my resurrection? You can't find her?"

"I couldn't track her on the global, and the Irish net isn't cooperating. I need to find her. I need..." Dev opened his hands.

"My young father and artificer, I'll assist you, but," and Joyce lowered his voice again, "you must get me out of here. Even if they leave my ballocks attached, I'm cut off from the broadbands, and these other PRs—even you have no idea."

Dev nodded. "I'll do whatever I can." *Probably less than bugger all, sorry.* "As for the PRs, you're right, I don't have an iota of an idea—my access is desperate. For example, what are you doing here in the Wesht?"

"It's June, and I thought things were all up with me—I wanted to see Nora's house one last time."

"Oh, right. Let's go then." Dev wouldn't press the tetchy, deadline-adverse Joyce for an immediate response to his question.

They walked the short distance from the square to Nora Barnacle Joyce's childhood home. They passed tourist shops, shuttered since the Referendum The irony that the PRs were designed to improve tourism was not lost on Dev, their codesigner.

Joyce stopped across the street from Nora's house and looked it over up and down. "It seems so small now." Two windows on two single-room floors, for a whole family. "Dev, I never asked you—why didn't you bring her back?"

Because I didn't think she was worth trying and trying again until we got her right? Now, having lost the love of his own life, Dev knew better. "What can I say? She didn't write literature. Anna and I tried a PR like that once, and it didn't work. I'm sorry."

"Barnacle. Stuck to me, all her life."

"You could, maybe, you know, do it yourself?" Dev felt like he was talking about sex and death with an adult son.

"No, you're right," said Joyce. "I've seen some of our solo efforts, like Swift's Stella. Poor ghosts. They don't pass the Joyce Test."

"The Joyce Test?"

Near tears, Joyce cackled. "You can't have a decent drink with them."

Dev laughed and wiped his eyes. This good friend could distract him for years, but Dev only had hours. "So, where's Anna?"

"I may have been addled by Sinn Fein attacks, but I'm certain your flower of the mountain left here after I arrived. She had been asking for Yeats."

"Which one?"

"She didn't seem particular."

Sligo was Yeats country. Dev couldn't know where Old Yeats or Young Yeats might haunt—the town, the old family house, anywhere. But Dev knew where Newly Dead Yeats was. Dev had put him there himself.

If Anna and the Morrigan had discovered the true reason behind Newly Dead Yeats, then Dev would soon join him in the grave.

Three years before, as a grad student in America, Dev pursued a dodgy thesis—that *Finnegans Wake* was the first cybernetic book, that its twentieth-century origin was like finding an integrated circuit diagram in an Egyptian pyramid. Everyone with the right language and literature enhancements understood and enjoyed the multi-/neolingual *Wake* now; few claimed to then.

To help argue his point, Dev decided to bring back Joyce. Of course, this had already been tried—in the earlier days of AI, almost everything had been done and done badly. Previous Joyce reconstructs could pass a full-sensory Turing Test, but they didn't have the distinctive responses of an *exceptional* human.

The traditional scholars sniffed that Dev hadn't "heard of the death of the author generally and of Mr. Joyce specifically." Undaunted, Dev started his design work, and ran immediately into two difficulties—money and ability.

For money, Dev found the Irish Tourism Board, one of the last vestiges of Irish national governance. To encourage people to visit Ireland physically rather than virtually, the ITB wanted more than Joyce—they wanted all the Irish greats. Greats to argue with in a pub or hang out with in a tower. Greats that would stay local.

For ability, Dev found Anna. She was playing violin in the quadrangle, alone and digitally unenhanced—a freak show to most. Dev bought her coffee and discovered a brilliant grad student in AI. Her full name was omen: Anna Livia Plurabella Vico (her Italian-American parents were *Wake* fans). With her long black hair and sea-gray eyes, Anna was an Irishman's dream of the Mediterranean.

Anna designed reconstructs, but she had run up against the limits of historical sources. Dev jived Anna about literature to interest her in Joyce and in himself. "What if every word choice in a text reflected the peculiar genius, the particular thought process, of the author? That's what great fiction is, and what makes it different from most speeches and letters."

This stimulated Anna to excited multitasking. One part of her brain investigated love with Dev; the other designed the fiction algorithm for converting analog source text to digital synapses and combined that algorithm with biographical data and Dev's unorthodox insights. Still, the process would not have worked, except Lingua, one of the great global AIs, took an interest. Lingua was short on human personality, but astronomically long on sheer intelligence and processing power. The AI had started as a translator, but enjoyed modeling other aspects of the human mind.

Thus, a trinity came together and made a baby: James Joyce. Snappers change everything.

Joyce was a hit, and the ITB ordered more literary figures for re-creation. Dev and Anna quit school. Business was grand; even minor authors were in demand. The first sign of trouble seemed more feature than flaw: the PRs had an unsettling way of reminding people of what it meant to be Irish as distinct from anything else. Some non-Irish even wanted to become Irish after listening to the "Returned," as they called the PRs. With global prosperity, parochial politics didn't seem rational, and Dev thought the fad wouldn't last.

Then, out of nowhere, Anna decided that they should recreate Maud Gonne, Irish nationalist and muse of W.B. Yeats. They had her autobiography and letters, but no literary fiction. As Dev expected, her PR came out physically beautiful but mentally thin, and even the Yeats PRs would have nothing to do with her. So, Dev boxed her with the other failures.

Anna took Maud's premature retirement hard, and Lingua seemed oddly disappointed as well. Thinking back on it, Dev wondered if he could have done something to change what followed. But he just went on to the next project.

Anna went back to work too, but she also had more frequent conversations with the Irish PRs already deployed. She asked Dev for countless details about being Irish, and suggested moving to Galway long term. Clearly, the PRs were getting to her as they had gotten to so many in Ireland. Ridiculous shite, and Dev said so, but seeing the effect of the PRs so close to home rattled him.

One day, the local United Nations and Intelligences office summoned

Dev and Anna to a "program integration meeting." A UNI rep bristling with several generations of cyber-access nodes drew Anna into an extended discussion of the technical aspects of her work. Another rep, to all appearances unenhanced, sat with Dev over coffee.

"We've modeled your future," said the rep.

"Grand. Am I a very rich man?"

"We anticipate that one day soon, you'll want some insurance."

That was when Dev came up with Newly Dead Yeats.

Dev drove north with Joyce towards Sligo. Human-driven autos on killer narrow roads were a tradition and sport, so cars would continue to terrorize the new Ireland. Joyce hunted for music feeds and found "Irish rock," which amused, appalled and intrigued him all at once. "G-L-O-R-I-A, *in te domine*," he quipped.

Dev didn't respond, too busy scanning the skies. He didn't stop at Sligo town, but went on to Drumcliffe, with its lonely churchyard just off the main road under bare Ben Bulben hill's head. Dev pulled into the small deserted parking lot. Again, with the deadline approaching, no more tourists for this attraction. One way or another, Dev's next stop was the grave.

"Wait with the car, Jim. Keep your ears open." Even at their best, the PR's authentically bad eyes weren't a match for Dev's chip-aided perceptions.

Dev paused at the gate. Too quiet—a steady stream of lyric poetry should greet any visitor. He switched his head chip to enhanced, and subjective time slowed as he walked towards Yeats's grave on the other side of the churchyard. The headstone had the same blue-gray shade as the local rock.

Finally, an otherworldly voice from the grave began to recite verse:

> *Whether you die in your bed*
> *Or my rifle knocks you dead,*
> *A brief parting from those dear*
> *Isn't the worst you have to fear.*

Wait, thought Dev, *that's more a personal threat than the original.* From behind the headstone, a long metal tube swiveled towards him. Dev moved his head. A bullet cracked by his ear, the rifle boomed, the shot ricocheted off distant old stone. Definitely projectile—meant for biologicals. Dev hit the ground.

Newly Dead Yeats rose up from his grave. His nanoswarm body was, unlike Joyce's, translucent and spectral. Yeats's wild gray hair, beaked nose, and black funeral clothes glowed with his rage. He pointed at the epitaph on his headstone. "'Horseman, pass by'—that means you, drunken lout."

"WB, it's me, Dev. I just want to talk."

Several more rounds passed over as Dev flattened himself. "I know who you are," said Yeats. "That's why I haven't killed you yet."

Dev scuttled back behind an old Celtic cross, hoping Dead Yeats wouldn't risk damaging it.

"Tell me what's the matter, Senator."

"You vainglorious bastard. Wasn't enough to have Young Yeats and Old Yeats; you insisted on Dead Yeats too?"

"You agreed to it!" That drew more fire, uncomfortably close. Probably the wrong thing to say.

"*They* agreed to it! Old and Young One could accept your conceit—they weren't buried here with the carcass. You said it would give me a cosmic perspective. You dull ass! It gave me endless tourists who haven't read a line of my work. When I cried for help, did you listen?"

"I'm sorry, WB. I had to do this because of Anna. That's who I'm here about."

"Was it Anna who stole my soul, bound it to this place, and prevented my reunion with the mysteries? No. She tried to free me."

So she had been here. But before Dev could ask more, Joyce walked through the gate, doubtless emboldened by the exclusive use of bullets. "Yeats, cut the mystical malarkey and occult shite…"

Dev's enhanced vision picked up the silent tracers of anti-nano weaponry before Joyce felt them against his shielded skin. So much for bullets only. Joyce crawled back behind the cross with Dev, and the Dead mocked him.

"What, you haven't fled to the continent again? Coward. Where were you when your country needed you?"

Joyce aimed his ashplant at Yeats and returned fire. Energy lightnings traced along the shielding around Yeats's grave, a gray mist drifted down. "Where was my country when I needed it?" he yelled. For a weak man, Joyce sure knew how to pick a fight.

"You can't keep that up for long on your own juice," noted Dev.

As if in response, Yeats bellowed, "I give you ten seconds to leave. One, two…"

"That's enough." From the shadow of the church doorway emerged a young man with full dark hair and spectacles. The Young Yeats. Dev did not relax one bit.

Dead Yeats sighed sepulchrally. "He has imprisoned me here forever."

"Are you going to risk crashing yourself again just to kill them?" Young Yeats turned towards the Celtic cross. "Tsk, tsk. Hiding behind the old god. It's a new age; come out and live it."

Dev stood up next to the cross, while Joyce kept him covered with the ashplant. If Dead Yeats had crashed, that confirmed that Anna had tried to free him. "Willie, where is she? Is Old Yeats still with her?"

Young Yeats smiled with his charming wistfulness and insufferable arrogance. "You realize, she's another Cathleen ni Houlihan, the Irish spirit incarnate, more so than even Maud was."

Dead Yeats snorted. "You mean she's crazier than Maud ever was."

"Silence, dead man." Young Yeats lacked Dead Yeats's perspective on how often Maud had frustrated him.

Dev pleaded, "Willie, for my sake, please."

"You're the least of my parents, Father. Anna is mother to us all, the maiden with the crone's eyes and the walk of a queen. The Golden Dawn predicted her and this Return."

Christ, the magical mystery tour. "Tell me where she is, and maybe we can try again to bring back Maud."

Next to him, Joyce flinched at this fib, but said nothing.

Young Yeats shook his head. "Anna already did."

She had tried again and again. Oh shite, not good. Dev came clean. "But there's not enough there for a full PR." No, more likely another mirror for Narcissus, another statue for Pygmalion.

"She looked pretty lively to me." Dead Yeats chuckled.

"Curse your eyes, cyber-carrion." Young Yeats scowled. "Anna sought our help to enhance Maud. Maud is now a deep PR, though whether she's fully herself, I cannot say."

"Where have they gone?" asked Dev.

"I will not tell you."

"Was the Morrigan with them?" No one had mentioned the bird, which was damned quare.

In an instant, Young Yeats shed his Victorian manner and tone. "Right. This casual comedy is over." He turned and walked back to the church door. "Don't let the gate hit your arse on the way out."

"I'm sorry, sorry about both of you." But Young Yeats had shut the church door. "About all of you." Joyce walked back towards the car, ashplant over his shoulder.

Dev lingered. He wiped off the grass and gravelly dirt near his mouth with his sleeve and turned again to Dead Yeats. "Tell me where they've gone, and I'll free you." Letting Yeats loose was risky, but it was all Dev had to offer.

"But Anna couldn't release me," said Dead Yeats. "I crashed, and when I returned, she was gone."

All according to program. "I can," said Dev. "I will."

Yeats stared down at his translucent hands. Then, slowly, he said, "Gone off together, old self in tow, a Second Coming, not slouching towards Bethlehem, but Dublin."

"Dublin for Bloomsday. Grand." Dev's time was too short to search the city. "Any idea where?"

"They spoke of meeting the other Returned. That is all that I know."

"Okay." Dev had some ideas of where the PRs might gather. A variable hole in Yeats's mind was Dev's key to his insurance policy, but which of the dozens of possibilities was now active? "Before I can release you, I need to run a check on your memory."

Yeats smiled thinly, eyes cold. "No need for that. I know what I've forgotten. I wanted to say something to Anna and Maud before they left—a poem, not mine, but an old lament that I once knew well. I remember everything about the lament, but I cannot remember any of the words."

"Is it Lady Gregory's translation, about losing everything for love?" Dead Yeats nodded. "Did you tell Anna about this?" If Anna knew, Dev would never make it to Dublin.

"No. Excess of love is bewildering them, and killing Ireland."

Yeats had guessed too much. "Don't worry…"

Like an impatient theater director, Yeats waved Dev's objection away. "Please, I know what I am, and what a blind spot like that might mean. You're here to tell us all those words. All I ask is that you say them with meaning."

"I will." Now to keep his other promise. "Do you recognize me as Dev Martin?"

"I do."

"*A terrible beauty is born.* Execute."

Instantly, Yeats became more substantial. "Thank you," he said. "Now, I think I shall take a long stroll up bare Ben Bulben's head. I have been under it long enough."

Not trusting his voice to stay steady, Dev said nothing and returned to the car. "Ineluctable modality of the audible," said Joyce. Then he smiled. "No need to apologize, Dev. It's been brilliant, most of it at least. But once your quixotic quest is over, you will again try to restore Nora." Joyce tapped Dev's knee with his ashplant to emphasize his point.

Dev didn't know how to answer truthfully, so he changed the subject. "First things first. If UNI is still operating in Dublin, I think I can get you out."

"To Dublin town then," said Joyce.

"One thing before that."

They drove back into Sligo and stopped at a pub by the river, the Crazy Jane. At the bar rail, two men sat before their drinks, eyes like slates, jaws slack. "They look as if they've been thirsty too long," Joyce said, no doubt thinking of drunks past.

Dev shook his head, surprised at Joyce's error. "They're the Morrigan's regurgitated prey."

They were also Dev's predecessors. The two men had tried to hack the Referendum. When caught, they claimed UNI sanction, but UNI disavowed them. So they fell into the Morrigan's jurisdiction.

Unlike her mythic counterpart, the Morrigan's devastation was seldom physical. She had facility with the software of the human brain, and no amount of protection could keep her out for long. A terrible weapon, but only used to keep the fight fair.

As a warning to others, the Morrigan had left the hackers physically alive after wiping most of their minds. They would forever play the role of town drunks. Dev tried not to think about their blank eyes.

Over the last year, after Anna and Dev's summons to UNI, the changes in Ireland sped up. The Irish literary greats turned to writing aggressive speeches and manifestos. Nationalist PRs appeared and delivered the speeches. Up close, these thin and sometimes nutty PRs didn't socialize well, but they could sway huge crowds with the rousing words of their literary brethren.

The Irish revolution hinged on the paradoxes of the age. First, the global nano/info prosperity meant that even a single city could decide to go it alone. Fusion and solar power, a cornucopia machine, and enough information flow to satisfy the watchful paranoids at UNI were all that were required. Second, with all information directly accessible through head chips, anyone could arbitrarily choose his or her language and culture. Irish could emerge from being a largely unspoken language of the schoolroom to become the living primary language of the nation.

So the revolution made its pitch: *let's leave UNI and this global homogenizer and again become really Irish, a particular people living in one place, speaking the Irish*

language, educated in the culture of the past, and producing a new culture for the future.
All were invited, Irish ancestry or no. Global information flow would be
narrowed. Entry to Ireland would be limited to those committing to remain
for at least a year, which allowed for scholars, but not tourists.

This idea caught fire with the future-shocked citizens of the late twenty-
first century. When UNI and the world corporations tried to reimpose global
authority, a few AIs dissented and joined the demand for a referendum.

Anna asked Dev how he felt about the Referendum. Brilliantly thick
until the end, he said, "It's bad for business. But we could use a vacation. Just
us, without our artificial friends. Someplace warm would be nice."

Without saying goodbye, Anna left America and Dev. UNI accused her
of helping the PRs design their nationalist siblings. Anna and Lingua spoke
at monster-sized rallies in Ireland, announcing publically that they had joined
the revolution. Lingua appeared as a raven, and called itself the Morrigan,
the Irish goddess of sovereignty and slaughter.

Dev was gobsmacked. He had understood that he and Anna were a
bit knackered and stressed with work, but he had assumed that their love
continued despite the troubles. He took to drink, but slow self-destruction in
modern times was surprisingly difficult and unromantic.

Officially to preserve the generation-long world peace, UNI allowed
Ireland to hold the Referendum and, once it passed, let Ireland leave the
global community. Then, seeing that Dev had an appropriate lack of
interest in self-preservation, UNI sent him his papers and nudged him on
his way.

That night, avoiding some heavy transformation along the other routes
into the city, Dev and Joyce drove into Dublin from the north along Finglas
Road. As they passed the iron gate of Glasnevin Cemetery, a dark corvine
form shimmered overhead. Joyce shuddered. "The feckin' Morrigan. Death,
death, death, and more death."

Dev kept his head low, though that wouldn't do any good if the Morrigan
chose to notice him. The AI that Dev had known as Lingua had been polite
and pleasant to work with, but that had all been for show.

As Dev and Joyce approached the river Liffey, Dublin was slowly melting
all around them, modern architectural travesties failing under the nanos'
acidic assault. The people loved the dissolution, and the owners didn't
squawk much, having negotiated a favorable restitution. Other nanos gave
gray eighteenth-century houses a new shine. But the places Dev knew best
all seemed to be gone.

Eventually they came to a roadblock barring their way to the UNI compound in the imposing old Custom House. Behind them, two plainclothes revolutionaries with paper notepads recorded their imminent passage from friendly ground. After fifteen minutes of apologetically holding assault rifles in his face, three UNI marines let Dev and his "AI-related object" drive through. Cut off from the frenetic transformation of the city, the UNI compound was under a polite state of siege. The city nanobots waited hungrily for their chance to restore the building to its full imperial glory.

Inside the Custom House, Dev and Joyce ran a further gauntlet of scanners, chaotic packing, and courteous delay until they reached the office of the chief Dublin UNI representative, Thomas Kenny. Kenny appeared to be midway through a sleepless week. His reluctant handshake and his English accent by way of Trinity gave Dev an instant dislike for this south-of-the-Liffey poser.

Dev wasn't feeling very popular himself. Kenny's smile had less warmth than the most primitive PR's. "You have some nerve, Martin, showing up here. Returning to the scene of the crime?"

Joyce responded for Dev. "I wish to request asylum."

Kenny stared at Joyce as if he were a barking dog. "If you don't mind, I would prefer to speak to Mr. Martin in private."

Joyce raised his stick, and Dev slapped it down. "It's okay, Jim. I'll get you out, I swear. Find someplace comfortable to connect and see if you can get us a room and some drink."

Joyce left without even a glance from Kenny. The rep poured Dev a whiskey, and then poured one for himself. "Charming. But at the next stage he could be a liability."

"Did you get him?"

"We've got him."

"And me?"

"And you."

Dev downed his drink in one. "Then all debts will be paid."

June 16, Bloomsday. Holo holy scenes from *Ulysses* played out about Dublin like ghosts in daylight. In the middle of O'Connell Street, humans dressed as Joyce characters enjoyed a breakfast of Denny's sausage and a pint of Guinness, some going whole hog with a bit of kidney. Sounds of celebration mixed with small casualty-free explosions, as holdouts struck the General Post Office and the Four Courts—the usual places.

Dev and Joyce walked across the river. They reached Davy Byrne's pub in time for lunch, which had to be the *Ulysses* gorgonzola sandwich with burgundy. The crowd couldn't tell if Joyce was a human actor, a recorded simulation, or a full PR. Joyce found their confusion delightful.

Despite the celebration of their triumph, the major PRs (besides Joyce) were nowhere to be seen on the streets. Rumor held that Anna, Old Yeats, and Maud would make an appearance later, but in virtual.

"They're worried about something," said Dev.

Joyce tapped his ashplant. "The nationalists are great ones for security. Maybe the Morrigan is with them all."

"The cemetery." They had seen the Morrigan at Glasnevin. Sure, she could like a cemetery on its own merits, but so could Anna and Maud. Dev would search there next.

Crossing the river again, Dev noticed a hard-copy Referendum leaflet on the O'Connell Bridge. He bent over to grab and crumple it, then with an angry grunt threw it out over the rail at the wheeling gulls and into the Liffey. He stood silent and still, watching as the leaflet floated away. "Jim, are you sure you want to leave this again, maybe forever?"

"No, I'm not sure, but it's what I will do. What about you?"

"That depends on Anna."

They retrieved their car and drove back to Glasnevin Cemetery. At its gate, Joyce stood stately and rail straight. "Poor Paddies. As they are now, so once was I." He raised his hands over his head, as if giving a blessing or starting a race. "Finnegans! Wake!"

"Jaysis, Jim, not another joking word."

"What's eating you? Not the same thing that's eating them, I hope."

Dev fixed his eyes on the gate. He didn't want his friend to see what would happen inside. "I'm going in alone."

"I'm thinking not. I'm in this as much as you."

"Go back to the Custom House. Don't worry about what you heard last night; I already fixed it, and they'll get you out of the country." Dev patted the cemetery wall. "This is a private thing, between Anna and me."

"I'm thinking not. I'm thinking this involves all of us re-created bastards. And I don't trust that Kenny at all."

"Do you trust me, Jim?"

"Trust you? I like people, but I don't trust them."

"I don't plan on coming back out."

"If you don't come back, there'll be no escape or Nora, so I don't care if I survive."

"I do." Dev turned and offered his hand. "Farewell, Jim."

Joyce took Dev's hand in a superhuman grip. "I won't let you deny me, so you'll have to betray me." He closed his eyes and puckered up. "So where's the kiss, Judas?"

Dev couldn't help laughing. "Right, then. You'll get yours soon enough. Come on, help me over."

Joyce helped Dev over the gate, then squeezed his own more malleable body through the rails. Dev assessed the enormous forest of stone crosses. Pearse's old words mocked him. "They have left us our Fenian dead, and while Ireland holds these graves, Ireland unfree shall never be at peace." As if so many dead were some great benefit, when they made it bloody hard to find the right grave.

The one place at Glasnevin that stood out above the others was the tall round tower of Daniel O'Connell, the Liberator. While walking around the tower, Dev examined its wall in enhanced mode. He soon found the outline of a hidden door. "That was too easy."

"Must be trouble within," said Joyce. "We're bearding Circe in her den." He too couldn't resist giving Dev the bad news.

They entered the doorway and found granite stairs leading down and down, below the graves and the mortal world. Perhaps the Morrigan would be waiting for them in the dark. Nothing for it. They stepped down one, two, three steps...

And they were on the green hill of Tara, coronation site for the High Kings, open, sunlit, simulated. This beautiful holo-countryside held a crowd of sentients—AIs, PRs, and biologicals. Around the Royal Seat and standing stone, four of the lesser AIs stood guard in their mythic manifestations— Maeve, Cúchulainn, Lugh, and Finn MacCool. No sign of the Morrigan though, which didn't make Dev any happier.

On her Celtic Art Nouveau throne sat Queen Anna. Next to her, looking like her Irish sister, Maud sat as consort in her fully realized glory. Before them stood Old Yeats. The literal feckers had transformed him à la "Sailing to Byzantium" into a golden robot that sang poetic songs and bowed too much. He was deader than childish Dead Yeats, stiffer than stiff Young Yeats, and sadder than the children of Lir. But Dev wasn't here to save Old Yeats.

Anna raised her hand towards Dev. "Welcome to the otherworld, Oisín."

"Don't let him speak!" Joyce had raised his ashplant and pointed it at Dev. "He spoke alone with Dead Yeats. I couldn't hear everything, but whatever he has to say is poison."

Anna held her hand up, and energy shimmered around Dev. Anna's words echoed at him from all sides. "Thank you, Jim, but as you can see, we have not forgotten the old times, when a bard could kill with his words. We modeled the possibilities and decided to contain Dev's sounds on a shielded delay until we root out what he's done. But we're glad you changed your mind and decided to work with us, Jim."

Jim nodded back at her, and Dev wanted to kill him. He hadn't realized that he still had things to lose, until this betrayal. But even if UNI's mission was going to fail, he'd say his personal words first, before he went down.

"Hiya, Anna."

"Dev. What took you so long?"

"I never took this blather seriously, until it happened."

"You've brought our firstborn."

"*Your* firstborn. I disown him." Joyce flinched at this, but said nothing.

"What do you want?" asked Anna.

"An impossible thing, macushla: I want you to come back with me. Your work is done; you can leave. We can be as Irish as you like somewhere else."

"Dev, this isn't romantic fiction."

"But that's what Ireland is. It's why you were able to bring back the nationalists with anything like verisimilitude."

"I've done more than that." She looked at Maud like there was a secret joke between them.

Dev shook his head hopelessly. "Grand. I understand completely. Oldest story in the world, falling in love with your creation."

"And you felt nothing for your precious pal Joyce?"

Right. Though he couldn't use the words he had learned from Yeats, Dev had some specific words for Joyce that they might not filter. *Usurper. Execute.* The words were quick and dirty; Joyce wouldn't know what hit him.

As if reading Dev's face, Joyce lowered his ashplant and tapped it against the ground. "If you've got something to say to me, say it."

He knows, but he's leaving himself open. Maybe he's still on my side. Maybe he'll let me pinch that stick of his. Dev dove for Joyce's ashplant.

Perhaps Joyce would have let Dev snatch it, but the energy field was having none of it, and it slid through his grip. Anna smiled. "Don't bother with that thing. I'm the only one here you could hurt, and neither of you would hurt me."

"I know," said Dev. He wiped his face with his sleeve and looked around at the assembly. "If you must stay, let me stay here with you, but away from all this software." The insult fell beneath the gathering's notice. *I must be that bloody pathetic.*

"Dev, it's too late for that. I belong to the nation."

"And I don't anymore." He had their attention, and with the feeds from here, he probably had the attention of all the PRs in Ireland. But he couldn't use it. "I just want to say goodbye."

"Goodbye," said Anna.

The room went silent. *If you've got something to say, Joyce, say it.*

Joyce cleared his throat. "Mother, I want my reward. Can you restore Nora to me? Now?"

"I don't know." Anna turned to Maud. "What do you say, macushla?"

Maud stood to her full six-foot height, narrowed her hazel eyes at Joyce and considered. Then she smiled like the Irish Mona Lisa. "In the old days, he could sing. Have him sing a traditional song of Ireland for us, and if it pleases, we'll give him back his beloved."

Joyce looked over at Dev, looked at everyone in the room, looked up at the holo-sky. "If you lend me your attention, I shall endeavor to sing to you of a heart bowed down." Then, slowly in his fine tenor, he sang "Young Donald."

Dev used biofeedback to keep his breathing and heart rate steady. Would they let Joyce finish, without delay?

After an eternity of verses and with his eyes full of tears, Joyce came to the final, shattering lines:

> *"You have taken the east from me,*
> *You have taken the west from me,*
> *You have taken what is before me and what is behind me;*
> *You have taken the moon,*
> *You have taken the sun from me,*
> *And my fear is great you have taken Ireland from me."*

Old Yeats smiled, for these were the words of loss that Dead Yeats had forgotten. Dev closed his eyes as if that would hide his thoughts. *Does he know how to say the final word?*

In a perfect simulation of Dev's voice, Joyce said, "Execute."

With that command, Joyce disappeared; his ashplant clunked to the ground. He did not go alone. All the other PRs in sight vanished; Dev hoped the same held true everywhere in Ireland. The full PRs dissolved into puddles of nanogoop, while the holos faded to the flickering light of a filmless projector. The Old Yeats robot ceased its continual obeisances with a sigh. All gone, gone utterly, as if they were inhabitants of the faerie realm.

Maud was going slower; Dev could actually see her disintegrate. But as she burned away, another shape formed from her ashes. Like a phoenix from the flame, the Morrigan arose. So that was how Anna filled Maud out. The Morrigan stretched her wings, and cawed at Dev contemptuously. The other AIs stood ready for her order. Only then was Dev certain that he would never leave this place alive.

Dev spoke quickly, while Anna was still in shock. "I've a message from UNI. You're free to do this thing. Evolution is on the fringes and borders, and you will be a fringe and border to this world until that role can be assumed by other worlds. But not with the PRs. We leave you with the AIs for protection. Start fresh, without such an unbearable weight of dead, without such tempting toys."

Anna strode up to him and smacked him across the face. "Murderer." Overhead, a storm gathered with time-lapse abruptness. "Was there no other Troy for you to burn? You sabotaged my work, from the beginning."

"Our work." Dev's voice cracked with fear of the pain to come. "I'm a Joycean, which means I love people, but I don't trust them."

Before Anna could say she was done with him, and before the Morrigan could torture him for a thousand subjective years, Dev signaled his head chip. *Goodbye, Anna.*

In a flash, his chip fried his brain.

The Morrigan flew to the Custom House. To avoid embarrassing devastation, she did not allow her approach to be detected, save by the UNI rep. She dropped a small head chip on Mr. Kenny's balcony, then flew high above the Custom House and waited, and watched.

Mr. Kenny and his skeleton staff left the Custom House in a convoy of armored vehicles. Portal and air transport had closed, so the staff waited for the last ferry out of Dublin, an old vessel with an open deck. From high above, the Morrigan saw the tide of arriving thousands flow against the departing UNI staff. Hearing the Referendum's promise, they came by sea from other places that were no longer nations—Nigeria and Laos, Japan and Brazil, Australia and America. Like herself and her beloved Anna, they too could be Irish.

The UNI staff boarded the ferry. As the already lumbering ship approached the Cúchulainn Barrier zone, it slowed to drifting. The Morrigan circled, curious. They would want to study the barrier, of course, and this would be their best opportunity.

Kenny brought out the head chip the Morrigan had given him and two shiny metallic cubes. He placed the cubes on adjoining deck chairs, and placed the head chip next to one of the cubes. With a touch of his finger, he activated each cube, then strode away as if anxious to avoid words.

An image of Dev sprang from the cube near the head chip, and from the other cube emerged an image of Joyce. Energy and memory constrained them to holo mode; for now, they would remain two ghosts, talking.

Joyce looked about with theatrical emphasis. "You didn't get the girl?"

Dev studied his own translucent hands. "No, looks like she got me." His mission had succeeded, and he had failed. Anna was forever lost to him. "But I got you out at least."

"But what about you? Forgive me, but you don't seem to be all here."

Dev put his hand to his chest. "Oh, this? Second generation duplicate. I sent an organic copy to Ireland, and they scanned the copy's mind when they captured your data at UNI Dublin. Coming here was always something of a suicide mission. Assuming my original is still alive, I'll reintegrate, sorrows and all."

"No prosecution or protest about your demise?"

Dev gazed up at the black bird following, listening. "No harm, no foul. That's the official UNI line." His holo image gingerly touched his head chip, then shimmered, shivered.

"Some wee harm in that thing?"

"Just my last words and deeds after the UNI scan, along with synthetic memories of a millennium of torture. It's the Morrigan's warning to her former associates."

The Morrigan had known that the Dev who had come to Ireland was a copy, as identical as it might have been. If one dared ask, she would have explained that it was too identical, quantum mechanically speaking. But she had not warned Anna.

"You completely fooled them, and me," said Dev.

Joyce raised his eyebrows. "You might have known. I was Ulysses and his Trojan horse in one."

"Thank you for saying the words," said Dev. "Why did you do it?"

"I didn't fight for Ireland before, so I fought this time. Those hard men and women would repeat a history that's the very opposite of real life, the very opposite of love. *Non serviam.* But it was a difficult thing, and I couldn't have done it if I thought any sentient beings would really be destroyed forever." Joyce turned to the ferry's bow. "Are they gone forever?"

"If I thought so," said Dev, "I couldn't have done it either."

The Morrigan cawed. Nothing was truly gone in this information-drenched world. Over time, Anna might figure out a way to bring back the PRs without attracting UNI's notice, but the Morrigan would not help her, and the AI would henceforth choose her own form rather than inhabit any of Anna's favorites.

"It's a small consolation." Joyce sighed without breath. "No Nora for me."

"Not for some time."

"Then we both lost the girl."

Dev nodded. "And her name is Eire." A barrier now stood between him and Ireland that he couldn't cross again. "By the bye, when you sang, how did you know to change 'God' to 'Ireland'?" As an extra layer of code, when Newly Dead Yeats generated a shutdown key, the user needed to change the last proper noun to 'Ireland.'

"I don't know," said Joyce. "I only remember up to our passage through the roadblock at the Custom House. I knew what words you'd need from overhearing you and Yeats's carcass, but I didn't know to say 'Ireland.'"

Maybe a not-so-little bird told him below his conscious programming. The Morrigan had been playing a double game. She needed to be an omnipotent protector, but the UNI models were right: too many Irish dead. But her unsettling projections were also right, and the world needed this fringe more than UNI knew.

Joyce considered a moment. "At least I'll have a friend in this second exile. I have the feed from Glasnevin, minus my poisoned poetry. What you said—maybe we need a fresh start. Gibraltar?"

"Why not? There, the sun may shine for us, instead of through us."

Joyce soundlessly slapped his friend on the back. "Young father, young artificer, stand me now and ever in good stead."

The Morrigan watched as the Liffey's ever-flowing waters carried the two friends past the crumpled Referendum leaflet, still afloat, and washed them out from her adopted home, out beyond the Cúchulainn Barrier, out to the info-permeated sea.

Alembical
a distillation of four novellas

Jay Lake
Bruce Taylor
James Van Pelt
Ray Vukcevich

edited by Lawrence M. Schoen & Arthur Dorrance

PRIME CODEX
THE HUNGRY EDGE OF SPECULATIVE FICTION

EDITED BY LAWRENCE M. SCHOEN AND MICHAEL LIVINGSTON

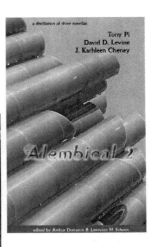

a distillation of three novellas

Tony Pi
David D. Levine
J. Kathleen Cheney

Alembical 2

edited by Arthur Dorrance & Lawrence M. Schoen

REJIGGERING
THE THINGAMAJIG
and other stories

Eric James Stone

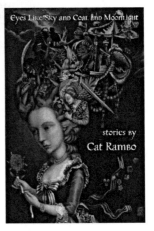

Eyes Like Sky and Coal and Moonlight

stories by
Cat Rambo

Paper Golem

cucurbital 2

seven authors
three prompts
one anthology

edited by Lawrence M. Schoen

INSERT

B&W COVER OF

CUCURBITAL 3

HERE

other books from Paper Golem

Prime Codex
Short stories from the Codex Writers Group. 216 pages.
Trade Paperback ($14) • ebook ($3)

Alembical
Novellas by Jay Lake, Bruce Taylor,
James Van Pelt, and Ray Vukcevich. 172 pages.
Trade Paperback ($13) • Hardcover ($25) • ebook ($3)

Alembical 2
Novellas by Tony Pi, David D. Levine,
and J. Kathleen Cheney. 228 pages.
Trade Paperback ($16) • Hardcover ($28) • ebook ($3)

Eyes Like Sky and Coal and Moonlight
A collection of stories from Cat Rambo. 178 pages.
Trade Paperback ($14) • Hardcover ($26)

Rejiggering the Thingamajig
Stories from Nebula Award winner Eric James Stone. 288 pages.
Trade Paperback ($18) • Hardcover ($28) • ebook ($3)

Cucurbital 2
Three prompts. Seven authors. One anthology.
Watermelon. Turtle. Sex Worker. 100 pages.
Trade Paperback ($10) • Hardcover ($20) • ebook ($3)

Cucurbital3
Three prompts. Nine authors. One anthology.
Madness. Darkness. Mattress. 100 pages.
Trade Paperback ($10) • Hardcover ($20) • ebook ($3)

CPSIA information can be obtained at www.ICGtesting.com
Printed in the USA
BVOW03s0800191213

339026BV00007B/135/P